NO GOING BACK

Anna Patrick

This is a work of fiction, based in large part
on the memories of the author's mother.

Matador
9 Priory Business Park,
Wistow Road, Kibworth Beauchamp,
Leicestershire. LE8 0RX
Tel: 0116 279 2299
Email: books@troubador.co.uk
Web: www.troubador.co.uk/matador
Twitter: @matadorbooks

ISBN 978 1838590 550

British Library Cataloguing in Publication Data.
A catalogue record for this book is available from the British Library.

Printed and bound in the UK by T J International, Padstow, Cornwall
Typeset in 11pt Sabon MT by Troubador Publishing Ltd, Leicester, UK

Matador is an imprint of Troubador Publishing Ltd

To Mike, for everything.

LONDON
1998

We are in the psychiatrist's chair: my mother and I. She is there for treatment of the anxiety and depression that have dogged her for most of her adult life; I am there to act as her spokesperson – after two or three mini strokes, her ability to communicate is something of a lottery. The psychiatrist does not like this arrangement. He wanted to see her on her own, but I insisted. He asks her a question; I start to answer. An angry glance and impatient gesture silence me. I lean back in the armchair and look around the room. I hear my mother answer in fragments; he needs the whole picture, but it is not forthcoming.

'The Road Less Travelled' by M. Scott Peck nestles among psychiatric tomes, also an autobiography by Leslie Thomas. I am pleasantly surprised though I have read neither book. There are two prints on the wall: the one opposite me is a beach scene in pleasing pastels; I glance at the other, but its colours are angry, the scene menacing. This is the picture facing my mother.

He asks another question. This time my mother turns to me in despair. I summarise my mother's problems: her frustrations at not being able to communicate properly;

the loss of her friends; the intellectual isolation; the world closing in on her.

'Exactly,' she cries. I have been faithful in my interpretation of her grief. I do not look at the psychiatrist while I speak, but I sense that he has understood the need for my presence. Then he says: 'The important thing at the first meeting is not to have too much information.'

I cannot believe the stupidity of this remark and want to leave. I re-examine our surroundings while, unexpectedly, he starts to ask for more details of her depression. Perhaps he expressed himself clumsily. He is doing better now, honing his questions, grasping the point of what is being said and what is being left out.

Sotto voce and in her native tongue, my mother says: 'I've had enough. Let's go now.'

I smile, but we both know we're here for the duration, for whatever £175 buys of this man's time.

More acute questions follow. She is being put on the spot and does not like it. While he writes his notes, she continues to plead with me to go. He catches her speaking and asks what she is saying.

'I didn't say anything,' lies my mother, picking imaginary fluff off her skirt and winking at me.

It is a bravura performance and I love her for it. I know she is looking forward to coming away for the weekend and wants to be out of here. Now she is sharp, verging on rude in her answers. He asks about her friends.

'I used to have friends,' she says, 'but they died.'

'All of them?'

'No, one by one.'

He asks her what she does during the day, whether she goes out, what interests her. She is negative in her replies. She doesn't want to take responsibility for her happiness or her life. There are pills to take care of that if only she can find the right ones or persuade him to give them to her.

'I'm a hard nut to crack,' she volunteers.

He summarises the situation as he sees it. She does not appear to be in the depths of depression. She disagrees immediately: she is in the very depths of depression and despair.

He is willing to help her with additional medication, he says, and we have a break in proceedings because she thinks he has suggested meditation, a path she has been down before. I have to raise my voice to get her to understand. At nearly 80 she is more than a little deaf and doesn't wear hearing aids.

He continues; he knows of her traumatic past but does not think this is the problem now. He needs her to participate in her own treatment, to work as a team with him. He knows she has been brave in the past and he wants her to be brave now by making an effort. He says she is lazy and focused on herself.

She has stiffened in surprise. Such forthright opinions from a stranger are a shock, but she does not disagree with his analysis.

'You may not like me for saying this,' he says.

She laughs and with an almost coquettish air indicates that this is not so. He is not fooled.

'You may say otherwise once you leave here.'

He has gained her respect which is not easily done. He wants to see her again, together with me – my turn for surprise – in six weeks' time. In the interim, he wants her to have cognitive therapy with a young, bright therapist.

I explain cognitive therapy to her briefly and tell her I think it would be helpful. He gives her a prescription for some additional tablets and we say our goodbyes.

As we wait to pay in the reception, she gives her assessment in loud Polish.

'He's not very sympathetic, but he's far from stupid.'

This is high praise indeed.

'I was a little shocked by what he said and embarrassed really.'

This is promising; no indeed, it is amazing. I allow myself a little hope, but who am I kidding? The cognitive therapy never happens; the return visit is endlessly postponed.

KRAKOW
1944

1

MARTA DRAGGED HER FEET, resisting the marching pace set by the guards. Her eyes scanned the passers-by, some now gathered into groups watching the prisoners go; others hurried about their business, their faces averted as if misfortune were contagious.

Was he here? Would she see him one last time before… what exactly? What did the future hold? Fear shuddered through her.

'Good luck,' someone shouted.

'We will pray for you,' called another.

The blood drained from her face and she swallowed hard to stop herself being sick.

He wasn't here. Why would he be? He would be at work and might not know they had transported her for days or weeks, perhaps not until they returned his next parcel… if they returned it.

She bit her lip to control her emotions, but tears coursed down her cheeks.

Somebody hummed the national anthem, but she didn't join in. Everything around her blurred, and she stumbled on the cobbles once, twice, until friendly arms locked into hers and pulled her along.

At the station, one of those women, lined face compassionate, voice stern, cupped her head.

'Take control of yourself, girl. Whatever courage you have inside, find it now and keep hold of it. Only then will you survive.'

She looked away, frowning. Her lower lip jutted out.

'It's so unfair.'

The old woman shrugged.

'And when was life ever fair?'

Marta sat down on the platform, arms and legs crossed; other prisoners sat down nearby, but nobody engaged her in conversation. She was glad.

Her act of love wasn't meant to end like this. She was meant to go home, put her books on the window sill, wait for the sound of a key in the door, rush into his arms and swing round and round, laughing, crying.

She had set out with such *élan*. Everything was going to be fine.

And if it went wrong? She would show those Germans, hoodwink them. She was clever, so much cleverer than they were. And when she had convinced them of her innocence, they would let her go. What a bloody fool she was.

A short blast on a steam whistle and the burning smell of heavy braking mixed with the fustiness of an engine coal fire punctured her mood. She was a little girl jumping up and down on the platform waiting for relatives to emerge through the billowing white clouds and shower her with kisses, and, best of all, gifts. Now she was all grown up, dressed in the latest Parisian fashion, a cigarette alight in its ebony holder, ankles crossed, as she travelled in opulent carriages with sumptuous upholstery or took refreshment in the busy dining car with its sparkling glasses and gleaming plates. Happy days.

An SS officer strode down the platform and the guards sprang into action, yelling and marshalling them onto the train with shoves and shouts.

Caged with a stranger, she clutched at the wire netting separating the two of them from the other prisoners.

'At least it's not a cattle truck,' she said, turning around.

'Oh? You an expert on prisoner transportation?'

'No, but these cells are weird. What's it used for? Mailbags? Parcels?'

'Lady, I don't care.'

'Oh.'

Her mouth dropped open, and she blushed. She looked around but didn't recognise anyone inside the rest of the carriage. She sighed and watched as her companion sat down and huddled her knees. It would be a long journey. She decided to introduce herself.

'My name's Marta Paciorkowska.'

There was a flicker of fear followed by a sigh of resignation.

'Rachel Goldstein.'

'Oh, you're…' She didn't want to say the word out loud.

'Brilliant deduction.'

'I'm sorry.'

'So am I, believe me.'

'How did you manage to…?'

'Survive this long? How do you think? I hid.'

Marta's face turned bright red.

'Sorry.'

'So you said.'

The train moved off with a jerk, catching her unawares and she staggered. Rachel glowered, fists clenched.

'For the love of God will you sit down and shut up.'

She slid to the dusty floor. The mention of God reminded her of the prayer and she touched the folded piece of paper in her pocket. Now wasn't the time to share it.

The guards were talking nearby, ribbing each other and laughing. There was nothing to do but wait.

Four weeks earlier, on an airless June night, her beloved Ludek had tossed and turned and moaned in the few snatches of unconsciousness. One minute too hot, the next too cold, they found no comfort in each other or sleep. When Sunday morning came, neither of them wanted to get up. Eventually, Marta forced herself out of bed. Dressing as a saucepan came to the boil, she cut two slices from the stale loaf, made two glasses of weak tea and brought their breakfast over to the bed.

Ludek clutched his stomach, his face pale and perspiring.

'Do you remember when we used to eat butter on our bread? You always piled it on as thick as the bread itself, while I just scraped it on to add a bit of colour, well that and a bit of taste.'

She looked at Ludek; there was no response.

'I'm going to look out for Maria at the market next week; her mother always used to keep some butter to one side for us, but I haven't seen her for ages. I know she had a soft spot for me after that incident with the policeman, but I haven't been able to find out what happened to her. Maria always has a long queue to her stall, but she might be willing to part with some. If only I could find something to sell, but I don't think she'd be too impressed with the stuff I've got left.'

She chattered away, the words falling like snow on rock.

'What is it, Ludek? Something is obviously worrying you. You hardly slept all night and your eyes are haunted by something. Tell me about it, maybe I can help?'

He shook his head, but as usual she persisted.

'You don't have to give me details, just the gist of what's troubling you.' On and on, she continued, persuasive, insistent, demanding, cajoling, until finally he relented.

'All right, all right, I'll tell you. I have to deliver a gun today. It's for... no, nothing, forget it.'

Chewing pallid lips, his hand combed through his hair.

'Something is wrong, Marta. I can feel it in my guts, but I know it's got to be done.'

She nodded, a plan already forming.

Ludek had been a member of the resistance, the Home Army, since the start of the war. They never discussed the struggle. What was the point? Fear for his safety would never dissuade him from fighting for Poland's liberation.

'Has anything specific happened? Have the Gestapo caught anyone?'

'No, all's been quiet, almost too quiet. The last operation was a dream and the cell's been lying low since...'

His voice trailed away.

He tapped fingers against lips before gnawing at his knuckles. Perspiration covered his forehead.

'I can't let my colleagues down.'

'You won't. I'll do the delivery in your place.'

'You? But you're not...'

'Not what? Not trained? Not patriotic enough? What am I not?'

'Nothing. Would you really do that for me?'

'I would do anything for you.'

She had been chewing on the slice of bread, making every crumb last, but now it was finished.

'Where is the rendezvous?'

'The Planty park, along from the theatre where we used to meet up with Andrzej. Any bench around the oak tree.'

'What time?'

'10am.'

'Better get moving then. Shall I change into something more appropriate?'

'Appropriate? A postman's uniform, perhaps?'

'Perhaps.'

They smiled. Their love for each other was so deep, and had been so bitterly tested, that communication between them was as strong in silence as in the words they enjoyed pitching back and forth.

'Hell, I don't know, Tusik,' he said, using her diminutive name. 'It's a terrible risk.'

'Everything is a terrible risk these days. I could go shopping and they could arrest me in a street round-up. Look, I have no bad feelings. You do. So it makes perfect sense to swap places.'

'Are you sure you're happy about this? No bad dreams?'

'None.'

Marta was generally optimistic about life; only one thing caused her to falter, and that was any dream featuring meat, especially raw meat. The dreams brought bad news in their wake and were never wrong.

Days before war erupted, she woke up in the early hours of the morning sweating and gasping for breath. Heart pounding, eyes wide open, the nightmare scene refused to dissipate: fat men in fancy uniforms jabbed fingers at a map of Europe which transformed into a raw steak, the size of a table. They tore at the flesh and crammed pieces into their mouths, the blood running down their chins, as they turned to look at her.

The scene made her shiver every time it came to mind.

She went to get dressed endeavouring to look smart and efficient with a hint of frivolity. A favourite blouse trimmed with lace, a dark skirt and enough heel to give her additional height but to enable the fast walking she preferred to strolling. She would have loved some jewellery to add to the outfit, a string of pearls perhaps, or a gold chain with a simple cross, but, like everyone else, she had sold the few pieces she owned long ago for bread and other essentials. A glance in the mirror made her frown. No, it was too demure, too secretarial. She went to the wardrobe and pulled out a flowered skirt she had made herself and put that on instead. Although June was invariably hot in Poland, she decided to take a cardigan with her and placed one ready on the bed.

She pirouetted into the room and stopped. Never had she seen him look so sad.

'You are so beautiful.'

'Yes, Pinocchio, that is clear to see.'

'Maybe you don't see it, but I do. I always have and I always will.'

'Especially when I'm old, wrinkled and cantankerous.'

'So, only two things to get used to then.'

'Pah.' She turned away in mock offence, but he pulled her towards him and kissed her, fondling her ears, melting her inside. He looked deep into her eyes.

'Are you absolutely sure about this?'

'Yes, don't keep going on. When will I see you again?' She took hold of his hands and entwined her fingers with his.

'Tonight, I hope.'

'How will I let you know I'm safe?'

'Put something in the window. I'll be able to see it from the street.'

'Mm, I'll put the green vase there. It's tall enough.'

'Oh God, if you do that, then I won't know whether to laugh with joy at your safety or cry with shame at its ugliness. Why don't you get rid of it?'

'Because it's not my vase as you very well know and I'm not about to pay money for replacing it, when my landlady notices it's gone.'

'What about a pile of your beloved books?'

'Good idea. I might even do it tidily.'

'Miracles, I don't expect.'

They both smiled, acknowledging the one difference between them that threatened their domestic harmony.

Ludek moved away to the bed, reached under it and pulled out a parcel wrapped in brown paper and tied up with string.

She stepped back.

'You brought it home last night?'

'Yes, it was safer that way.'

Her face flushed as she glared at him. How dare he decide what was and wasn't safe without consulting her?

'I can't believe I've been sleeping on a gun. What on earth possessed you? What if we'd had a police visit? Didn't you think you were endangering both of us by bringing it here?'

'Marta, this is who I am. This is what I do. It's not a game. I endanger you every time I come here, more so when I spend the night. Would you prefer me to stay away?'

'No, of course not.' But she spoke through clenched teeth and her arms tightened their grip around her.

'Have there been other parcels before?'

'No.'

Her eyebrows shot up.

'Trust me, there have been no other parcels. Look, I had to think on my feet. There was a drunk next to the hiding place who was starting to attract the attention of the police. It really wasn't the best time to say "Excuse me, Officers, may I leave this parcel here?" and then walk away.'

Ludek started prancing around the room, mimicking the actions of a polite fool, negotiating with the police before they frogmarched him away, one arm up behind his back. Annoyed as she was, she giggled, and the tension between them evaporated as quickly as it had developed.

He hugged and kissed her again.

'Thank you for doing this for me. Now I'd better get moving before your landlady returns. Good luck, my darling, I'll be with you the whole time.'

Ludek checked papers and other belongings and glanced round the room to make sure he'd left nothing.

The door closed, and she listened for him going down the stairs, but he was always so quiet she never heard his steps. She opened the drawers of her desk, scrambling through the contents: old notebooks, some receipts, an empty perfume bottle without a stopper, a fountain pen with a broken nib. Eventually, she found it: a small knitted bag containing a mirrored compact, lipstick and mascara.

Teeth brushed at the kitchen sink, she scraped the last bit of lipstick onto her finger and coloured her lips. She spat into the mascara tablet, mixed it around with the brush and applied it.

Satisfied with her appearance, she organised her belongings. Identification papers fitted into one pocket, cigarettes into the other. She rummaged around her bag for some coins; she thought she might treat herself to a coffee at one of the local cafés when the pick-up was complete. Then she draped the cardigan around her shoulders, ran across to the desk and picked up a small box of matches she had been given by a friend visiting Berlin before the war; it bore the name of a famous nightclub and featured a stylised black cat winking against a red background.

Perfect, she thought, picked up the parcel and left. As she ran down the stairs, she kept having to stop to adjust her cardigan as it slipped off her shoulders. Exasperated, she came to a halt and put it on just as the door to one of the ground floor apartments opened.

'Miss Paciorkowska, do you have a minute?'

Damn, thought Marta, just my luck.

'Mrs Wisniewska, you must forgive me, I'm in a terrible hurry and I think I'm going to be late. Mass is at 10 o'clock at the Church of the Holy Trinity, is it not?'

'Oh, well, yes, I believe it is. Another time, perhaps?'

Marta smiled her most charming and regretful smile and left the building feeling a little guilty at her duplicity although glad she hadn't lied. After all, she argued with herself, I didn't say I was actually going to mass at the Holy Trinity. Head held high, shoulders back, she walked briskly, overtaking dawdlers, until she reached the Planty, a green walkway of seamless gardens and open spaces encircling the old town. Krakow was busy with families and especially the elderly making their way to church and for a moment she felt a pang of regret that she wasn't joining them.

She and Ludek no longer practised their faith; the Pope's unwillingness to condemn Hitler and the atrocities he was inflicting on their country appalled them both, but even before that, they had vigorously debated religion in all its forms and even questioned the existence of God.

She pondered how crises seemed to affect people in opposite directions: some turning to the figure of Christ on the cross for comfort while others rejected, with bitterness and anger, the very notion of a loving Creator. But she couldn't completely abandon a faith she had been brought up in and which had sustained her in difficult times; she wondered, ruefully, if her own rejection of religion wasn't down to laziness and enjoying an extra hour in bed.

Once inside the Planty, she walked straight to the rendezvous, chose an empty bench and sat down. There was plenty of time. Nobody appeared to be looking for her. A light breeze caught a strand of hair and blew it into her eyes. She moved it aside and thought about Ludek and the love they shared.

She grinned. The party was buzzing when he walked in, but she noticed him straightaway. Had it been love at first sight? It certainly seemed that way to her, but wait, now she thought about it, she remembered that when they had first been introduced, the attraction, on her part at least, had not been instantaneous. He was handsome enough, blond with sparkling eyes that held your attention, but she remembered thinking he was flawed by a receding hairline which lengthened his face.

Yet, within minutes, she was entranced and would have argued he was perfection itself. Intelligent, funny, sensitive, he made her laugh and made her think and unsettled her in every way. The conversation ranged from literature to art to politics to religion and back again. They talked for hours, sometimes on their own, sometimes inveigling friends to agree with the points they were making: 'Andrzej listen to this nonsense, Tusik claims....' or 'Wanda, can you believe Ludek has never read...' It was intoxicating and when, in the early hours of the morning, Ludek took hold of her hand they had both leapt apart, so electric was the connection between them.

They left the party together and never seemed apart. She marvelled at the way she sensed his presence even when he wasn't there. He was her twin, her soulmate.

The bells from a nearby church struck the hour. Engrossed in happy memories she took a moment to remember why she was sitting in the park with a parcel on her lap. She wanted a cigarette and as she reached into her pocket saw them: two Gestapo officers walking towards her, unmistakable even in their civilian clothes.

2

SHE FROZE. HEART POUNDING, ears thrumming, she took deep breaths. So this was it. Ludek had been right. There had been a tipoff, a leak in security, who knows what human frailty or deliberate evil. She would have to brazen it out.

'Papers.'

'Good morning, gentlemen,' she replied politely in German, reached into her pocket for her papers and handed them over. With a pleasant smile, she continued to calm her breathing and appear unconcerned.

The older man, mid to late 50s, had a natural air of authority. He wasn't tall and showed signs of middle-aged spread, but his posture was good and there was an economy in his movements that made him appear calm, unruffled by life's vicissitudes. The younger one, still suffering from acne, towered over him. He belonged in a classroom; long limbs and a scowling face beneath an unruly mop of hair added to the impression of a schoolboy let loose to create havoc with his mates.

'What's in the parcel?'

'I have no idea. It's a present.'

'A present? That's a new one,' said the youngster with a cackle.

'Hand over the parcel. Now come with us,' said the older man.

'Why? I haven't done anything. My papers are in order.'

'Be quiet.' The younger man snarled.

'We need to ask you some questions. I'm sure you would want to assist in our enquiries.'

'Well, it's not what I planned for my Sunday off, but if you insist.'

'We do.'

She nodded by way of acquiescence and stood up. The men stepped either side of her and they left the park. A black Mercedes was waiting in the street and they manhandled her into the back.

The car moved swiftly through the streets. The musty smell of leather mingled with unwashed armpits as she sank into the leather seats and looked through the windows. Two German officers, talking on a street corner, turned to look, but most people ignored the car and its occupants.

'Goodness, there's Halina. I haven't seen her for ages.' Marta beamed and tried to peer round the guard to see her imaginary friend. He did not react and did not even glance at her.

The car turned into Pomorska Street and stopped outside a tall, five-storey building: Gestapo headquarters. Before the war students from Upper Silesia used to live there and filled the rooms with talk and laughter, arguments and passion.

'Get out.'

She did so, without undue haste, smoothed down her skirt and looked at the building with as much interest as if she were being escorted on a sightseeing tour.

'Don't forget the parcel,' she said, turning and smiling at the older man who was carrying the box.

'Get inside.'

The younger man led her across a hall furnished with swastika banners to a door marked "Duty Officer". He knocked and marched inside. Heil Hitlers echoed into the hall. The older man scrutinised her, head at a slight angle.

Minutes later she stood before a uniformed officer and looked around the room, maintaining an air of insouciance. Instinct told her not to show fear.

'Full name?'

'Marta Antonina Paciorkowska.'

'Address?'

She gave it and sighed.

'Date of birth?'

'29th of September 1919.'

'Religion?'

'Exactly as stated on my papers.'

'Answer my questions without your arrogance, Polish bitch.'

She straightened and lifted her chin as he completed the paperwork.

'The charge?'

'Carrying weapons for the resistance.'

'What?'

Her eyes popped and her head shot forward as if she couldn't believe her ears.

'What are you saying? I'm not in the resistance. Show me the parcel.'

Her voice was getting louder; her hands had come up to her chest and were forming fists as if she would fight them.

'Shut up.'

The uniformed officer got up and yelled. He must have been twice her size, but she stared him down and said through clenched teeth:

'I am not and never have been in the resistance.'

This much was accurate and she hoped her words rang true to their ears.

'I insist you show me the parcel.'

The older man continued to look. She held his gaze with grim determination. After a long pause, he reached over for scissors, cut the string and revealed a box of chocolates made by the renowned Polish firm, Wedel.

'There, see. What a waste of time. Resistance indeed.'

Without taking his eyes off her, he opened the lid of the box and offered her the contents.

'Chocolate, young lady?'

'Thank you.' Marta smiled at him and looked down at the selection to find a handgun wedged into the box.

'Oh, my God. I don't believe it. Tell me it's not true.' She stared at the gun and shook her head, mouth gaped open.

'What do you want to do Inspector?' asked the Duty Officer. 'I can send her over to Monte and we can all get some Sunday rest.'

'Thank you, Karl, but Henni has taken the children to visit relatives so there's no hot meal waiting for me. I may as well start the investigation today.'

'As you wish, Inspector. Take the prisoner.'

The youth gripped her arm and pulled her out of the room.

'Let go. I am not a criminal and have nothing to fear from your questions.'

He pushed her into an adjoining room where a civilian blinked rapidly at the sight of them.

'Photographs and prints and be quick about it.'

'Of course, Sir. At once, Sir.'

The clerk, a slight figure of a man in his mid-forties, collided with the furniture and dropped things as he prepared the equipment. She stared at him. What hold did they have over the poor creature? He asked her to face to the front, to the side and then in-between. When she hesitated, uncertain of his meaning, he reached up with feminine hands and with a soft touch moved her head to give a three quarters view.

Photographs taken, he indicated the ink pad. His actions mesmerised her as he inked each digit and transferred the image onto a printed sheet. It was a strangely intimate procedure.

'Finished, Sir.'

The youth nodded his approval, took Marta roughly by the arm and marched her along before kicking open the door to a small room. The sickly sweet smell of blood tinged with something more acrid pervaded the air.

'Dear God in heaven, what have you done to people in here?'

'You'll find out soon enough,' he said before locking the door.

Tears welling, she noted the stains on the walls, on the floor, on the table, everywhere. She knew only too well what they did to people in here.

'Dear God,' she whispered. 'Be with your people in their hour of need.'

Then she took hold of herself. This is deliberate, she thought. This is designed to break you before they have even started. You must take control of the situation. She closed her eyes, focused her thoughts on Ludek's face and his heart-melting smile and forced herself to relax.

A desk stood in the room, two wooden chairs on one side, a metal one on the other. She pulled out a wooden chair and crossed her legs. Cigarette lit, she breathed what little nicotine it contained deep into her lungs and positioned the packet and the box of matches on the table.

She heard footsteps in the corridor, but they passed by her door. She was halfway through her cigarette and deep in thought when she heard the door being unlocked and the Inspector walked in. He halted and covered his mouth.

'Wait here.'

Sounding exasperated, he left the room and shouted down the corridor.

'Guard the prisoner while I go to the office.'

Many minutes passed before he came back, accompanied by a different uniformed officer and an elderly peasant woman dressed in black from headscarf to flat shoes. The poor woman looked terrified.

'Clean it.' The officer pointed at the table.

Nothing happened.

He shouted the order again and whipped out his pistol, pointing it at the shaking woman.

'May I translate?' Marta asked the Inspector and at a nod did so.

'They want you to clean the table.'

The woman made a hurried sign of the cross and whispered, 'What with?'

She shrugged as she removed her stuff from the table. The woman hesitated, took off her headscarf and proceeded to wipe down the table, spitting at the stains as she bustled round.

Marta saw the horrified expression on the officer's face and had a sudden urge to laugh. How ridiculous he was, disgusted by one bodily fluid when he must know how the table had become stained with another. But the thought of the suffering people had undergone within these four walls sobered her instantly.

Finally, the officer appeared to be satisfied with the woman's cleaning efforts and, after checking with the Inspector, told her to stop and get out.

'You can stop now. You are free to go.'

'May God protect you. I will pray for you.' She made another sign of the cross and fled from the room.

'Now, Miss Paciorkowska...' The Inspector mangled her surname.

'If you would be so kind as to sit opposite we shall proceed.'

Marta stubbed out the remainder of her cigarette on the floor and without saying a word moved across to the metal chair and again placed her cigarettes and the box of matches on the table. She watched as he sat down and settled his papers on the table.

'My name is Criminal Inspector Bauer and I shall be in charge of this investigation.'

'May I smoke?'

'No, Miss Paciorkowska, you may not.'

The tone was stern, but he did not raise his voice as he again mispronounced her surname.

'A cigarette would help mask the nasty smell in here and please call me Marta. It will be easier for you and I don't mind. After all, you have given up your Sunday to interview me and it seems I have given up my Sunday to be interviewed, so we may as well make the situation as pleasant as possible.'

She knew she was taking a risk answering back, but the way he had behaved so far suggested a human being rather than the monsters she knew the Gestapo to be.

There was silence as he considered the matter.

'Be very clear that I am here to ask questions and you are here to answer them. I do most sincerely suggest you co-operate in every way you can, Marta. It will be to your benefit.'

She nodded like an eager pupil, attentive and serious.

'Perhaps you would like to begin by telling me how you came to be carrying a gun.'

'I didn't know I was.'

'And now that you do know?'

'Then I shall do everything I can to assist you.'

'Go on.'

'A man called Artur asked me to do him a favour.'

'Surname?'

'Sorry, I don't know.'

Bauer raised an eyebrow but said nothing, believing from experience that most people, when given enough rope, would hang themselves.

'Continue.'

'Artur wanted me to deliver a present for his mother and promised to get me some butter as a thank you. Well, you can imagine how happy I was to oblige. Butter has been missing from my life for such a long time and wartime bread is so disgusting to eat without it. Mm I do so enjoy butter on my bread.'

She smiled wistfully and looked at him.

'Where and when did you pick up the parcel from this man, Artur?'

'He said someone would deliver it to my home and sure enough I was going out to work yesterday morning and when I opened the door, the parcel was there on the doorstep. There was a little note from Artur asking me to take it to the park today and wait for his cousin who would arrive at around 10am.'

'Not his mother?'

'Oh no, she lives in the countryside somewhere. Besides it's not much of a present if you have to collect it yourself. He mentioned something about her being unwell and wanting to cheer her up.'

'Did you keep the note?'

'I think so. Or wait, did I use it to light the cooker? It's a bit temperamental, my cooker, so I prefer to use a taper rather than matches. I'm not sure. If I didn't use it, then it's still at home.'

'How were you to recognise his cousin?'

'Oh, God, I never even considered that. I imagined he would introduce himself as Artur's cousin and that would be that.'

She giggled.

'Not much of a conspirator, am I? It's that butter you see: the promise of it addled my brain.'

'Describe him.'

'Tall, about the height of the duty officer; dark blond hair and eyes which are a most unusual shade of blue, almost grey; darker around the pupil and lighter towards the edges. He is clean shaven and wears glasses for reading.'

She gave an accurate description of a student friend killed in the first days of the war.

'Anything else.'

'Um, yes, a little scar just beneath his right eye which he got in a fight at school.'

'Where did you meet this Artur?'

'Funnily enough, in the same park where you found me today, possibly even on the same bench. God, that would be ironic.'

'Go on.'

'I was trying to light a cigarette on a windy day and having problems with the matches. Artur came along and offered me a light from his lighter. We talked, and we agreed to meet for a coffee after work that evening.'

'And did you?'

'Meet for coffee? Yes, we did.'

'Where did you go?'

'Oh dear, I don't remember… it was months ago now. Probably at one of the cafés in the main market square, I mean Adolf Hitler Platz, or at the milk bar in Haupstrasse.'

'Where does he work?'

'Sorry, I never asked.'

'How often did you meet?'

'Now and then, once or twice a month.'

'Would you describe him as a friend?'

'No, I wouldn't describe any of them as friends, but I liked him well enough, and he was useful; he introduced me to several German officers.'

'He was familiar with German officers?'

'Oh yes. He seemed so friendly with them I wondered if he was in some kind of black market racket.'

'Are you suggesting officers of the Third Reich would undertake criminal activities?'

'Heaven forbid, no.'

She widened her eyes to look appalled at the suggestion but caught the glimmer of a smile on Bauer's face.

'I only meant that Artur seemed wealthy considering he's a Pole. Although perhaps he has German ancestors and counts as one of your honorary Germans or Volksdeutsche. They're allowed butter as part of their rations, aren't they?'

'If he wasn't a friend, how would you describe him?'

'A client.'

'A client? What do you mean?'

'Somebody you would entertain.'

Bauer raised an eyebrow.

'Perhaps you had better explain.'

'This is embarrassing, Inspector, especially as you are a family man.'

She stared at the floor and remembered an occasion when she had behaved so badly towards a dear friend it always made her cheeks flush. The memory did not fail her now, and her face reddened.

'The first time it happened my landlord was threatening to evict me because I was behind with the rent. This was in Warsaw before I moved here. A German soldier offered to buy me a drink, and I agreed. He was a nice person, hated the war, seemed to sympathise with our plight as an occupied nation. He was handsome too and interested in the finer things of life: music and art and suchlike. One drink led to another and then one thing led to another. Then, afterwards, he paid me. At first I didn't want to take the money, but his cash saved me from eviction. And if they'd thrown me out on the streets, perhaps I would have to do this for a living.'

'And you don't now?'

'No, it's quite a bit different to that.'

Dear God, what would her sainted mother, her beloved Mamusia, have said to witness her debase herself like this and tell these hideous lies?

She bit her lower lip and blinked back tears. He had been watching her, but now cleared his throat and returned to making notes.

'This was supposed to be a gift, but it wasn't very well wrapped, just some old, crinkled brown paper. Didn't that make you suspicious?'

'Not really. Most people reuse any paper they've got. I would be more suspicious if it had fancy new wrapping and I wouldn't have been comfortable carrying it. Nobody wants to draw attention to themselves on the streets.'

'Did it not strike you as odd he would ask you to pass on a package to his cousin to give to his mother? Why didn't he visit her himself when he had gone to the trouble of buying her a gift?'

'Yes, that does seem odd.'

Marta frowned as she considered the matter.

'All I can say is that he made it sound entirely plausible. He had business to attend to, would visit her later but wanted to show he cared about her in the meantime. Something like that. I wasn't suspicious for a second and I was certain he would be as good as his word about the butter so I didn't much care if he was telling the truth or not.'

'And what about you? Are you telling the truth?'

'I think you know the answer to that, Inspector.'

She looked at him without blinking and without further comment for what was probably seconds but seemed like minutes. Eventually, she lowered her gaze suspecting that any more emphasis on her truthfulness would be counterproductive.

The Inspector put down his pen and leaned back.

'Your German is remarkably fluent. Did you learn it at school?'

'Oh no, I didn't learn German until life resumed a degree of normality.'

'Normality? That seems a strange word to use in the circumstances.'

'It means I couldn't see the point of learning anything while your troops were bombing the hell out of my city.'

'You don't regard Krakow as your city?'

'Now it is, but Warsaw was where I was born and grew up. People have a special attachment, or perhaps you would call it nostalgia, towards a place they grew up in and it is, or what's left of it, a beautiful city.'

'So why did you move here?'

'When I was visiting friends, the chance of a permanent job came up. It was difficult to find work in Warsaw and it seemed too good an opportunity to turn down.'

Inspector Bauer looked at his notes.

'You work as a tram conductress.'

'That's right.'

'A lowly job for a university graduate.'

'I didn't graduate. The war saw to that.' A mixture of sadness and bitterness filled her voice.

'What were you studying?'

'Psychology. I wanted to work with problem children.'

'Perhaps one day you will.'

The throwaway comment inspired her to make an impassioned case for being allowed to return to her studies. She had to take every opportunity to make Bauer think of her as a human being with thoughts and feelings, ambitions and desires, rather than just a case with a number and no hope.

'How does it help the Third Reich to prevent people fulfilling their potential? War causes so much suffering in all the nations involved. How many children in Germany have suffered bereavement because their fathers died at the front? Death, particularly violent death, is not good for the psyche and children are the ones who suffer most.

'So it makes sense to allow psychologists to practise their healing wherever they exist, be that in Germany or elsewhere in Germany's empire. The children need to heal if they are not to develop psychological problems. It is such a waste to stop trained people working and equally wasteful to stop students completing their studies in vital subjects. Wouldn't you agree?'

Inspector Bauer had been leaning back in his chair, hands intertwined behind his neck and staring up at the ceiling, when a sudden realisation hit him with the force of a punch. What made him assume he was safe here in these unfamiliar Gestapo headquarters? Prying eyes and ears alert for disloyalty, hid everywhere. He barked his response.

'Don't be ridiculous young lady. First, the Fuehrer thoroughly disapproves of psychologists. The books of Jewish mind doctors fuelled the bonfires first and rightly so. Second, German families will look after German children with no help from Jews or Slavs, thank you very much.'

'Oh,' she said and her mouth remained open.

There was a knock at the door and the officer who had supervised the cleaning stepped inside.

'Excuse me, Inspector Bauer, but Criminal Director Fuchs would like a word.'

'It seems everyone is giving up their Sunday,' said Bauer as he gathered his papers and followed the officer.

Seconds later she jumped up, punched the air and grinned. She lit up and inhaled. Smoke enveloped her as she puffed away, replaying the conversation from the beginning. She squinted as her tongue played with a strand of tobacco. Had the interrogation gone well or badly? She frowned as she chewed her lower lip.

3

CRIMINAL DIRECTOR FUCHS RADIATED good humour. Lubricated by coffee and cognac, he planned an extended lunch. Visiting the office, as he did at odd moments to keep everyone on their toes, he beamed to find his newly acquired inspector hard at work.

'Come in, come in', he called out. Bauer found him leaning back in his comfortable chair, small feet up on his desk, with small hands folded over his substantial stomach. He looked like an upturned toad. He responded to Bauer's crisp Heil Hitler with a giggly voice and half-hearted gesture, never shifting from his chair.

'What have you been up to this morning?'

Bauer summarized Marta's arrest and interrogation.

'Is she on our list?'

'No, Sir.'

'Is she beautiful? Slav women can be stunning.'

'She's attractive, but not what I would call a conventional beauty,' said Bauer, wondering where this line of questioning was leading.

'They say beauty is in the eye of the beholder.' He mopped his brow with a handkerchief; his thinning hair drenched with sweat.

'You should have seen some of the Jews we rounded up in Krakow at the beginning. There was one in particular: dark hair, olive green eyes, perfect skin with the faintest blush of colour on her high cheek bones.'

He had pulled rank on the officer in charge and taken her away for questioning.

Bauer noticed the bulge developing and dismissed his boss as another middle-aged lecher.

'Still, weeds can be very attractive, can't they? I'm fond of dandelions. Used to spend hours as a child telling the time with them. Have you ever done that?'

His face assumed a childlike quality.

'My grandmother used to look after me and taught me the game. Blow on the seed head, Willie, and tell me the time. I must have blown thousands of seeds all over the place–a complete nightmare for any gardener.'

He laughed and Bauer nodded as enthusiastically as seemed polite but couldn't take his eyes off Fuchs's tiny childlike teeth. Stuck between thick pink lips they looked obscene and reminded him of piranha fish devouring bait in Berlin's aquarium.

'Are you a gardener, Bauer? No? Me neither. Anyway, where was I? Oh yes, weeds. No matter how pleasing to the eye you wouldn't hesitate to root them out and throw them on the compost heap, would you? Not when you're trying to establish the most perfect garden in the world. Weeds in paradise? Perish the thought.'

He ordered his driver to take them to a clearing in the forest, made her strip at gunpoint. Revelling in her beauty, he took his time raping her. When he finished, she spat in his face. She would never do that again.

Fuchs moved his feet off the desk and rearranged the pens on his desk in a businesslike manner. His voice hardened and took on a menacing edge.

'So what do you make of this woman?'

'Mm, it's difficult to say at this stage.' Bauer didn't want to commit himself too early.

'But your gut feel? Your famous gut feel?'

Bauer exhaled, forcing out his lips and turned to look at Fuchs. The man's eyes had narrowed to dark slits stressed by his florid face. Swastika colours. He had to tread carefully but also needed to show trust.

'I think someone has set her up.'

'A lover who's tired of her, perhaps, and wants us to do their dirty work. It happens.'

'As you say, it happens.' Bauer's tone was deferential, although his meaning had been different. 'How do you want me to proceed, Sir?'

'Carry on with the investigation. Bring Friedman in on it. Have you met Friedman? No, that's right, he's away on leave for some family matter or other, back next week if memory serves me right. The man's keen on promotion so let him have his head on this one, under your direction.'

'Yes, Sir.'

'And now you must join me for lunch. I shall show you the delights of the Hotel Imperium.'

'And the prisoner?'

'Leave her where she is. We're not expecting any more visitors today so the room won't be required. We could always do with more information and a period of solitude in our little sanatorium may yet loosen her tongue.'

'Thank you. Henni has taken the children to visit relatives, so I wasn't expecting a proper meal today.'

'Yes, Karl mentioned it. Well, I recommend the pork escalope and the wine is exceptional, unless you're more of a beer man.'

'Oh I'm keen on beer and wine.'

'Excellent,' replied Fuchs, his volatile mood once again sociable and expansive.

The two men left the building together, chatting about the best meals they had consumed.

They walked for the best part of an hour. Fuchs, who was grossly overweight, kept stopping to point out landmarks or share gossip or catch his breath. Both men were hungry when they entered the bustling interior.

The hotel manager greeted Fuchs effusively and showed them to a table by the long windows overlooking the gardens. Fuchs excused himself to talk with friends at another table while Bauer took in his surroundings with a practised eye.

The ubiquitous swastika banners hung from the walls and a portrait of Hitler, flatteringly painted in oils, dominated the space over a large baroque fireplace. Crisp white linen covered the round tables placed discreetly apart and laid with crystal glasses, monogrammed plates and silver cutlery.

It was a high-class establishment and red leather bindings with gold lettering and golden tassels revealed an extensive menu and wine list. He hadn't eaten in such an exclusive restaurant since taking Henni out to celebrate their first wedding anniversary in Berlin all those years ago.

He had already noted the exit points of the restaurant, an automatic response from his policing days. Now he turned his attention to his fellow diners: SS men; members of the German army; businessmen and half a dozen wives or mistresses and one or two girls of easy virtue as his mother would have called them.

Watching these prostitutes from a distance made him reassess his prisoner. Was she what she claimed to be? Or was she leading him a merry dance? She was, as he had told Fuchs, attractive without being a conventional beauty. Luminous brown eyes were her most noticeable feature that and thick chestnut brown hair cut just above her shoulders; she had an aquiline nose and a small gap between her front teeth. Even in the confines of an interrogation cell she was an animated companion and seemed unaware of the danger she was in.

He had noticed the careful make-up, the colourful skirt and neat blouse, the slight heels on well-polished, if worn, shoes. They all suggested class. Well, why not? Not every prostitute had to be the blowzy, loud-mouthed specimens the police picked up off the streets; the ones in the dining room today were probably from decent homes. Goodness knows, the war had forced people into all manner of compromises and although illegal it wouldn't have remained the oldest profession without the connivance of his male colleagues.

The wholesome beauty of his wife Henni and their shared joy in their children left Bauer pretty much immune to the sexual charms of other women, but he recognised that his prisoner had possibilities in that department, especially if the man wanted something more than just a physical release, such as intelligent conversation, humour, companionship.

He was inclined to believe her story and rely on his gut instinct, the famous gut instinct as Fuchs had sarcastically described it. Now what did he mean by that? His new boss worried him. Mercurial by nature and concealing what Bauer suspected was a cruel streak, he could prove an enemy he didn't need in his new situation. He would have to play this one carefully.

Minutes later Fuchs returned to his seat. A waiter, scanning the room as he went about his duties, came to take their orders. Beers and a fine bottle of wine soon graced their table, followed by generous, appetising dishes of meats and vegetables.

'This is a magnificent place; I could get used to eating here,' said Bauer.

'Enjoy it while you can.'

Bauer raised an eyebrow and inclined his head forward, certain that a confidence would be forthcoming. Fuchs did not disappoint him.

'The Tommies are making headway in France.'

'Ah.' Bauer leant back and nodded. This wasn't the place, or the chosen companion, to offer his analysis of the war. Fuchs was unperturbed, however, whether from an excess of brandy or because he regarded the hotel as his natural stamping ground and lectured his subordinate on the shortcomings of current military strategy.

'We should have left Brother Ivan alone and invaded Britain first. They're not a bright people, the British. I swear we've got more intelligent cleaners in our smallest villages than they have brains in their entire government. Maybe not Churchill but aside from him there's nobody. They're cowards too, couldn't manage anything on their own, need the bloody Americans behind them.'

Bauer shifted in his chair. He had seen Tommy courage at first hand during the Great War, but he wasn't going to disagree with his new boss. Nodding approval of his invective seemed the safest policy; he filled the man's glass with wine as soon as it was empty and chewed his own food to prevent a two-way conversation.

By the end of the meal Bauer was exhausted, not only by the onslaught on his ears but also the necessity, as he saw it, of preventing his boss making a fool of himself in public. Although he now regarded Fuchs as dangerous, he knew any humiliation would reflect just as badly on him. He suppressed a yawn and rubbed his eyes.

Desperate to change the subject, he remembered his boss's lascivious nature and pointed out one or two of the more attractive females. Fuchs responded with a clownish wink at his companion.

'You've got a good eye, Bauer, I'll give you that. Or should I call it your gut instinct? Or does it come lower than that?'

Fuchs roared with laughter and gave Bauer a playful poke in the ribs. One or two diners looked round but were quick to smile at Fuchs's infectious enjoyment of his own wit. Bauer played along with a broad grin and an embarrassed shake of his head.

The waiter reappeared at that moment to ask if the gentlemen would like to order anything else and the interruption enabled Bauer to say he needed to be getting home as Henni and the children would be back and expecting him. He offered to pay for the lunch but

Fuchs, still smiling and in high good humour, waved him away.

'No, no, the treat is all mine. I'll just have a brandy and then I'll be setting off for home too. Give my warmest regards to your wife.'

'Thank you, Sir. It's been a real pleasure.'

Once in the hotel foyer, he asked to use the telephone and told the operator to put him through to Gestapo headquarters.

'Duty Officer.'

'Is that you, Karl? It's Bauer here. Would you arrange to send my prisoner to the holding prison? Yes, that's right. No, don't order a car, she can wait until one becomes available. Yes, that will be all. Thank you, Karl. Heil Hitler.'

He asked the doorman to point him in the right direction for Wawel Castle and set off at a brisk walk. The family's large apartment was a stone's throw from the castle, now used as the headquarters of the Central Government.

Henni was supervising the children's tea when Bauer turned his key in the lock.

'Papa!' There were squeals of delight from his two youngest children as they threw themselves at him; only his eldest was more restrained in her greeting which she followed with an earnest Heil Hitler.

'Papa?'

'Yes, Monika.'

'I've been wondering…'

'Yes?'

'We don't have a portrait of the Fuehrer in our apartment here. We should get another one, just like the one we had back home in Berlin, don't you agree, Papa?'

'Ah yes, that was a superb portrait, wasn't it? Your mother purchased it in Berlin and that's a long way to go. We must ask her to find another one in Krakow.'

'Uncle Albrecht and Aunty Magda have an enormous one hanging in their living room. I'm sure they'll be able to tell Mama where to buy one.'

'Didn't you ask them yourself while you were there today?'

'No.' She sounded disappointed in herself.

'Don't worry, Monika. I'm sure your mother will find out. Now will you take the younger children into the other room and play with them so I can talk to your mother in peace and quiet?'

'Yes, Papa.'

'Thank you, Monika, and close the door behind you please.'

Bauer had one eyebrow raised as he went to greet his wife.

'How was Albrecht? And Magda?'

'We had a lovely day. The children enjoyed it.' Henni waited until the door closed on the children and she heard the piano being played before she relaxed enough to speak as frankly as she dared.

'Oh Heinz, Albrecht has become a stranger to me. We've led such different lives for so many years now. I used to have a real connection with him but not anymore. Still, one thing hasn't changed: it's still the Fuehrer this and the Fuehrer that, all said with complete loyalty and conviction.'

'Just as it should be.'

'Yes. And it seems we need not worry about the outcome of the war or anything else because Hitler has our future safe in his hands.'

'Good, that is reassuring.'

'Oh and guess what? Magda is pregnant again. Their eighth baby in almost as many years.'

'Goodness, well I must remember to congratulate them when I see them,' he said, hoping the occasion would never arise. 'Eight? That must be the gold cross, then.'

'Yes, she's already got the bronze and silver on display for everyone to admire.'

Bauer rubbed his wife's shoulder. 'I'm sorry, my love, perhaps if we were younger.'

'Oh never mind about that. There are worse things to worry about, like my parents.'

'Oh?'

Bauer realised that age and anxiety were catching up with his beloved wife. A deep frown marked her forehead and little lines edged her cornflower blue eyes while grey hairs were dulling her golden locks. He noticed too little pouches under her eyes but rather than be repulsed, he loved her all the more and wanted to take her in his arms and protect her from the world.

'We spent quite a lot of time talking about them and Albrecht doesn't appreciate how old they are or how difficult they're finding it to manage on the farm.'

'That worries you, doesn't it?'

'Yes. In fact I've been wondering if there's anything we can do about it.'

'Such as...'

'Early retirement.'

'Albrecht's? I don't imagine he'll agree to that for a single second.'

'No, silly, yours.'

Bauer smiled. 'Yes, I did rather suppose you meant me. I can't do anything for a while. We can't let Albrecht down when he's been kind enough to help us.'

'No, I understand that, but they must release people on compassionate grounds.'

'Well, like I said, I'll look into it. I enjoyed helping your father when I stopped with you at Christmas. If he's still able to keep running things, then I could provide the labour.'

'Yes, and I could do my bit, besides helping Mama around the house, and the older Tomas gets the more useful he'll be around the farm and he does so love being there.'

'Yes, he's a young farmer in the making.'

'Thank you, Heinz. You're a good man.'

'Am I? In that case, why don't you join me on the sofa, with a small glass of schnapps, while we watch the children play?'

'Give me five minutes to clear up and I'll be through to join you.'

Together, enjoying their children's sense of fun, Henni felt a small spark of hope they might escape the surrounding madness. Let the Albrechts and Magdas of this world continue Hitler's vision; she wanted none of it anymore.

She blushed at the naïve entries she'd made in her diary just a few months ago; how she had hoped her Jewish friend, Mrs Rose, had found somewhere nice to go to. Could she have been that stupid?

In her diary she had wanted answers to questions she didn't dare ask out loud, but Albrecht had provided all the answers, without even being asked. She didn't want to talk to Heinz about the horrors her brother had described without compunction; there would be time enough for that when the war was over. She prayed Heinz was unaware of all these orders Hitler had issued because she wasn't sure how such knowledge would affect their marriage and her feelings for him. Sometimes it was better not to know.

4

It was late when they ordered her out of the foul, airless cell and manhandled her into another make of car which smelt of pee and worse. She slumped in the back and couldn't stop yawning, great ungainly yawns she barely covered with her hand. A high wall topped with barbed wire and broken glass surrounded Montelupich prison, a place she had hoped never to see again. She groaned and tried to stretch, bracing herself for the next interview. The sleepless night with Ludek, the strain of maintaining an act of injured innocence, the hours of waiting, no wonder she felt shot. She craved a bed and oblivion.

Gates opened. They marched her up to the red-bricked building and pushed her inside the door. The prison's duty officer turned out to be a small, dapper man, with slicked back, dark brown hair and glasses he kept pushing up his thin nose, accompanying every push with a little sniff. Was it a cold from the damp surroundings or an affectation? He kept a running commentary as he noted her details in black ink in a large black book.

'Do you have a bag, my dear?'

'No.'

'Empty the contents of your pockets.'

She handed over the keys to her flat, loose change and the remaining matches. The black cat continued to wink at her but the Inspector never noticed their German origin.

'Everything looks innocent, my dear. No doubt you are innocent; prisoners always are, I find, not that I listen to a word they say, but I want to keep things pleasant while I can.'

A burly woman entered the room through a side door and stood, arms folded across her formidable chest.

'Ah yes, Klara, thank you. Strip search the prisoner.'

She gasped. The woman gave a mocking laugh and moved towards her. Marta stepped back.

'Not in here, Klara.'

Klara stopped. She moved like a robot.

'Follow her please.'

Legs turned to cement. Surely there hadn't been a strip search last time?

An almighty thwack of wood against metal made her jump: 'Move right now or you'll regret it.'

In a separate room filled with filing cabinets, the automaton ordered her to remove her clothes. Face coloured scarlet, she held back tears. Nakedness in front of strangers was unbearable.

She handed over her cardigan and Klara checked the seams turning the sleeves inside out.

'Why are you waiting? Take off your clothes.'

'But it's cold in here.'

Klara narrowed her eyes: 'Do I care?'

She examined every item of clothing, dropping it onto a pile on the floor. Marta watched every movement to make sure she didn't find anything. At a dismissive nod, she grabbed the clothes and dressed in seconds.

'Find anything?'

'No.'

'In that case we'll find you a nice room for the night in our lovely little hotel.' He winked at her as he waved a big bunch of keys in her face.

Her stomach flipped wondering if he had seen her humiliation through a peep hole. She did not react to his feigned humour and stood aside to let him pass.

'This way, my dear.'

They stopped outside a cell which unlocked to show a long, narrow room with a tiny, barred window. Her spirits sank to a new low as she noted a dirty mattress on the floor, a pail with a tin lid in the corner by the door.

'Well, good night, my dear.'

The mattress gave off a musty, unpleasant odour of sweat and soiled linen. Her stomach grumbled, but she longed instead for another cigarette. Crouched on the bedding, she prayed for Ludek's safety but her mind remained uneasy. How bad was the betrayal? Had they captured him too? Was this deception in vain?

And the interrogation? What changed its mood? What made an ordinary man with a sense of humour explode into a grim, hard voiced, gimlet eyed disciple of Hitler? Did it mean the end of polite conversation and the start of... torture?

She shivered, hands clammy. Eighteen months earlier brutal suffering racked her body as she went into induced labour weeks after her due date. But it was already too late. Sweat poured off her body as she writhed on the bed and screamed like a wild animal. Excruciating, unfathomable pain tore her apart. She clutched the sides of the bed as she roared for mercy. The nurses and doctors, appearing and disappearing from the bedside, tried to help with their limited resources. They darted ominous looks at each other which she registered somewhere deep in her delirious state. An injection made her black out. When she regained consciousness Ludek was there clasping her hand. She didn't need to ask: his red-eyed, blotchy face said everything.

'A boy, a beautiful boy.'

'Bring him to me.'

'Tusik, I can't. They've taken him away.'

She gripped his hand with the strength of a maniac.

'Bring him here if it's the last thing you do on this earth.'

Frightened by her reaction, he ran out.

An hour passed while she moaned at every movement.

Ludek returned empty-handed.

'They..um..Oh God, Tusik, a nurse will fetch him from…'

'Where?'

'Nothing.'

She cradled the dead child in her arms, smoothing the blond hair, kissing his eyelids, his lips, his cheeks, his forehead, his cold, oh so cold hands.

The physical pain continued for weeks but nothing compared to the mental anguish. Swollen eyes gushed rivers of tears; they clung to each other in grief, despair, bewilderment and love. Ludek stayed at her side, the resistance forgotten, as he sought to comfort her and she him. Whole days passed in a dense fog where movement slowed to a stop and time held no meaning.

Friends rallied round with food and practical help and kindness shown in a hundred different ways until slowly, imperceptibly, body and soul started to heal; the tears flowed less readily; the mind looked forward; they began to hope. They even talked of having another baby, not yet, but in a better, brighter future.

She never forgot the fair-haired, blue-eyed boy they removed from her exhausted body but in moments of clarity consoled herself that fate had spared them a greater grief.

The Nazis abducted Aryan looking babies, even ripping them from their mothers' breasts, sending them to Germany. Her broken heart would mend: other mothers suffered far greater torments than her own.

Guards switched off the bare light bulb hanging from the ceiling. Sleep overwhelmed her and the night passed.

* * *

She squatted over the bucket in the semi-light; when she heard movement and voices in the corridor, she finished her business quickly and stood alongside the mattress. Two men, prisoners, filled a metal cup with steaming fluid from a cauldron and handed her a piece of thick, grey bread.

'Polish?' asked one man.

'When did they bring you in?'

'Last night.'

'Good luck to you. Enjoy the so-called coffee.'

'You don't have a cigarette by any chance?'

'Sorry. We'll try to get hold of one.'

Their kindness sent a warm wave through her.

Dipping the bread in ditch coloured water, she chewed it a morsel at a time, eating to stay alert.

The day stretched out. Monday. She worked the late shift. Would the Gestapo inform the tramways of her arrest? Should she ask? Would anybody care? Did she care?

Oh heavens. To be so helpless and so alone. There was nothing to do. She walked the length and breadth of her cell several times. Twice as long as wide. Then as sunlight streamed in through the window, she noticed the markings on the wall.

Men's names; women's names; dates of arrest; updates such as 'sent to Auschwitz' or 'executed by the enemy, date unknown' caught her eye. How long had people been incarcerated in here, she wondered, as her fingers traced the entire Lord's Prayer carved in neat, capital letters on the pitted surface?

In another place, she found Poland's national anthem, written in pencil in a flowing, cursive hand, as if penned on expensive notepaper instead of a rough wall.

Poland has not perished yet
So long as we still live.
That which foreign force has seized
We at sword point shall retrieve.
March, march, Dabrowski!
From Italy to our Polish land.
Let us now unite the nation
Under Thy command.

She sang the words imagining the Polish legions created in Italy in 1797 and commanded by General Dabrowski. Under Napoleon's leadership they believed they were fighting for Poland's independence. It was not to be.

The never-ending desire for freedom choked her. What a fraud she was sharing this space with true patriots. She loved her country, she did not doubt it, and sought inspiration in the sacrifices of her fellow countrymen, but she was a coward. Love for Ludek had brought her here not love of country.

She hated the Nazis and everything they stood for and yet she never joined the resistance. Did resistance in small ways count? Free rides on the tram when nobody watched, was that in the same league as blowing up communication stations or couriering vital information to the Allies? Hardly.

At university in Warsaw her outrage knew no bounds when Poland tried to introduce the segregation of Jewish students. She fought against the authorities with a passion equal to those of her friends. Whether from determination or sheer numbers, they won: Jew and non-Jew continued to attend the psychology lectures side by side.

Perhaps that was the problem: treacherous people lived in every country. That didn't lessen the evil of occupation, but it made her less inclined to view any nation, even her own, as right. After all, she recollected with a sudden flare of anger, wasn't it a Pole who had brought her to Montelupich three years ago?

God how furious she had been, stopped on the streets of Krakow, by a Polish policeman dressed in the navy blue uniform that gave them their nickname of 'Navy Blues' or 'Granatowy'. A much too well-fed, boiled potato face, gave away his political leanings without the additional swastika badges on his uniform. There appeared to be something wrong with his watery blue eyes, which never stopped moving as he accosted her.

'Madam, you are an Israelite.'

'What are you saying?' She sounded as puzzled by the turn of phrase as the accusation itself.

'Come, my little Jewish maiden, I know just the place for you.'

With that he grabbed her arm with one hand and placed the other on his holster.

'And don't even think about running away. Nothing would give me greater pleasure than to shoot you and save us a lot of trouble.'

He marched her down the street as she berated him all the way. She demanded his name and when he wouldn't give it to her, used the number on his uniform.

'So, Mr 165, is this the way you earn your living? You round up innocent citizens as they go about their business? You're not fit to be a policeman, let alone a Pole, how dare you dishonour your nation?'

On and on she went, driven by fury rather than fear, until they arrived at the police station.

'Found another one, Sergeant, walking the streets in broad daylight. Unbelievable, isn't it? Build them a nice ghetto where they can be together and look how they thank us. They are the limit.'

'Well your timing is impeccable There's transport out the back ready to leave as soon as Adam's finished his tea.'

With the mention of transport, Marta swallowed hard, her heart thumped and her guts tightened.

'Where are you taking me? I am not a Jew.'

Both men looked at her bemused.

Through clenched teeth, she repeated: 'I am not a Jew. Why won't you listen?'

'Dear lady, please calm yourself. If you are not Jewish, you have nothing to fear. They will check your papers and let you go.' The oily tone did nothing to reassure her.

Potato face sneered.

'Not Jewish? I can sniff out your lot with a blocked up nose. You stink.'

'I told you. I am not a Jew.'

'Know what? If you look like a Jew and walk like a Jew and smell like a Jew, the chances are you are a bleeding Jew.'

Both men guffawed. Sick to the pit of her stomach, she lurched sideways and leant against a wall. The realisation her immediate future, possibly her entire fate, lay in the stupidity and malevolence of men such as these made her scalp prickle and dried her mouth to ash.

Inside the sharp-edged, rusty prison van, she sat on a splintered bench alongside three other women; two sat on the opposite side. One clutched a rosary and rocked back and forth while moving her fingers through the beads much too fast. Similar shades of blonde made her wonder if they shared the same hairdresser and then, more grimly, how soon their dark roots would show. The doors shut, and their eyes adjusted to darkness. The driver moved off like a rally driver and they crashed into each other at every corner and braced themselves with their feet and arms. They arrived bruised and shaken.

They took her papers and belongings while they screamed at her for not responding fast enough to their questions and orders. One woman translated their demands until they told her to shut her mouth and slapped her so hard Marta blanched in horror. Minutes later they shoved them through a door into a large room.

The lock-up was in semi darkness with no windows and only one bare lightbulb lit the space. As her eyes became accustomed to the gloom, she discerned twenty or thirty women. There was another door half way down one wall and in the furthest corner buckets she assumed to be the source of the stench.

Some inmates looked at the new arrivals, others carried on their whispered conversations without a glance; the atmosphere in the room vibrated quiet despair. Most of the inmates were Jewish, she was certain of that. She turned to the woman who now sported a bright red mark on her cheek.

'Thank you for trying to help me. I am so sorry they did that to you.'

'It's nothing to what they have done to others in here.'

'Have you been here before?'

'No, but it's not a secret.'

She fell silent as shame and regret flooded through her. Everyone knew life for Jewish people had become unbearably hard. From the beginning of the occupation, those wearing the Star of David invited ridicule at best or a sadistic beating at worst and every shade of humiliation in between.

But what could she have done in the circumstances? She would never have turned away someone asking for her help, she felt sure of that, but to pay too much attention to what was going on, or comment on it, or actually intervene, was to guarantee the same treatment for yourself.

Like everyone else, she was desperate to survive.

When they set up the ghettos and started the transports and the rumours circulated about their ultimate destination, then pity abounded but the courage to do more, in her case at least, proved lacking. Difficult enough to risk your own life, but if they caught you, they rounded up and killed your entire family. It wasn't a decision anyone took lightly.

An organisation called Zegota and countless individuals sought to help them. Although she always donated money – and God knows she had little enough of that – she didn't get involved. And now here she was sharing their fate. Would she have done differently if she had known she would end up here? On balance she thought not and shame overwhelmed her.

The other prisoner sensed her inner turmoil.

'What's your name?' Her voice was matter-of-fact but not unfriendly.

'Marta. And yours?'

'Pola.'

5

'LISTEN, MARTA, LET ME give you some advice. Try to learn German if you can. When they interrogate you, they will make you pay for a translator and you'll never know if they've allocated you a decent human being or one who has sold his soul to our new masters and will say anything to please them. If you're familiar with the language, you stand a better chance.'

'Pay for a translator? But what if you have no money?'

'They go after family or friends. They always get what they want.'

'Will you teach me?'

Pola said nothing for a moment.

'Please and if there is anything I can do to help you, I will do it.'

'Help the others. They need it more than me, but I will teach you as much as I can.'

'Thank you. Can we start now?'

'Goodness, you're keen.' Pola laughed, attracting attention from the prisoners nearby and then she spoke loudly enough to be heard across the room.

'German lessons starting here for anyone interested.'

Somebody spat and muttered an expletive, but several came alongside as Pola sat down with Marta.

'We'll start with the obvious commands such as empty your pockets, hand over your papers, stand over there.'

They spent the next few hours learning by rote.

'Enough. Absorb what you have learned so far. We'll continue again tomorrow.'

Marta thanked her again and stood up, stretching arms and legs. She felt tired and desperate for a cigarette but pleased at how much they had managed to cover. As she walked around the room, she noticed the woman from the prison van clutching her rosary.

Kneeling down, she said: 'Excuse me, Madam. My name is Marta and I don't have my rosary. May I use yours while we pray together?'

The woman looked with narrowed eyes and her grip tightened.

'I won't steal it from you.'

The woman shrugged and looked away, as if to say what did it matter when they had already stolen everything of value, but she held out the rosary.

Marta took it reverently and holding the crucifix, made the sign of the cross saying, 'In the name of the Father and of the Son and of the Holy Ghost, Amen.' The woman imitated the actions in silence.

Still holding onto the crucifix, she said the Apostles' Creed. No reaction. When she moved onto the first bead the woman joined in. As she said the words, the familiar rocking motion began and Marta moved a hand across to stop her.

When they finished the prayer, she moved onto the next bead and they both said the Hail Mary in unison. She was humbled to see how many women were joining in the prayers.

When they finished, the woman waited until the small crowd dispersed, then held the crucifix.

'The sign of the cross and then?'

'The Apostles' Creed,' she said and taught her the words. She was a diligent pupil and by nightfall was reciting the creed in full.

'Will you come and pray with me tomorrow?'

'Yes, of course.' Sympathy spread through her body as she vowed to do more.

Pola was deep in conversation with another prisoner, heads bent towards each other. Something drew her to the older woman's open, round face and the way she held herself, upright without being stiff like a sunflower turning to the light. She estimated her to be in her late thirties, or early forties, and was certain that the long, caramel coloured hair, plaited down her back, was genuine, matching darker eyebrows and blue-grey eyes.

Not wanting to interrupt, she looked for a place to settle. There was a small space alongside one wall and she sat down, leaning back against the damp brickwork; eyes closed, she repeated the German words and phrases.

The door was unlocked and against the brighter light of the corridor she watched as two burly men threw in a ragged bundle which smacked to the floor. Pola was the first up.

'What is it?'

'Not what, but who?'

With gentle care, Pola lifted away bloody rags. When she revealed the bloody, swollen face, eyes closed in purple pouches, tears welled in Marta's eyes.

'Oh God,' she whispered.

'Not now, Marta, you can pray later. Help make her more comfortable.'

Pola's voice broached no argument and Marta pulled herself together and did as she was directed. She took off her cardigan and folded it as a pillow beneath the woman's head lifting it a fraction with the same infinite care she had seen Pola use. She helped to arrange her arms and legs to aid recovery and covered her with a shawl donated by another prisoner.

'That's all we can do. We'll assess the damage when she comes round.'

Marta nodded, unable to speak. A short while later, the door opened again, and the guards pointed to two women.

Not again, she thought, unable to bear it. But the callout turned out to be routine as they left to collect the prisoners' supper of bread and an urn with two metal cups to share out the contents.

She waited and received a small piece of bread and some lukewarm brown liquid that could have been anything. Unable to forget the image of the swollen face, she ate mechanically. Sleep did not come easily that night, and she tossed and turned on the hard floor, often blinking eyes wide open in terror, conscious of a constricting lump in her throat and a weight pressing down on her chest.

When morning came, a deep sleep brought vague, terrifying images and a sense of foreboding.

Somebody shook her shoulders, and she awoke startled. Pola was sitting next to her with a steaming mug and a piece of bread.

'Here, drink it while it's hot. It'll do you good. Don't linger over it or they'll get annoyed about the mug.'

The warm liquid seeped into her stomach. She gave back the mug and chewed the bread. Pola handed back her cardigan.

'She didn't make it. The internal injuries were too grievous.'

'Oh.' Deflated she made the sign of the cross and prayed.

Later that morning, Pola announced her German lessons, and a harsh voiced old woman answered from the other side of the room.

'What the hell's the point you stupid bitch? Do you think they'll think twice about beating you up because you speak their God-forsaken language?'

The intemperate language shocked Marta, but she had to admit she had a point. The brutal death had unsettled the whole group; those who had forgotten about their plight for long enough to chat about family and friends now sat motionless and silent; among others she could sense an almost palpable tension and, she realised, a mutinous hatred.

She made the effort to move across to Pola. A few more joined them but they were a smaller group than before. The atmosphere affected Pola. Instead of giving a lesson she sang a beautiful German lullaby.

Marta understood little but enjoyed the haunting melody convinced Pola's voice was soothing all of them.

A sudden buzz of anger like a hive disturbed and a scrabbling movement in the far corner proved her wrong. Two women were trying to get up and being pulled down by friends, but they wrenched themselves free and marched across to Pola.

'How do you say 'I am Jewish' in German?'

'Please don't,' said Pola, but the prisoners were adamant.

'If you don't tell us, we'll say it wrong and we don't want that. Help us say it in perfect German, help us show them we're better than they are, help us be who we are, instead of these frightened rats they've turned us into.'

One of Pola's pupils stood up and responding to the madness raised her chin.

'Wir sind judische Frauen'.

Beaming, the three sauntered to the door arm in arm, shouting out 'Wir sind jüdische Frauen.' They pounded fists against the door, repeating their proud declaration again and again. The rest of the room looked on horrified until the door opened and they walked past an open-mouthed guard.

Nobody spoke for a long time; nobody moved for a long time except to wipe away tears; nobody could believe what they had witnessed, and each gave the action their own interpretation which erupted in whispered debate.

'Such courage,' said one.

'Such stupidity,' countered another.

'Well, I'm proud of them.'

'Me too, I wish I had the courage to do the same.'

'You shouldn't be proud. There's no courage in suicide and that was suicide pure and simple.'

'The act of a madman.'

'Did you see those faces? They looked euphoric.'

'Bewitched, more like.'

'Plain crazy.'

Pola sat holding her head in her hands.

'What do you think will happen to them?'

'If...' she hesitated a moment. 'If they are lucky, the guards will shoot them.'

Hours passed. The mood in the room remained sombre. Marta gathered herself to find her prayer companion and knelt down to say the rosary with many others joining in.

'Looks like you've got more pupils than I have.' Pola joked as they sat together eating supper.

'Have they told you their favourite prayer yet?'

'No, what is that?'

'Our Lady's Dream.'

'I'm not familiar with that one.'

'Someone found it scribbled onto a piece of paper and left on the altar of the Church of the Three Crosses in Warsaw, not long after the Germans moved into the capital.'

'I used to attend that church. What are the words?'

'Perhaps I should let them tell you. There can't be many things they can teach you, so I'm sure it would please them.'

'Oh, Pola, don't tease me. I'll pretend I've never heard it before and I'd much rather know in case they never share it with me.'

'I'm sure they won't do that, but I will recite for you:

Our Lady's Dream

Lord Jesus came to her and asked:

'Mother, are you asleep?'

'I fell asleep,' says the Virgin Mary, 'but you, dear Son, awakened me. I saw you in the Garden of Gethsemane, stripped of your garments, when they spat on your Holy Face, when they crowned You with thorns, when they

nailed You to the Cross. They pierced Your side with a spear, whence flowed water and Your Sacred Blood. Then they took Your Body down from the Cross and laid it in my arms.'

And the Virgin Mary wept.

Jesus replied most tenderly:

'Most Holy Mother, whoever recites this dream or listens to it or carries it upon his person will gain 100 days remission from purgatory and on that day he will not die a violent death without having received My Sacred Body and Blood. And whoever asks anything of You, or Me, Mother, will OBTAIN it.'

(This is where you make your petition, explained Pola.)

'Whoever recites this prayer, listens to it or carries it on his person, neither while travelling, nor in war nor in any other place will evil befall him. In whichever house he finds himself neither fire nor water will harm him nor any other harm come to him.'

We offer up these 100 days indulgence for the souls of all the faithful departed and they in their turn will watch over us. Eternal rest grant unto them, O Lord, and let perpetual light shine upon them. Amen.'

'Oh that is beautiful. Perhaps this is blasphemous, but I've never liked the Hail Mary. It strikes me as cheating to use the words of the Angel Gabriel…'

'And Saint Elizabeth…'

'And Saint Elizabeth inspired by the Holy Spirit.'

'Well, at least we can recite our catechism.'

'Will you stop interrupting me?'

Pola grinned in amusement.

'Now you were saying or was it blaspheming?'

'Agh stop it.' But she was grinning too.

'Anyway, I don't find it easy to say except for the last part. Our Lady's Dream is so evocative. It's powerful because it's telling a story and you're aware it's not a dream but the future facing her beloved son and you empathise with a mother's pain.'

'Oh? And there I was thinking it was all about saving your skin and getting your petition granted.'

'That is outrageously cynical.'

Pola chuckled, and they sat like two naughty pupils who had defied the priest in a confirmation class.

The friendship blossomed and Pola spent many hours talking to her in German, stopping to translate whenever she could not follow and correcting her increasingly fluid attempts to converse with her.

'You're not Jewish, are you?' Marta asked her one day. 'So why are you here?'

'The jealousy of neighbours.'

She frowned and tilted her head.

'I have an easy life. I speak German like a native so communication is not a problem. My job as a waitress gets me tips and a good meal every day. That makes a few of my neighbours spit. They watch me with pinched lips and clenched teeth and mutter under their breath as I walk past.

'Someone must have reported me to the authorities for helping Jews. I cover my tracks so I don't think they have any proof but who knows? The trouble is I doubt they'll keep my job open for me and the arrest alone will have tainted me in the eyes of potential employers. It's surprising how word gets around even in a large town like Krakow.'

'How did you learn German?'

'My mother died giving birth. My father was a doctor who specialised in tuberculosis, work that saw him travel abroad to various hospitals and clinics. He was away when she started labour early and the news of her death reached him by telegram. When he came back, it was with a German wet nurse who stayed beyond her contract and ended up being our housekeeper. She was a good woman. I loved her very much.'

'What happened to her own child?'

'Stillborn. She used to say "You saved my life, and I saved yours, so we're quits." It was like a little nursery rhyme but I didn't understand the significance until much later.'

'What happened to her?'

'She returned to Germany to nurse her dying mother when I was twelve. Later she wrote to say she was getting married. After about a year she gave birth to a baby boy called Hans. Communication was sporadic after that and they returned the last letter we sent.'

Pola lowered her head and pressed hands against eyes. She sighed.

'Why did she have a son? He must be in his early twenties now and I can't help wondering if he's one of my customers.'

'That would be an extraordinary coincidence.'

'Yes, but not impossible, and the thought turns my blood cold. If he's an ordinary soldier I can cope with that, but what if he's in the Gestapo or the SS? What if he's responsible for torture or murder? You saved my life, I saved yours and now instead of being quits your son is killing both of us. Oh hell. It upsets me so much.'

'What about your father?'

'He was a lot older than my mother but very hale and hearty. He died in 1934. We'd had our evening meal together as usual and he went to sit in front of the fire with a newspaper. I was doing paperwork in the study, trying to concentrate and he was snoring. I even called out: "Tatusiu, stop snoring!" But it was death rattling in his throat.'

'I'm so sorry,' said Marta, reaching for her friend's hand.

'Thank you. Yet I'm glad he died when he did and he didn't have to see any of this horror. He was such a good and noble man that if he hadn't died, I think Nazism would have killed him.'

Two days after their conversation, a guard called Pola out for interrogation. She did not return. Marta hoped and prayed that all had gone well for her; she missed her easy going friendship and assuaged her loneliness by continuing to talk to her in her head, practising her German at the same time. During the day she helped the other prisoners, telling them all she remembered about Catholic doctrine and practice. As Pola had predicted they shared their love of Our Lady's Dream with her and she often said the prayer asking for their safe release.

The prison became crowded as they arrested more women. The brutality of certain interrogations continued. There were no more deaths, but the injuries inflicted on some prisoners so appalled her she shook as she lay down to sleep.

Twice they called her out to empty the slop buckets and once to collect the prisoners' food where she watched, sickened, as her companion stuffed bread into her pocket for her own private consumption.

'Go on, you may as well stuff your own pockets, they all do it.'

But Marta shook her head and let her get on with it. At least it explained why people were as eager to volunteer for the food run as they were to avoid the slop run.

Once a fortnight they used the communal washroom. The first time they showered, Pola returned with the rag-like towel concealed under her dress.

'Why on earth?'

'And what will you do when your period comes?'

'Oh Lord, I never thought of that.'

'No, good thing I did.'

Pola tore the towel into strips and distributed them.

'Try to pinch a towel next time you shower, but be careful not to get caught. You don't want to get beaten up over a sanitary towel.'

'Don't you want any?'

'No need. I had fibroids in my twenties that resulted in a hysterectomy. Poor Tata cried because I would never experience the joys of motherhood, but I was delighted to be rid of my periods and with my mother dying in childbirth I could never understand why he was so upset, knowing I would avoid that danger for ever.'

'Did you never want children?

'No. I'm sure they bring great joy but they can also bring great sorrow.'

In the days that followed, Marta often remembered their conversation and wondered at her friend's equanimity when she was so certain she wanted children. What would she have done if a surgeon's knife had made her barren? It was a fate she couldn't imagine.

Six weeks into her captivity, the door opened, and they called her name. A guard escorted her into a small office where a German official sat at his desk while an obsequious man hovered in the background.

'This is your interpreter,' the official said, waving a dismissive hand towards the stooge.

'No interpreter, thank you. I speak German.'

'Very well,' responded the official while the redundant interpreter threw her an evil look.

The question-and-answer session that followed went through her family set up. He noted the names and last known addresses of her parents and grandparents. She confirmed her current address and gave the name of two of her parents' friends as additional referees, not wanting to implicate her friends in Krakow.

With the forms filled in, the official put down his pen and asked her to recite the Lord's Prayer.

'Our Father, who art in heaven...' Her mind emptied.

'Our Father, who art in heaven,' she repeated and swallowed for no further words came.

'I'm sorry, my mind is a blank.'

The official raised his eyebrow and looked disgusted.

'Guard. Take her back.'

Once inside the lock-up, she burst into tears. Her rosary companion came up and hugged her.

'I couldn't remember the Lord's Prayer. I couldn't remember the words.'

Her sobs subsided, and she sat down, wretched with a hopelessness as dark as her surroundings. The days passed in a monotonous sludge of despair, a hollowness of spirit she had never experienced before.

One morning, she awoke to find herself surrounded by her prayer pupils, all kneeling and reciting Our Lady's Dream. When they came to making their petition, they all, as one, asked God to give her the strength to carry on.

Embarrassed by their show of faith in a religion that wasn't even their own, she knelt alongside them.

'Thank you for showing me the way. I will never forget this moment and I will never stop praying for all of you.'

They blushed and rolled their eyes, moving back to their places. From that moment she redoubled her efforts to be helpful and even stole a towel when they next showered.

Two weeks after her disastrous interview, they called her out again. As she left, a chorus of voices proclaimed the Lord's Prayer, to boost her on her way.

Inside the official's office, she beamed as she said 'Good morning' and waited for his instructions, confident of finding the words to every prayer.

'You're free to go.'

'What?'

'I said you're free to go. My colleagues in Warsaw have checked your credentials and you are free of the taint of Judaism at least as far back as your grandparents, which is all we require at present. Here are your papers. Now leave and make sure you don't waste our time again.'

Fuming at the slur, she had enough sense to say nothing.

'Guard. Show this woman out.'

Once on the streets she ran, oblivious of the looks she was attracting, until she reached the home of her friend Wanda Szymanska. Breathless, she banged on the door and when it opened, fell crying into her outstretched arms.

When they stopped hugging, she said: 'Please say there's enough hot water for a bath. I'm desperate for one, that and a cigarette.'

'This would be a good time to give up for good.'

'Deaf. Must be a blockage. Only cigarette smoke will unplug it.'

'I give up. There's a packet on the kitchen table.'

They sat up half the night as Marta told her story.

'They're not human beings, Wanda, they can't be to torture people like that. When they threw people into the cell, they were so bloodied and bruised we couldn't see which end was which.'

'Yet, there is one good thing about the Germans.'

'Oh, what's that?'

'Their rule book efficiency set you free.'

'My God, you're right. It makes little sense when you think about it. They despise Poles as much as Jews so why go to all the trouble of checking my details? They could have left me there or sent me out on the next transport.'

'Precisely and yet they didn't because rules are rules.'

In the weeks that followed her release from Montelupich, life returned to normal. They had filled her job on the trams, but it wasn't long before they offered her shifts on a different route and she was soon back in full-time employment. On her days off, she tried to find Pola but as they had never exchanged addresses, it proved a difficult task. Then she met Ludek and nothing else seemed important.

6

LUDEK GOLAB SAT PINNED to the chair, shoulders drooped, head bowed. Wanda paced up and down, banging cupboards, slamming down glasses and spoons as she made tea. She tutted and shot dagger glances at him. Shaking, she spilt the boiling water and splashed her hand.

'Ow. See what you've made me do?'

'I'm sorry. Do you want me to leave?'

She groaned and collapsed in a chair.

'I'm worried sick.'

'This is all my fault. I sensed danger, yet I let her go. What does that make me? A coward and an idiot. Why didn't I keep my big mouth shut?'

She clapped her fists together; the hollow sound reverberated around the kitchen. Desperate to keep active she plaited her strawberry blond hair and pinned it up around her head.

'She has form, Ludek. Madcap actions were her speciality at school. Oh the stupid, stupid girl.'

'But why did I agree to it? Did I lose my sanity? God in heaven, what possessed me?'

The same thoughts ricocheted through Wanda's head

but seeing Ludek berate himself in such heartfelt fashion abated her anger.

'Marta is so determined nobody can stop her if she believes she is doing the right thing.'

'Regret is pointless. I'll invent a story, hand myself in and take the consequences.'

There was a new glint of determination.

'That is insane. Do you imagine they would release her just because you turned up in a suit of shining armour waving a banner of righteousness?

'Take me; let my beloved go!' She waved in a dramatic flourish.

'The first thing they'll look for is any inconsistencies in your stories and then you're both done for.'

Ludek pinched his nose and averted his face.

She slammed her fist on the table, jade eyes blazing.

'Don't you dare play the martyr? Go to the Gestapo and you jeopardise Marta and your resistance cell. Have you any idea how they torture people?'

'I would never betray them.'

'Nobody knows how they would react to torture.'

'I'd lie.'

'By the time they finished you wouldn't know the difference between the truth and a lie.'

'Maybe you're right.' His eyes widened.

'Oh my God, is that what they are doing to Tusik? Right now? It's unbearable. What can I do to help her? I love her so much.'

He sobbed.

'Does Marek know?' His older brother had brought him up after their parents' death and remained a stalwart influence.

'Not yet.'

'Listen. In Warsaw, Marta would already be dead. We are lucky the regime is more relaxed here. The chances are they interrogated her and she satisfied them with her story. She's as safe as she can be in Gestapo hands. You'll be able to help her once they transfer her to Montelupich.'

'How?'

'By sending parcels. No, don't react like that. Imagine what it means to a prisoner? To know somebody on the outside is thinking about them and doing whatever they can for them?'

'Yes, I suppose so.'

'I'll go to the prison, check she is there and ask what you're allowed to send and how often. Now is there anything else?'

He shook his head, still numbed by the enormity of his actions, then mumbled something about visitors.

'What was that?'

'I don't suppose they would allow her visitors.'

'Highly unlikely and dangerous,' said Wanda, in a businesslike manner. 'Now you'd better go. What time is your shift tomorrow?'

Ludek worked as a machinist in a wood mill outside Krakow.

'I'm on early shift so I need to be there for six.'

'Come when you've finished work. I should be here by then.'

Arrangements made, they hugged.

'Be brave.'

'If anything happens…'

'I will. You don't have to ask.'

They both knew nobody left their home in the morning confident of returning safely in the evening. Too many things could go wrong from street round-ups to reprisal shootings to a sudden bullet in the head for showing insufficient respect to a German officer who had passed you on the pavement. No wonder fear held your hand every step of the way.

Ludek left the building and for a moment desperately, childishly, wanted to run all the way home to his brother just as he had done when they were growing up. Running wasn't a crime, yet, but it attracted attention and it was never wise to do that; so instead he set himself a steady pace and tried hard to keep control of his emotions while remaining alert for danger.

He lived on the southern side of Krakow in the parental apartment where three of the rooms were now let out to supplement their meagre income. Marek was eight years older and had effectively brought up his younger brother following the long illness and then death of their mother when Ludek was just ten years old; their father, having died on army service in 1919, was just a distant memory.

Ludek loved his brother without question but also respected him as the head of the household. He never forgot what he owed his brother who worked so hard at his job in local government – a job he found no pleasure in – just to keep them going; but more than financial security, he knew that any happiness and emotional security he had experienced growing up was down to his brother's unfailing patience and brotherly love. Marek had become for him a father and a mother rolled into one. He, in turn, took his responsibilities seriously and tried to provide everything he thought his younger brother needed to grow up a rounded human being.

It was with this ambition in mind that he had taken fourteen-year-old Ludek to the theatre to celebrate his birthday. The schoolboy's face was alight; he fidgeted in his seat and observed everything, nudging Marek whenever he spotted someone famous. When the orchestra tuned up and an expectant hush fell over the audience, he leaned forward, goggle-eyed, lips parted. The colourful costumes and spellbinding words mesmerised him. During the interval, he stood sipping a drink, eyes glazed. Marek shook him to get a response to his questions. When the play ended he shot up and clapped and cheered.

'Bravo. Encore.'

The leading actress spotted him and curtseyed towards the young fan giving them a standing ovation. From that day his only ambition was to become an actor and play to audiences throughout the land.

Marek, however sympathetic he was to his brother's dreams, put his foot down and insisted on proper qualifications first. Many late into the night arguments followed.

'Yes, I appreciate art is important, even vital to life. It is indeed the expression of our nation's soul… I am aware of all that. What neither of us knows is whether you have the talent to make it your career.'

'But there's only one way to find out, and that's letting me try.'

'Not without something to fall back on. I don't want to deprive you of finding joy in your work. That's the last thing I want.'

Ludek blushed to be pursuing his argument when his brother loathed his job, but reasoned there was no point in both being miserable.

'If I don't make it, I will find another career. I want to earn my living and not rely on you for the rest of my life.'

Marek sighed. These endless discussions exhausted him.

'University is a must. If you train as an actor, you will miss the opportunity to get a degree forcing you into a rubbish job with too little money to enjoy anything, let alone the theatre.'

Inspired, he tried a different tack.

'As you're such an argumentative so and so, why don't you study the law? With a legal degree you can try acting and if that doesn't work out you can perform in the courts. Everyone says you need to be a convincing actor to be a successful lawyer whether you're trying to defend a criminal or prosecute one.'

His brother's lips twitched as he considered the idea.

'I have faith in you, little brother, but I also need to see you established in a career. You see that, don't you?'

But Ludek was already in court. Your Honour, this long and painful case would have strained the patience of Job. Brother Marek here insists on a career in the law while this beating heart desires artistic freedom like a flowering plant seeks water. He continued in this vein while he strutted, gesticulated and moved the judge to tears. When he finished, the room was empty.

'You win,' he whispered, rubbing his hands together and grinning.

After university, he trained as an actor and proved talented enough to enjoy regular work and favourable mentions by theatre critics. All the reviews and souvenir programmes, listing his name alongside the famous actors of the pre-war period, lived in a suitcase under the bed.

The occupation ended all artistic or intellectual employment and he was lucky to get manual work. Ironically, a carpenter who used to build stage sets found him the job.

At home he found Marek reading a book in the bedroom they now shared to maximise the income from lodgers.

'What's happened? Your face is ashen.'

'It's Tusik. The Gestapo arrested her this morning, and it's all my fault. Oh Marek, I'm such a bloody fool.' Hands gripped the bedstead as he stood shaking.

'Tell me what's happened.' Seated on the bed, they could have passed for twins, having the same strong chin, long straight nose and high forehead.

Between sobs and self-recrimination, Ludek related the whole sorry story.

Marek paced the green walled room, frowning and chewing his lips. After all these years protecting his brother, he was helpless. Just hearing the word Gestapo knotted his stomach and made him sweat.

Could he send Ludek away? Could he hide him somewhere until the situation became clear? But where? And would he go? He could be stubborn as hell and he was no longer a child. The thoughts swirled in his brain until he was nauseous with the effort of finding a solution.

Marta's courage moved him. Much as he loved him, he didn't think Ludek would cope well under interrogation. As he recalled her large brown eyes shining with intelligence and her sparkling wit, he calmed down. Please God, let her be lucky. As he prayed, a sense of peace flowed through him.

'Marta is a resourceful woman who will never betray her love. Panic is the last thing she needs. You must go to work tomorrow as normal, behave as normal. Nobody must suspect anything. Do you understand?'

He nodded.

'Now I will go to evening mass to pray for Marta. Do you want to come with me?'

That would hardly be normal, he thought, but he didn't want to be alone in the apartment and if prayer could help then, whatever his thoughts about religion, he would kneel humbly and contritely and ask for God's help and the Blessed Virgin Mary's intercession.

Later that night, lying in his bed, he watched his brother kneel and recite the rosary. Marek had never married; never had a girlfriend. Was he destined for the priesthood? A vocation would explain his monastic lifestyle. He would have to ask him, but no sooner had the question formed itself in his head, he fell into an exhausted and dreamless sleep.

The next morning he set off for the mill with the warning to behave normally at the forefront of his mind. He greeted the foreman, checked the work schedule and settled down to machining planks of wood, careful to go neither too fast nor too slow. The order was for crates again.

When he started at the mill, he assumed the crates were for weapons or machine parts to send to the front and considered ways of sabotaging the finished product. The prospect of a crate coming apart as it was being loaded onto a lorry or rail wagon, perhaps damaging the contents beyond repair, amused him. He speculated on whether the man nailing the planks together shared similar thoughts; in reality both jobs lacked the complexity to mask any deliberate faults in production or assembly.

When he discovered they were using the crates to transport art works into Germany, his attitude changed. He wanted none of the country's heritage damaged, because one day this madness would end and they would get back the plundered paintings and sculptures, porcelain and silverwork.

'What's up, Golab?' The foreman raised his voice above the sound of machinery.

'What do you mean?' said Ludek, not looking the foreman in the eye.

'It's nearly nine o'clock and you haven't tried to sneak off for a quick smoke.'

'Ha,' said Ludek with a laugh. He finished machining the plank and inhaled the scent of fresh wood.

'Like a fool I finished my cigarettes last night, so I'm stuck without until I can nip out during the break.'

'Must be why your hands are shaking like that.'

He thrust them into his pockets.

'Here, take one of mine. I know what it's like to be desperate for a fag. Be quick though.'

'Thanks. I appreciate that.'

An outside toilet doubled as a smoking hut and he lit up and inhaled the smoke; tension eased and made him lightheaded.

As he knelt in church the previous night, he vowed to give up smoking, partly as a sacrifice so that, God willing, they would release Marta and partly to afford cigarettes for the parcels he intended to send. Now he realised he would have to keep smoking, at least at work, to avoid the withdrawal symptoms he'd displayed this morning. This conclusion didn't afford him any pleasure, however; he would have much preferred to make a clean break and suffer wholeheartedly.

With a packet of cigarettes purchased from the local kiosk during his lunch break, the rest of the shift passed without incident. As he walked home, Marta's plight loomed large; tears welled up, and he clenched his jaws to master himself. Not for the first time since her arrest he considered the premonition haunting him for days beforehand.

He recollected his training: the emphasis was on reliability, on not letting colleagues down, on carrying out the task without considering the consequences. Like any army, they taught you to trust your superior officers: their plan was the right plan; they assessed all the risks and tested all the components, human and mechanical.

Once the job was completed, you moved on. If disaster struck, then there were clear protocols to follow: he knew, for however long it took, he had to lie low; he knew he should make no attempt to contact anybody and that nobody would contact him until they confirmed the all clear; he knew drop-off points and hiding places would all be scrapped and new ones found. He knew all that, but he still didn't know what he was supposed to do when his instructions said one thing and his heart said no.

He whipped round certain somebody had whispered the word betrayal in his ear. There was nobody behind him. He shook his head and moved on.

So what went wrong? What gave rise to the foreboding, to that gut-wrenching sensation that something wasn't right? Were there clues he picked up without realising? He re-examined his last contacts with cell members and leader. Was there anything strange? Was that when the premonition started? And now insidious thoughts mushroomed: they wanted him arrested; he was to be a lure for the Gestapo while others escaped; it had all gone according to plan. Oh God, was he really the victim of such treachery? But then it wasn't him, was it? It was Marta, his beloved, his soul-mate, his everything.

Ludek turned into the street where she lived and realised his mistake. He wasn't afraid of being recognised; he had always taken such care when he visited Marta to enter and leave her apartment without being seen. He knew her landlady's routine which changed little from day to day and anybody watching the building would have seen a variety of male visitors, not one of them looking as he did now. He had used his actor's training to assume characters as different from one another as suggested by a change of gait or posture, a cap or a hat.

On the other side of the road, a Gestapo officer left the building, a black Mercedes parked outside. His mouth went dry as he glanced at him and hurried home.

7

INSPECTOR BAUER PAUSED AT the bottom of the entrance steps and considered his next move. He turned to look up at the dilapidated building and wondered what secrets it held. Had he missed anything? A question he asked on every investigation.

The search of the prisoner's rooms revealed little of importance; there were plenty of books lying around, a few clothes hanging in the wardrobe, several more scattered about the bedroom, a yellowing newspaper in the desk, several photographs of family or friends, but nothing to offend or incriminate, certainly nothing to suggest she was a member of the resistance.

A junior officer remained behind to collect the material he'd indicated while he headed back down to the landlady's apartment. The door was ajar, and he smiled; most people would have shut it as quickly as possible after a Gestapo visit.

He found her sitting proud and tight-lipped in a hard-backed chair, still wearing her raincoat, as if she'd second guessed his intentions. She was an attractive woman, in her late forties or early fifties; her brown hair streaked with grey; her eyes a penetrating shade of amber.

Deciding against another long day at work, he tore out a page from his notebook and handed over his written instructions. She raised an eyebrow and with the slightest nod acknowledged his order. She replaced her coat on a hook in the hallway and held the door open.

Impressed by her quiet courage he said 'Auf Wiedersehen' respectfully before leaving her home.

His assistant came down the stairs carrying a box of evidence and stood waiting for Bauer's orders.

'Did you lock the door behind you?'

'Yes, Sir.'

'Good, put the box in the boot and we'll be off.'

The next morning at ten o'clock precisely Mrs Wisniewska, accompanied by her parish priest, arrived at Pomorska Street. After a short delay they were both escorted to Inspector Bauer's office.

'Good morning,' said the priest, in fluent though heavily accented German. 'Father Michal Nowakowski from the Church of St Teresa. I hope you don't mind my attending this meeting, but my knowledge of German might be helpful to you.'

'We welcome any assistance offered to the Gestapo,' replied Bauer, smoothly. He had been so convinced the landlady would turn up with her own translator he hadn't bothered to organise one.

'At this stage of our enquiries my interest is less in your parishioner than in her tenant, Marta Paciorkowska, even though that may change as more information becomes available.'

Bauer trusted the implied threat would ensure co-operation.

'If you would translate my questions and your parishioner's answers, we can proceed. When did Miss Paciorkowska become your tenant?'

'About a year ago.'

'Why did she move to your establishment?'

'I didn't enquire.'

'That seems strange.'

'Why? She was looking for an apartment and I had one available. It was a straightforward transaction.'

'Don't you check your tenants' backgrounds or demand references?'

'Not if they are Polish.'

'What do you know about Miss Paciorkowska?'

'She is a polite young lady who pays the rent on time and works on the trams. That's all I know.'

'Did you know she also works as a prostitute?'

Bauer had maintained eye contact as his questions were being translated, but this one did not provoke the shocked response he expected.

'No, I didn't and I don't believe it.'

This wasn't immediately translated although Bauer understood the response well enough. The priest spoke to her in Polish.

'Stop. As you are here to translate into German, kindly do so.'

'Apologies, Inspector Bauer, I only added, as a priest to his parishioner, that we must not judge others.'

Curious, thought Bauer, she doesn't believe it and yet he does.

'I see. Tell me, Father, is Miss Paciorkowska your parishioner as well?'

'No, not as far as I'm aware.'

'Are there many prostitutes in your parish?'

'I... I don't know.'

He enjoyed putting this scrawny, bald priest on the spot.

'Oh, but surely they come to you for confession, do they not?'

Bauer raised his hand to silence the priest as he protested about the sanctity of the confessional.

'I'm not interested in what they say to you, merely pointing out you must have a feel for the number you deal with, purely on a professional, or should I say pastoral, basis.'

'Well, maybe a handful of women have lost their way.'

'A handful? What four or five? Less than ten?'

'Yes, I would say less than ten.'

'How many churches are there in Krakow? Ninety? A hundred? So you have something between nine hundred and a thousand women breaking the law in the capital of the Central Government. Perhaps we need to do something, what do you suggest Father? A suitable fine for each parish, how does that sound?'

The priest sat silent, chewing his lower lip, fearful of unleashing further retribution on his beloved church.

'Well, leaving that aside for the moment, would you ask your parishioner when she last saw her tenant?'

'Sunday morning.'

'What time?'

'Shortly before ten.'

'That's very precise.'

'Yes.'

'Why?'

'Because she told me, she would be late for mass at the Church of the Holy Trinity which starts at ten.'

'Was she a regular churchgoer?'

'I would imagine so.'

'Was she carrying anything?'

Mrs Wisniewska frowned, then closed her eyes trying to remember the encounter.

'Yes, a brown paper parcel.'

'Did she have many visitors to her apartment?'

'No, I don't recall seeing a single visitor.'

'Didn't that strike you as strange? A young woman with no visitors?'

'Inspector, perhaps you are under the misapprehension I have nothing better to do than spy on my tenants. I lead my life while they lead theirs. As long as they pay their rent I leave them alone.'

'And yet you seem unwilling to accept your tenant is a prostitute?'

'Well, that would require visitors, wouldn't you say?'

Bauer allowed himself a small smile.

'So tell me about your life.'

'I work for the butcher's in Jacob Strasse. I start early and finish late unless the Gestapo come visiting.'

'Would you have preferred us to break down the door to Miss Paciorkowska's apartment? Some of my esteemed colleagues are keen on that approach.'

Mrs Wisniewska pursed her lips.

'Please continue.'

'On Sundays I attend early morning mass at St Teresa's. Then I relax: take a walk in the park, read a book, listen to music.'

'What does your job entail?'

'Serving customers; scrubbing counters; sweeping floors; balancing the ledger. I do whatever needs doing.'

'Are you married?'

'Widowed.'

'What did you do before?'

'I was a teacher of mathematics.'

'And your husband?'

'He was a professor at the university. He died at Sachsenhausen.'

Aktion Krakau to rid the city of its intellectuals had prompted international protest and Bauer looked away as he cleared his throat.

'Are we finished here?'

'Not yet. How did you acquire your premises? I cannot imagine academic salaries would run to the purchase of a three-storey house.'

'It belonged to my husband's family. When his parents died, we had the building adapted into separate apartments.'

'Why?'

'We had no children, so the house was too big. We wanted to supplement our income by letting out rooms and enjoy an early retirement.'

'Before you go, I would like you to write the names of all the tenants in your building and a brief description of them: age, occupation and anything else of interest.'

'Surely all this information is at your fingertips. You had no problem finding me.'

'Indulge me,' said Bauer, pushing a pen and paper across the desk.

She sighed heavily.

He glanced at the translated sheet; as he expected it contained minimal information.

'There is one thing that surprises me, Mrs Wisniewska,' he said, as he showed them to the door.

She waited, head to one side, eyes sceptical, chin jutting out.

'You have never once asked why we arrested your tenant.'

This time she didn't wait for her translator and said: 'Warum?'

'She was carrying a gun for the resistance.'

He closed the door. It amused him to imagine their reactions and their private conversations as they returned home. One of his skills as a detective was judging when to release information; he had known people reveal far more than they ever intended because a fact, mentioned almost in passing, had completely unnerved them.

Not that he expected this nugget to lead to anything. The Poles were much too proud and defiant, different from the Berliners he was used to, but at least maintaining his own approach to investigations gave him job satisfaction in a career he was no longer proud of.

Interrogations by his new colleagues in the Gestapo had dismayed him. Lacking any imagination or finesse, they endlessly repeated the same question while insisting that lying was futile as they had all the answers. Sometimes, he was loath to admit, the method worked and people, already weakened by pitiful conditions and solitary confinement, cracked under the constant pressure.

But he had no desire to appear omnipotent preferring to keep initial interrogations fluid. Set the hare running and watch where the dogs lead you, he explained to junior detectives while he was still a member of the Kripo. Now, despite the promise of a Thousand Year Reich, nobody had the time or patience to enjoy the craft of detecting. A pity when he remembered the many interesting investigations carried out in a previous life.

When his boss invited him to join the Gestapo, Bauer stalled. He guessed the career move would mean a better life for his family and he also suspected they might interpret refusal as criticism or showing insufficient enthusiasm for Hitler's policies. So he claimed to be interested and said he would talk it over with his wife that night.

Instead he took the tram to Tiergarten and walked the rest of the way to Birkenstrasse to meet up with retired Chief of Police, Ernst von Linden, his onetime mentor.

A maid answered the front door and showed him into a large drawing room with French windows onto a well-kept garden: neatly clipped shrubs and trees surrounded a central lawn while herbaceous borders filled with a variety of flowering plants made an impressive display.

Linden walked into the room unnoticed. He was a tall man who retained the Italianate good looks of his youth. Now in his seventies, his black hair was still dark and his steel-blue eyes bright with intelligence.

'Good evening, Bauer. You are admiring my garden.'

'Good evening, Sir, and yes it is a most delightful sight, even for someone who can't distinguish one flower from the next.'

Linden beamed and shook his protégé's hand warmly.

'Come and sit down. Will you join me in a glass of something?'

'I shall be glad to.'

'Good, a man shouldn't drink alone and I don't get as many visitors as I used to and when I do, they are not always as welcome as you are.'

'Thank you, Sir.'

With drinks in hand and mutual toasts made, they sat in comfortable armchairs on either side of the ornate fireplace.

'You are married now, I hear.'

'Yes, Sir, a wonderful woman called Henni, and we are now the proud parents of a beautiful daughter, Monika.'

'I am pleased for you, Bauer. A man should be married. I miss my dear wife every day. You must bring Henni to meet me. I'd like to see what kind of woman unshackled you from your desk.'

Bauer grinned and promised to do so. Linden refilled their glasses and became serious.

'When you rang me earlier today you said there was something you wanted to discuss?'

'Yes, Sir. They have invited me to join the Gestapo.'

'And?'

'I'm wondering whether I should.'

'Explain your thoughts.'

'I'm not sure they are coherent. There are criminals and there are policemen dedicated to tracking them down. I'm very comfortable with that…'

'And superb at it.'

'I appreciate the compliment, Sir.' He paused.

'I'm not sure I like a Secret State Police and with recent events I'm not sure we need one.'

'Ah, you mean the "Night of the Long Knives." Yes, I've heard that argument used since then, but I'm not convinced by it. Any state, particularly one as new as ours, will always have enemies and we have to be prepared to fight those enemies by any means.

'And if you remember your history lectures at police college, you'll know Prussia had a political police force from the mid-nineteenth century onwards and most of its members came from the criminal police force. So there's nothing new about your potential recruitment.'

Linden chuckled.

'It seems ironic now, but Department 1A kept a close eye on members of the Party during their rise to power as much as they did on the communists.'

'Is that so?'

'Yes, it's true. It's safe to say the watchers, and the watched, exist in every society on earth and in every period in history.'

Bauer was silent.

'Ah, of course, I remember now, you're not a political animal, are you Bauer? More's the pity. You could have progressed further in your career with a better understanding of office loyalties and manoeuvrings. Politics lies at the heart of everything we do whether in the office or in the wider world outside.'

'I'm beginning to appreciate that, Sir, and I have joined the Party.'

'Good. I wasn't convinced about Hitler at first, I don't mind admitting that, but he's proved himself a more than worthy leader. Take the purge of the storm troopers. Rohm was a personal friend of Hitler's yet he didn't hesitate to execute him for treason, for the good of the country, for the good of the German people.'

'But without a trial.'

'Desperate times demand desperate measures, Bauer. Do you realise Rohm had more storm troopers than our entire army? Imagine the mayhem he could have caused with a coup. You're not against the death penalty for treason, are you?'

'No.'

'Nor should you be. People who want democracy, God help them, can go and live elsewhere. Communists can go to hell or as we politely refer to it, Russia. Those who remain need to understand where their loyalties lie.'

'Yes, I suppose so.'

'You served in the Great War didn't you?'

Bauer nodded his assent.

'Life is simple as a soldier. You get your orders, you march and you fight. There's nothing to think about. Depending on your character, you are courageous or you are not. Police work, particularly political police work, isn't like that. You don't always see your enemy; they don't always wear a uniform or point a gun; but the damage they do can be just as lethal.'

'That is true.'

'But you're still not sure.'

'Perhaps I wish they didn't take so much pleasure in their brutal reputation.'

'Oh, come on, Bauer, are you getting soft in your old age? Do you mean to say you've never kneed a rapist in the balls? Or winded a murderer with an elbow to the solar plexus? I would say brutality is inevitable when you are dealing with an enemy, especially one as devious as you find in the political sphere. Would you rather be shooting them dead on a battlefield or roughing them up in a cell to get vital information that can secure your country's safety? It's a question of horses for courses, my boy, horses for courses.

'Come on, drink up and I'll show round the vegetable garden. Perhaps you'd like to take some produce home for Henni? There's nothing to beat fresh vegetables picked and cooked the same day.'

Half an hour later Bauer, carrying a bag of potatoes, carrots and beetroots, bid his host a warm goodbye.

'Remember Bauer, Kripo or Gestapo, you can do good wherever you are,' said Linden as he shook hands then raised his arm in salutation. He meant the advancement of National Socialism in all its manifestations, but Bauer interpreted the words as a moral imperative and it gladdened his heart and made him head for home lighter in mood and firmer in step. The next day he joined the Gestapo.

8

THREE DAYS OF SOLITARY confinement and Marta didn't know what to do with herself. Her jaws ached; her head boiled; it was like climbing in the highest mountains. She rehearsed her story until she was word perfect. Predicting their questions, she probed her responses for flaws. She paced up and down; stretched and jogged on the spot; searched everywhere to find something to write or scratch her own message. Then she did it all again. Nothing brought her any peace.

She had always loved life and everything it offered; every minute, every second counted as she explored the world in all its kaleidoscopic wonder. Art, friendship, dancing, poetry, her studies and her beloved fiction: these were like champagne and caviar. They fed her soul and made her soar.

To be dull, to be bourgeois, offended her sensibilities when she wanted to paint on the canvas of the world. She never wanted to go to sleep arguing that it was an appalling waste of time. During late-night conversations with friends, it was they who insisted on their slumbers, leaving her to wander off reluctantly to bed; at other times, when she was on her own, her body rebelled and forced her mind to shut down and she would wake up bewildered, her book fallen to the ground.

This endless waiting, hour after hour, and now, it seemed, day after day, she found intolerable. To see time, the essence of life, wasted like this was a form of torture. The very walls pressed in on her, taunting her as cruelly as a ticking clock.

She understood that this, too, was a way of breaking her down, of making her pliable to interrogation. A routine would help and she forced herself to organise a series of mental and physical activities to fill the day.

She tried to exclude Ludek from her thoughts; she didn't want his name lingering in her head, blurted out with disastrous consequences. Yet she continued to sense him; when she hugged herself and shut her eyes, his imagined embrace brought her comfort.

With a plan to cope with her imprisonment, she became calmer and more optimistic. She had been lucky so far. Then a new sense of resolve took hold of her: lucky be damned, she needed to show the same bravado as before. She hammered a shoe against the door and yelled for a guard. Minutes later, she heard footsteps in the corridor and the door was unlocked.

'What's all this racket about?' The guard was young and stupid looking.

'Get me the duty officer and be quick about it. What an appalling dereliction of duty.' A useful phrase she'd read in a German newspaper.

The guard stood nonplussed with his mouth open. He wasn't used to having prisoners speak to him like that and it threw him off balance.

'The duty officer,' repeated Marta. 'This will get back to SS Reichfuehrer Himmler if you don't get a move on.'

He had been contemplating thrusting his rifle butt into Marta's face but blanched at the name. Maybe this was no ordinary prisoner, no empty threat. Better to leave any decision to his superior officer than end up on a charge. He'd noticed everyone getting more jumpy since the Allied invasion of France.

'All right, get back inside your cell.'

Marta snorted in a mixture of delight, amazement and contempt. Fancy shaking these cowards by invoking the name of Himmler as if she stood any chance of communicating with him. Well, more fool them.

Minutes passed as she worked out what to say to the duty officer. He was brighter, probably; then again he was just as likely to fear upsetting Himmler. Let the game begin.

She strode along the corridor and arrived at the office with head held high. With a curt nod, she launched her attack:

'As you know, I am helping the Gestapo with an important enquiry and they had to imprison me for my own protection, but I am perfectly sure that Inspector Bauer had no wish to detain me in a cold, dark cell with nothing but bed bugs for company.'

Cold, grey eyes gave nothing away.

'I suggest you phone Inspector Bauer immediately and ascertain his wishes. There is no doubt in my mind that this is a dereliction of duty on the part of the prison authorities and, as such, a reportable offence to SS Reichfuehrer Himmler. I have been patient for long enough; I will not be any longer.'

There was silence as the duty officer reflected on her words.

'When did they bring you in?'

'Sunday night.'

'I see.'

He pulled out the black ledger containing her details. He wasn't prepared to ring this Inspector Bauer and face a dressing down in front of her. No prisoner of the Gestapo would dare to act like this unless there was more to the arrest than had been noted in the book. Of course, the Gestapo claimed 'protective custody' for all their prisoners but to make a point of mentioning it sounded ominous. Well, whatever, she wasn't his problem; the book said nothing about solitary confinement.

'Take the prisoner to the women's block. Follow the usual procedures for a transfer.'

Marta kept her face impassive. She thanked the duty officer with what she hoped was a convincing degree of satisfaction at a grave injustice corrected and followed the guard out. Inside she whirled round in a dance of delight, especially when they stopped at the showers. She put the tiniest sliver of soap to good use and relished being clean. They disinfected her clothes and returned them steaming.

The guard marched her to the women's block, a long building separated from the rest of the prison by linden trees. It was like an elixir to her soul to see the bright green leaves and feel the sun warming her face.

They took her to a large, bright room with two barred windows reaching up to the ceiling. Curious, friendly faces came up to her; the prisoners shook her hand and introduced themselves.

'Resistance?'

'No.'

'Why were you arrested then?'

No harm in telling them what she had told Inspector Bauer.

'The parcel I was delivering for someone turned out to be a gun.'

'You were delivering a gun, and you didn't know about it? Are you stupid? Do you think this is some sort of game?'

'No, not at all.'

She looked to the other women for support but could tell by their faces they considered her action unwise.

'Look, I was mad to do it, I admit it, but he was so plausible and he promised to get me some butter as a thank you.'

'Butter? Well that makes it all right then. Bloody hell. What kind of idiot are you?'

The woman stomped off muttering under her breath.

'Take no notice of Helena. A ferocious tongue belies a good heart.'

A feeble voice called out.

'Will you come over and meet Zofia? Our oldest inhabitant, she is our inspiration.'

The white-haired woman lay on a mattress in a pitiful condition; she had been mutilated and a kidney infection made movement painful.

Marta knelt down and introduced herself. Despite the pain etched on Zofia's face, her eyes were as deep and blue as the ocean and she gave Marta a searching look.

'Tell me about yourself.'

'There isn't a lot to tell. As you probably heard, I transported a gun without knowing it, so now the Gestapo assume I'm working for the resistance. I've been in solitary for the past three days and now, thank God, I'm here with other people.'

'Yes, it's hard to be on your own in prison.'

'What happened to you?' Marta's tone was timid.

'My interrogators enjoyed being unkind, shall we say? But then I am in the resistance so I knew the dangers facing me.'

'Where do you find the courage?'

A long pause followed.

'I don't regard it as courage: for me it is a simple question of life and how I am prepared to live it. Do I accept the jackboot? No. Do I accept the label of being a sub-human? No. Do I accept that I can die at the whim of others? No. I accept none of these and therefore to join the resistance, to do all I am asked to do to liberate my life and the life of others, is something I have to do in the same way I have to eat food to stay alive. There is no choice in my head. I am like a hungry man who reaches out for bread and I am sure that same hunger lies in the breast of every Pole.'

Marta crumpled. Yes, she experienced hunger for freedom, and yet, and yet…

'I'm sorry, Marta, I am exhausted. We will talk again.'

She would have loved to continue talking but realised she needed time to marshal her thoughts and understand her own position. The approach of a woman called Danuta curtailed her hope to consider their conversation in peace.

'May I join you?'

'Yes, of course.'

Marta could hardly complain about having company when she had longed for it so passionately, yet she could see that being stuck in one room with the same people, day in, day out, could become as tiresome as being on your own. Danuta had spent her childhood in Warsaw so the two exchanged memories of the capital and chatted until the evening.

After supper, all the prisoners, except for Zofia, lined up in two rows facing the door. The warden – a small, dumpy woman with down-turned mouth – entered.

'Cell number 14. All 20 prisoners present and correct, Frau Inspector.'

The warden walked a short distance into the room, looked around without changing her expression and went out locking the door. Marta who hadn't realised she had been holding her breath, let out a sigh and the atmosphere lightened. During the next few minutes they moved the mattresses, spreading them out on the ground.

She lay down. Zofia was a remarkable woman to have suffered so much and yet remain so resolute. Courage wasn't relevant to her; there had been no choice about the path she took through life. Was it really that simple? The decision to help Ludek was similar: the need to take his place was obvious. Would she have gone if she'd had a bad dream? Yes, though she might have been more circumspect, less inclined to suppose all would be well.

Her thoughts turned to Father Jan Zieja, her father's friend and childhood companion, a man whose love of God sustained him and encompassed everything he did. He saved the lives of Jews without thinking twice about it, knowing it was the right thing to do, the Christian thing to do, the will of God made clear. The baptismal certificates he signed provided new identities to thousands and his search for hiding places never ended. Offered a meal and a bed for the night, he would accept, and then turn up an hour later with two Jews in tow ready to take his place.

He never seemed to have any doubt about what he needed to do and always did it with boundless love, with a blessing for those he absorbed into his mission, with a kind and encouraging word for those whose courage failed them.

Love made things simple, she realised with sudden clarity; it took away the need for choices and decisions and weighing up pros and cons. Love of God and of his every neighbour gave Father Zieja his strength of purpose; love of freedom and of her countrymen gave Zofia that same strength; perhaps in her own case her love for Ludek would see her through this ordeal.

9

LUDEK ARRIVED HOME TO find the building empty. His brother, whose experience in local government had enabled him to find employment with the Central Welfare Council, was still at work and none of the lodgers was around. He made himself a glass of tea and waited until it was time to go to Wanda's apartment.

What had she found out? He lit a cigarette and drew on it several times before remembering his pledge to give them up. Annoyed with himself for forgetting, he decided not to waste it. He would need to ration the smoking around his work and worked out a schedule to avoid the shakes. By cutting right back he could put aside at least two packets of cigarettes a week.

Anxiety about Marta gnawed at his stomach. Would he ever hold her in his arms again? He needed to be strong for her sake and do everything to help her. Instead paranoia returned with a vengeance: find out how the bloody hell this happened. Thoughts screamed inside his head. Who did this to you? And why?

By the time Ludek set off again, he had worked himself up into a state of incoherent thoughts and aggression. Thumping on Wanda's door, he stormed inside and checked round all the rooms.

'What have you found out?'

Wanda looked horrified.

'Good evening, Ludek,' she said quietly. 'Is this how you enter the house of a friend?'

An equal horror overcame him and his body caved in.

'Oh God, my dear friend, I am so sorry. I don't know what came over me. Well, perhaps I do but let me talk about that later. Apologies for my behaviour. Please forgive me.'

With these words he took her gently by the hand and kissed it, his face expressing penitence.

'Forgotten already,' said Wanda. 'Now come and sit down and I'll tell you what I've found out. Marta *is* being held at Montelupich. A friendly guard told me prisoners receive Red Cross parcels regularly in the women's section. Unfortunately, Marta is still in the main prison. If we compensate him for his trouble, he will deliver private parcels. Although he wouldn't give a name, he told me when he was next on duty.'

'Thank you for doing this. It's a comfort she isn't being held at Pomorska Street. I don't suppose it's much better at Montelupich, but at least it isn't Gestapo headquarters. So, when do we send the first parcel?'

'Let's wait until they have transferred her to the women's section. I'm not sure why, but I feel we ought to be careful and find the right balance between helping Marta and not creating too much fuss that might be counterproductive to her well-being. Do you agree?'

'Yes, I guess so. Oh I do wish I'd asked her what she would say if they caught her, but I honestly never imagined it would happen. She seemed so confident she was just going to breeze through it, my beautiful girl.'

'Maybe she hadn't worked out what to say until the moment they arrested her. Sometimes a spontaneous reaction can be the most believable. One day soon, we'll find out.'

This was a lie, but Wanda didn't want Ludek dwelling on the past and getting himself agitated again.

'At the end of the week I'll go back and find out if she's there. Now, tell me what upset you so much that you forgot your normally beautiful manners.'

Ludek grimaced.

'Apologies again. It's just that I can't get the thought out of my head that someone betrayed me.'

'I don't understand. Someone did betray you. What else accounts for Marta's arrest?'

'I'm sorry, this doesn't make much sense to you, but it makes perfect sense to me. There has been a betrayal, but what I didn't think until now, is that the betrayal was aimed at me personally.'

'What do you mean?'

'Someone meant for me to get caught. Someone set me up as a lure for the Gestapo, to be sacrificed without my knowledge for a purpose I'm not aware of.'

'Ludek, you're still not making sense.'

'Not to you, but it is as clear as daylight to me. This wasn't some ordinary piece of bad luck but a betrayal from the top, the very top, downwards.'

Ludek leaned in, eyes blazing, cheeks tinged with colour.

'They didn't just find some unlucky partisan and torture him for information. They headed to the Planty hoping, intending, determined to find *me*.'

His voice rose to a falsetto.

'I was to be their prize. And I don't understand why.'

His head fell to his chest, and he kept shaking it from side to side.

'London. They're behind this, but why.'

Wanda was at a loss how to handle this. The Home Army took its orders from the Polish Government-in-Exile, based in London, but to suggest they had masterminded the betrayal of an individual agent was complete madness. Marta's arrest had unhinged Ludek. Should she play along with his theory or dismiss it out of hand? What would be the least damaging for him and for Marta?

'Have you ever heard of the resistance deliberately betraying one of their own?'

'No.'

'Well, then?'

'Doesn't mean it couldn't happen.'

'Ludek, you are overwrought. Marta's arrest has come as a devastating shock and your own feelings of guilt have twisted your brain into seeing enemies where they do not exist. Trust me, this is not how the resistance works; it never has and it never will. There is no doubt of your commitment to the cause of Poland's freedom and if the resistance wanted to sacrifice you, they would not have hesitated in asking you to make that sacrifice. And I am sure you would have done so willingly and proudly.'

Ludek nodded, his features at once serious and noble. Somehow Wanda had struck the right note.

'No more reflection on the matter is required, Ludek, nor is it profitable. Our one aim now is to help Marta survive. That must be the focus of all our efforts. Are we agreed?'

'Yes. Agreed.' Ludek smiled and looked optimistic.

'Before I came here, I had the most tremendous headache, worse than any I've experienced before, and it's only subsiding now.'

'When did you last have something to eat?'

'Breakfast or was it last night? No, I can't remember. Anyway, it doesn't matter.'

'Of course it matters. We have to keep ourselves fit and well to help Marta.'

She moved into the tiny galley kitchen and directed Ludek to help her.

'Now, if you open that cupboard, over there in the corner, you'll find two soup plates and the spoons are in that drawer, next to the stove.'

While he looked for the items and lay the table, Wanda set about warming the soup, stirring the contents and thinking about Marta.

She was about to ask Ludek to cut slices of bread, when the idea of him holding a sharp knife in his hands, made her turn queasy. She steadied herself against a cupboard and told herself not to be so foolish. This wretched occupation has shot all our nerves to pieces, she thought, but she still didn't ask him to cut the bread.

The soup was a hearty vegetable concoction to which Wanda added crumbled chunks of rye bread. At first, the silence between them seemed strained, but as the warm, nourishing soup filled their stomachs, they both relaxed and ate in companionable silence.

Ludek told her about his day and his attempts to give up smoking. His tone was light and amusing and before long Wanda was laughing at the tale, delighted to have the old Ludek back. She told him about her lucky escape from a street round-up that morning.

'It's the first time I've seen it happening with my own eyes. I really thought my end had come. Walking down Dietlowska Street I saw the trucks pull across the road; I did an about turn and ran when the next load of trucks shut off the other end. My knees just gave way, and I sank to the ground as the shouts and swearing and gunfire formed a kind of audible panorama around me. I honestly couldn't move and thought if they order me onto the trucks, they'll end up shooting me, because I can't move.

'Then a rough voice said "Young lady, get in here, quick." It was a workman with a little striped tent next to a hole in the ground. "They won't take me and they won't search my hut." Suddenly I was moving with no trouble at all. I made myself as small as a mouse inside his tent and he kept the flap open to avoid any suspicion he was hiding somebody. Then he wielded his pick axe rhythmically as if round-ups were no business of his.

'When the round-up was over, I went straight to the nearest church to pray for them. I spent my last coins to light candles for them and one for Marta.'

'Thank you, dear friend.'

'There's no need to thank me. I love her as much as you do and I would do anything to have her back with us.'

Ludek remained calm and reminisced happily about times he had spent with Marta and conversations they had had and outings they had enjoyed and the silly, joyful things they had said and done.

With the curfew fast approaching, Wanda invited him to stay the night on her couch, but he declined saying he wanted to update his brother. They agreed to meet up at the end of the week, when Ludek would bring a parcel of goods to deliver to the prison, and they hugged each other in a warm goodbye.

The brisk walk home energised Ludek, and he planned his next recital, scheduled for the following weekend. He took his resistance work for the Home Army seriously and with complete dedication, but this form of civil disobedience afforded him even greater pleasure. Performing plays, reciting poetry, reading extracts from the classical Polish writers, were ways he continued to practise his chosen career while cocking a snook at the Nazis.

Somebody usually brought a bottle or two of home-made vodka to the proceedings, but even without liquid refreshment, the atmosphere was always uplifting. People would sit on chairs, on stairways, on beds in adjoining rooms, anywhere they found a place to enjoy the performance. More often than not, their enthusiasm for the show resulted in people forgetting the curfew and having to bed down for the night on rugs and bare boards with folded towels and cushions for pillows.

The group he belonged to always appointed a Master of Ceremonies to ensure the audience did not get too rowdy or clap too enthusiastically, drawing unwelcome attention to their activities. But even the MC was part of the fun, wagging his finger ostentatiously, and goose-stepping his disapproval in the ridiculously small space available to them as a stage.

Just recently two of his friends had started performing satirical pieces of such devastating wit that the audience would gasp in appreciation. 'Last night I attended...' was a favourite when the performers took turns to be theatre critics of the latest 'Nazi show' which covered anything from military disasters to proclamations by Goebbels. The pieces were short but trenchant.

People came in from work looking haggard or deflated but within minutes you observed their spirits lifting, the pride returning. Even without the applause, Ludek always found the experience exhilarating. He would miss Marta's enthusiastic face in the audience but determined to do her proud with his performance.

The poetry of the 19th century poet Cyprian Norwid was his choice for the night; Norwid was her father's favourite poet, but Marta too relished his use of words, and found comfort in them.

He would peruse his brother's collection of poetry books. But even as he walked, lines of remembered poems came into his head: "Tenderness can be like a cry full of war" or "Oh! How sad and rare is deafness – When you hear the Word – but miss the punctuating notes."

His recitation would start with a quotation from the poet: 'Of this world only two things will remain: poetry and goodness... and nothing else...' It seemed appropriate.

He saw the light coming from their room. Motionless he whispered: 'Poetry and goodness, my dear brother, poetry and goodness.' Then he stepped inside.

10

On the Friday guards escorted Marta back to Pomorska Street. The interview took place in Inspector Bauer's office and he began by offering her a cigarette.

'Thank you, Inspector. I appreciate your thoughtfulness and I must say these surrounding are more conducive to civilised conversation than our previous meeting room.'

'Indeed, Miss Paciorkowska, my office was being renovated when we first met.'

'And you now say my name correctly. Well, I must congratulate you. Some Germans find Slavonic names almost impossible to pronounce, which must irritate the master race.'

Start as you mean to go on.

His eyebrows wiggled. While his phone might be tapped, there were no listening devices in the office so he let his feisty prisoner be free with her tongue.

'There are one or two matters I would like to clear up following the search of your rooms.'

'You searched my rooms?'

She stiffened and shook her head.

'Of course you searched my rooms, why would I expect any different?'

'That bothers you?'

'Yes, it's like a burglary. It's a violation to have strangers go through your possessions.'

'Yes, I imagine so.'

'Well, there it is; there is nothing I can do about it so please continue.'

'Thank you, that is most generous of you.'

He imagined relating the conversation to Henni and suppressed a smile.

'Perhaps you can identify the people on these photos?'

'That is a picture of my parents taken after their marriage. That is a group of friends from university days. That one is another friend, again from my days in Warsaw.'

'Names and addresses, please.'

Marta obliged as far as she was able.

'The young lady here looks Jewish.'

'Indeed.'

'Is she?'

'She was. Whether she is alive is quite another matter.'

'And you are not embarrassed to admit being friends with a Jewess?'

'No. She was one of my best friends, actually. An exceptionally beautiful and highly intelligent girl who went to Jerusalem to study medicine and made the mistake of visiting her family days before war broke out.'

'That was bad timing from her point of view.'

Marta agreed.

'Did you help her?'

'No.' She squirmed in her seat.

Bauer cleared his throat, pulling at his collar.

'Mm I dare say it wasn't easy.' He mumbled and straightened his papers

'Sorry?'

'Nothing.'

This was interesting. Did the Inspector have some connection with Jews? Was it something she could use?

He took the yellowing newspaper out of his file. 'This was in your desk. I wondered why.'

'I am sure you have worked that out, Inspector.'

'Maybe, but I would prefer to hear it in your own words.'

'The newspaper article is about the murder of three thousand Polish officers in the forest of Katyn. Each man had his hands tied behind his back, and a bullet put through the back of his head. One of those men was my father.'

Tears welled in her eyes as she remembered reading the news.

'The crème de la crème of Polish society: intelligent, creative, beautiful human beings whose lives were cut short in the most appalling way.'

'I agree that it was a most terrible crime perpetrated, as I am sure you are aware, by the Soviets.'

'Yes, the Soviets carried out the crime, but let's not pretend that your own countrymen haven't carried out similar atrocities.'

'Be careful, Miss Paciorkowska. While I can permit a certain amount of loose talk – it makes my job, a great deal more interesting – it would be unwise to push the boundaries too far.'

Marta raised an eyebrow but said nothing while Bauer made notes. She interrupted.

'Did you find the note from Artur?'

'No.'

'Oh, that's a pity.'

'There were various tapers, as you mentioned before, some by the cooker, some in the bin, one on top of the breadboard. Not a tidy person, are you?'

'No, you are correct. It's a terrible waste of time tidying up, but then so is looking for things because I haven't put them away.'

'You must be a nightmare to live with.' Bauer pictured his own home, kept pristine by Henni.

'Well, fortunately, I don't live with any of my clients.'

'Or anyone else?'

'Or anyone else.'

'Were you close to your father?'

'Yes, I loved him, but I also recognised that he was a great man – intelligent, erudite, witty, interested in all the arts, great fun to be with. I miss him.'

'And what would he have said about your current career?'

'Not a lot. If the Soviets hadn't murdered him, he would be in the same position as all Poles, looking for work wherever he could get it.'

'I wasn't referring to your tram work.'

'For goodness' sake, I don't consider what I do a career but an unfortunate necessity for my survival.'

Her tone was angry, impatient and dismissive.

'Do you possess an ashtray?'

He pulled one out of a drawer and she stubbed out the rest of her cigarette, crossed her arms and scowled.

'And your mother?'

'She died when I was 13 and before you ask I am sure she would spin in her grave at the thought of her beloved daughter reduced to these circumstances.'

'So why do it?'

With arms still folded, she turned to look at him, eyes flashing with anger.

'You don't understand what life is like for us, do you? People shot for no reason; towns and villages burnt to the ground; schools and universities closed down; professors and teachers murdered; forced labour; deportations; families torn apart; starvation rations while you grow fat on our labours. This isn't war; it's annihilation.'

'And yet you survive.'

'And yet we survive.' Pride surged through her, steeling her posture and illuminating her eyes.

'Not everybody turns to prostitution.'

Marta conceded the point with a turn of her head.

'We do what we need to do bearing in mind our individual circumstances. There is not one person who will judge me.'

'No, apparently not,' replied Bauer, remembering what the parish priest had said.

He continued making notes before resuming his questioning.

'What was your previous address here in Krakow?'

She gave it to him knowing it would be somewhere in the official records he had access to.

'Why did you move?'

'The new apartment suited me better. It's closer to work and bigger than the previous one.'

'No other reason?'

'No.'

She hoped she looked bored by this line of questioning because she didn't want him investigating her previous accommodation or, more specifically, the landlady who had evicted her, as soon as she was well enough to leave.

'Where do you carry out your entertainment of these men?'

'It varies. Artur, for example, used to go to his sister's apartment, but it's no good asking me where that is because he blindfolded me before we got there.'

She laughed before continuing.

'He said his sister would kill him if she found out what he was up to, so he had to take these precautions.'

'Did you mind?'

'No, not at all. I didn't want to get him into trouble.'

'Weren't you conspicuous wondering around with a blindfold on your head?'

'It wasn't the black mask you read about in cheap novels. It was a very pleasant, printed scarf of a type any woman might wear. And it's a funny thing, Inspector, but people see what they want to see. We were intertwined like lovers, my head nestling against his shoulder, my hand over my blindfold. I don't know if we passed other people or not, but I doubt anyone would have seen the blindfold. They would just have seen two lovers and in these dangerous times they would have done nothing but wish us luck.'

'How many times did you go to this apartment?'

'Four or five times.'

'In Krakow or outside?'

'In Krakow, I guess. He picked me up from the Planty and the journey didn't take that many minutes less than a quarter of an hour.'

'And did you nestle against his shoulder while he drove?'

'No, I would pretend to be asleep with my head resting against my arm like so.'

Marta showed her sleeping position.

'Did you go up steps to get inside the building?'

'Yes, and the apartment was on the first floor.'

'And what was the view from the window?'

'Sorry, Inspector, I kept the blindfold on until we got into the bedroom and only took it off once he'd closed the curtains.'

'Weren't you curious about the location?'

'No.'

'And what would happen after?'

'Same procedure. Blindfold back on and a short drive back towards the Planty. At some point Artur would say "You can take your blindfold off now." The joke is with my terrible sense of direction I could have done the journey without one, and still wouldn't have had a clue where we were.'

'What about other clients?'

'Please don't run away with the idea that there are dozens of clients. As I keep explaining this isn't a career but a way of supplementing my income to buy enough food to survive.'

'But he wasn't your only client so where else did you go?'

'Once or twice in the back of a car. A few times at the Hotel Europa. Sometimes out in the countryside.'

'What was the make of the cars?'

'Oh, Inspector, only a man would ask that. For me a car is a means of getting from A to B. While I might remember the colour, I wouldn't have a clue about the make.'

'And whereabouts in the countryside did you go?'

'My preference was always the Wolski forest. Do you know it?'

'All suitably vague.'

Marta said nothing.

'So that leaves the Hotel Europa. Where is it?'

'It was on Wehrmachtstrasse.'

'Was?'

'Yes, the resistance bombed it back in January and then it caught fire. It hasn't reopened yet.'

'How very convenient. An apartment you wouldn't be able to find, cars you can't identify and now a hotel whose records, I am sure we can assume, were destroyed in the attack.'

'Sorry, Inspector, I'm not trying to be unhelpful.'

'No? I wonder about that. What about your apartment? Did you ever bring anyone back there?'

'Certainly not. That's my home, my sanctuary, the place I can be myself and forget the terrible world we live in.'

'You read a lot.'

'Yes, it's a great consolation, an escape from the reality of our lives today.'

'What about friends? Do they visit you there?'

'I used to have friends, real friends, particularly in Warsaw, but most of them are dead now.'

'Who was the friend you came to visit in Krakow?'

'Henryk Skowronski.'

'And where does he live?'

'The last time I saw Henryk, he was hanging from a lamppost in Adolf Hitler Platz, along with five other Poles you murdered, in reprisal for a resistance attack.'

'And where did he live before they hung him?'

Bauer took the news of the death in his stride, much to Marta's disgust.

'In Gertrudenstrasse.'

'When we arrested you, you had caught sight of a friend in the street, a woman called Halina.'

'Yes. Halina is a prostitute. I can't in all honesty call her a friend but we smile, we chat when we see each other, we exchange moans and groans about men, but that's the extent of our friendship.'

'And no doubt you cannot tell me where she lives or plies her trade.'

'No, I'm sorry, I don't even know her surname.'

'You must be very lonely.'

'Not really. I'm an only child, so I am used to my own company. And then, when I am reading, I am in the company of thousands of different people who are sometimes more real than the people I meet or work with.'

'I still find it extraordinary you seem to have so few friends. You are a vivacious young woman. You had friends while at university and now, apparently, you have none.'

'That is because we live in extra-ordinary times, Inspector.'

'What about the people you work with?'

'Oh they're nice enough people but they are just that, people I work with. We don't socialise outside work.'

'All right, Miss Paciorkowska, we'll leave it at that for today.' The Inspector called for a guard who escorted her back to Montelupich.

11

'WHY ARE YOU FRIENDLY with that woman?'

'Who? Marta?'

'Yes.'

'I like her.'

'She's dangerous. For all we know she's a Gestapo spy.'

'Aren't you being paranoid?'

'She's been interrogated and there isn't a mark on her. Don't you think that's suspicious?'

'She was arrested on a Sunday. Perhaps they thought God wouldn't approve.'

'Like they have consciences. What do you talk about, anyway?'

'Not that it's any of your business but we share memories of Warsaw and we know some of the same people here in Krakow.'

'Humph.'

'Look she's funny, sensitive, probably the most intelligent person I've ever met. She's never given me any cause to doubt her.'

'Intelligent? Would you carry a parcel for someone without asking what it contained? She doesn't have an iota of common sense and that makes her dangerous if nothing else.'

'Well, I grant you, that wasn't particularly sensible, but that's typical of highly intelligent people: they often lack common sense.'

'If you want my advice, stay well clear of her.'

* * *

Back in Cell 14 Danuta greeted her like an old friend.

'Are you all right?'

'Yes, thank you.'

'How did it go?' asked the cell leader who dealt with the lugubrious warden at roll call.

'Not too unpleasant so far. I dare say it won't last.'

Everyone nodded except Helena.

'Do you want time on your own?'

'Yes, please, if you don't mind.'

'Girls, leave Marta in peace.'

With closed eyes, she went through the interview in her head. She had given so little information; would Bauer lose patience with her? The situation required a different strategy, and she needed to formulate one as soon as possible. So far, she had avoided mentioning Ludek or Wanda. It was vital to keep them out of the interrogation. Better by far to claim no friends than to deliver them to the Gestapo. But would she get away with it?

Ludek always insisted she kept nothing relating to him in the apartment. At the time she accused him of being over-scrupulous, but now she was grateful: it saved a lot of trouble during the interrogation. Imagine if she had kept his photo or the beautiful letter he had written after they first met.

'Tusik, these are just things, objects, property. They are not important in themselves, only in what they mean to you in your head and in your heart. Surely you can see that?'

'A photo wouldn't matter. I could always write somebody else's name on the back, somebody who died in the first days of the war.'

'Thanks, so now you want me to take on a dead man's name and character. How spooky is that? No, Tusik, whatever you did, or wrote, or said, it wouldn't stop the Gestapo releasing a "Wanted for Questioning" poster with that image and eventually they would track me down.'

He was so eloquent, so passionate, she let him talk long past the point he had convinced her. She didn't need a photo to remember what he looked like and she didn't need the letter to recite every word. She took a match to them and they had both watched them burn in an ashtray.

She calculated that, on balance, she had said enough to maintain her cover; the tragic death of Henryk Skowronski, a friend of Wanda's, had served her well, and she offered a prayer for his soul. Although she never saw his body, she'd seen others and knew the lump in her throat and the tears welling up during the interrogation were genuine.

After Henryk's death she accompanied Wanda to his apartment and helped pack away his things and return them to his family. Morbidly, she guessed Wanda would do the same for her if all this ended badly, but now wasn't the time to think about that. She yawned, exhausted at keeping one step ahead.

Somebody nearby lit up a cigarette, and she inhaled the smoke and pretended it was hers. Would they spare one? Better not to be a nuisance; there were worse things to endure than doing without nicotine. Zofia was a constant reminder of that.

According to the other prisoners, Zofia revealed nothing throughout her interrogations despite the mutilations and other tortures which turned her hair white overnight. When they finished, the Gestapo revealed all the information they had tried to extract from her.

Even that final insult did not break her, and she looked at her torturers with mocking eyes and sang the words of the national anthem until a blow to the head knocked her out. God, how they must hate her, although here at least everyone treated her with great respect; even the dour warden let her rest undisturbed at roll calls.

She considered how to approach her next interview and what lie to invent if Bauer checked her previous accommodation and discovered her pregnancy. She could claim it was an occupational hazard for prostitutes but a devoted father in attendance? Surely that didn't happen in real life?

The landlady had met Ludek and might give a reasonable description. She racked her brain to remember what name he used then. More importantly, how would she explain his current absence from her life? Bauer was unlikely to accept another death and he could easily check a convenient deportation.

The door to the cell opened and three new prisoners entered to the customary welcome. Marta didn't get up; there would be time enough to meet the women; in the meantime she needed to plan. By nightfall she was comfortable with her strategy of a wild goose chase and joined the rest of the group for a meagre supper.

12

'SO, YOU ARE A prostitute.' He spat it out leaving a glistening line of spittle on his lower lip.

'That is not a word I would use.'

'Really?' The scorn withered her, but she gathered herself.

'Perhaps you should reserve your disgust for the men who exploit prostitutes. The weakness is theirs, is it not?'

She kept her voice calm but winced as he cracked his knuckles again. The Inspector interrupted.

'We are not here to discuss ethics. Move on.'

'So how would you describe what you do?' Friedman's tone was chilling.

Bauer had introduced this rangy man as his assistant but allowed him to do all the questioning. She guessed the relationship strained both men, and when she glanced at Bauer, he was suppressing a yawn.

'I provide companionship. The men I meet are lonely. Some have lost their wives; others have parted from them, for whatever reason; others – and here she chuckled – can't stand them and want to be apart as much as possible. I talk to them. I make them laugh. And, please be clear, I have to enjoy their company otherwise "Goodbye." Life is far too short to spend time with bores even if I get a decent meal in the process.

'As for sex, we only proceed to that by mutual consent, attraction and respect.

'One client, a German officer as it happens, has never sought a physical side to our relationship. In fact, I rather suspect he is of a different persuasion.'

Marta observed her new interrogator. Coal-black eyes seldom blinked. The slightest twitch, in an otherwise granite face, gave her the opportunity she needed. No doubt he considered her beneath contempt, but a homosexual officer would be a real prize to pursue.

'I would never describe myself as a great beauty, but I am young and healthy. Does it not seem strange that a strong, handsome man with opportunity should be so reluctant to explore the possibilities?'

'Perhaps he finds sex with a prostitute too disgusting to contemplate.'

'Well that is a possibility, certainly, but if he's happy to wine and dine me in public then my suspicions seem more likely, wouldn't you say?'

'What is his name?'

'Ah. There you have me. He introduced himself as Hans, but I had the impression he was teasing me. It's quite a common name in Germany, isn't it? And he had a twinkle in his eye when he spoke.'

Marta's smile vanished; she leant on the desk, fingers steepled in front of her mouth.

Friedman recoiled. The scent of cologne wafted towards her.

'I've just remembered what led me to suspect he was homosexual. He possessed a beautiful cigarette case, made of silver, which must have cost the earth.'

Another twitch.

'On the outside it had the letters FJ or possibly SJ. The engraving was intricate and stylised so I wasn't sure about the first letter.

'But here's the strangest thing: inside, when he offered me a cigarette, the inscription struck me as false.'

'Go on.'

'It said: "To my beloved. In memory of days I will never forget." And that was it.'

'What's wrong with that?'

'Well, perhaps it's because I'm a woman, but I wouldn't choose an inscription like that. It would have my name on it or at the very least my initials.'

Lacking a response, she elaborated.

'Look, if he's the love of my life and I want him to remember the precious times we spent together, then I'll make sure he remembers we spent those moments together.

'On the other hand, if the world frowns upon our love, then I would seek to protect him by leaving out my name, and I would hesitate to add my initials in case there was already any suspicion of our relationship and the initials provided further evidence.'

She sat back triumphant at her clever bit of detective work. Then remembering the second twitch, remarked:

'I suppose it's the sort of thing rich people do automatically.'

'Describe this man.'

Yes, you petty official, joining the Gestapo made you important and now you've swallowed my bait.

'He is the Aryan ideal: tall, blond, blue eyes. No distinguishing features I can remember, no scars or anything like that. A strong face with a fairly high forehead, quite a prominent nose and thin lips. A manly look, not at all babyish.'

Marta looked into the middle distance and frowned slightly as if trying to conjure up an image.

'Sorry, is that helpful? I can visualise the man clearly and if I had any talent I could draw a picture?'

Unlike his boss, Friedman made no notes, and this unnerved her almost more than anything else about him. He was waiting for something and she didn't know what.

'Actually, he used to remind me of that English actor, the one who starred in "Gone With The Wind", but what was his name?' She bit her lower lip and played for time.

'No, it's no good. What was he called? Ashley, Ashley Wilkes, that's it. That was the character he played, but that's not his real name. They say it was a marvellous film, did you ever see it? I've only read the book but all the stars were featured in a German magazine once and they struck me as exactly the right people to play those characters.'

She looked enthusiastically from Friedman to Bauer but one merely narrowed his eyes while the other continued to stare out of the office window. There was a knock, and a secretary came in with coffee.

'Thank you, Brigitta, this interruption is most welcome, I must say. Please leave the tray on the desk.'

Marta folded her hands and gazed down, making herself as insignificant as possible. She need not have bothered; neither man paid attention as they stirred sugar into their coffee and conversed about their weekend activities.

The constant questioning throughout the morning had been exhausting, but she didn't dare lose concentration now and listened, careful not to show any reaction or interest.

They formed a strange pair: Bauer with a slight paunch and avuncular manner was at ease with himself while Friedman, towering over him, inwardly seethed with a nervous energy that betrayed itself with bursts of foot tapping or knuckle-cracking. As if his body rebelled against the unyielding features of his face.

The smell of coffee set her stomach rumbling. Eventually, Bauer called his secretary to remove the tray and asked if she had seen "Gone With The Wind".

'Yes, I saw it with friends. Actually, I went to see it three times in as many weeks. Every time another friend wanted to see it, I would volunteer to go as well. What a wonderful film. Even Hitler said it was brilliant.'

'Really, I didn't realise you were so close to our beloved Fuehrer.'

'Oh, Inspector, don't tease me.' Brigitta turned serious.

'The newspapers reported Hitler's love of the film and then those stupid Americans joined the British against us and so they banned it from the cinemas.'

'And do you remember the actors and actresses in it?'

'Yes, yes, there was Vivien Leigh – she was Scarlett O'Hara; there was Clark Gable – he was Rhett Butler; there was Olivia de Havilland – she was Melanie Hamilton; and Leslie Howard – he was Ashley Wilkes. Those were the main characters.'

Bauer glanced at Marta.

'Thank you, Brigitta, you have been most helpful.'

'Thank you, Sir, then perhaps you might also like to know that, only last year, our boys in the Luftwaffe shot down a plane returning to England from Lisbon and among the fatalities was Leslie Howard.'

Bauer burst out laughing.

Brigitta looked puzzled.

'Oh nothing, Brigitta, just a coincidence that amuses me. Thank you once again for sharing your knowledge with us. Actually, there is one more thing, could you get a picture of this Leslie Howard? It might prove helpful in our enquiries.'

'Yes, Sir, I'll do my best.'

Bauer shook his head as he contemplated the prisoner. She really was the kiss of death for everyone she mentioned in her evidence. He looked at Friedman who stared back, face devoid of emotion.

'Would you like to continue? You were in the middle of collecting information about a German officer.'

'Yes, Sir.'

Friedman resumed his seat opposite the prisoner.

'This German officer... what is his rank?'

'First Lieutenant.'

'How do you know this?'

'At one of restaurants we frequented, the maitre d'hotel welcomed him with 'Good Evening Herr Oberleutnant.'

'And how did he react?'

'He didn't. Oh, you mean was he troubled by the reference to his rank in front of me? No, not at all, but then we had known each other for a long time so he knew he could trust me.'

'And when did you last see him?'

'Oof. I'm not sure. Let me think.'

She tried to remember information Ludek had revealed about troop movements.

'Well?'

'Probably six months ago, shortly before they moved him to Warsaw.'

'He told you he was being transferred?'

'Yes, why shouldn't he? Like I said, he could trust me.'

'But not enough to give his real name.'

Let him have his little victory.

'You are right. Perhaps he didn't trust me as much as I thought.'

The Inspector ended the interrogation and called a guard to take her back to Montelupich.

* * *

Both men gathered up their papers and Bauer filed his away.

'So what are your initial impressions?'

'Of the prisoner, Sir?'

'Yes, Friedman, of the prisoner.'

'Stupid and morally disgusting but then I wouldn't expect anything else from a Slav.'

'And your thoughts on how best to proceed with the enquiry?'

'This German officer is our first priority. There isn't a great deal to go on, but we can't have homosexuals tainting the Fuehrer's army. The Polish bitch can wait.'

'Friedman, such dedication to the Fuehrer's wishes does you credit. What you *propose* would be an excellent use of your time.'

'Thank you, Sir. Heil Hitler.'

'Heil Hitler.'

Bauer responded with little enthusiasm. He disliked Friedman the instant he met him and hadn't increased his liking since.

He would have much preferred to deal with this investigation on his own, but Fuchs had been clear on Friedman's involvement. Perhaps he was his protégé? Maybe this search for a homosexual officer would keep him out of the way, at least for a while.

13

BAUER'S FACE WAS AS slack as a flat tyre; he rested his head against his palms and pushed thoughts to the back of his mind with a steady pulsing motion. Since the Allied invasion of France a sense of foreboding clung to him like damp clothing. The end was coming and there would be a reckoning; there always was. How would he fare? He tried to do good but the need to protect his family steered him back into the fold again and again. So many opportunities wasted and now it was too late. But what choice did he ever have?

The photo of his wife's carefree face softened the edges of his despair. He remembered taking it in the early days of their marriage: playing with a neighbour's dog, throwing sticks and laughing, she never noticed him standing behind a tree. The photo captured her essence, and he had it framed without showing her, knowing she would criticise her hair out of place and undignified pose. She would have insisted he take one of the studio shots they had done after their marriage and which she displayed in the centre of the credenza.

He met Henni Hoffmann on holiday when he was in his forties and fell in love. The daughter of a Bavarian farmer, she was easy-going, quick to smile and make the best of any situation, and for reasons he could only guess at, delighted to be with a man fourteen years her senior.

They married the year Hitler came to power and Henni produced three children in the first five years of their marriage. Two girls and a son filled the family home with laughter and fun; he could not imagine life without them.

The household was Henni's domain, and he never stopped being grateful for the haven she created for him. He knew from the mutterings of other men that a wife could make life hell, forever griping about some perceived failing, or pushing their husbands to go for promotion or demanding a move into better accommodation. The list of complaints seemed endless; he was a lucky man.

'Henni, you must miss the mountains,' he said, early on.

'Oh, we are where we are, Heinz,' she replied, stroking his arm, 'but thank you for noticing their absence.'

It seemed such a funny thing to say, but the remark often came back to him in the middle of an investigation; noticing an absence could be just as important as seeing what was in front of him.

They were still in the honeymoon months of their marriage when Henni's beloved younger brother Albrecht caused their one and only row. Impetuous, passionate and argumentative, he had been an early recruit to the National Socialist Party and as eager to recruit others as he was to rise in the ranks.

Bauer trod carefully and rather than express misgivings, explained that it was illegal for a policeman to be a member of any political party.

'No longer,' cried Albrecht holding up his arms in a Victory V. 'That's all changed under the Fuehrer. You can belong and you should. This is the future for all of us.'

'Maybe you're right. I'll check it out.'

'And you, Henni, you agree with me, don't you?'

'Of course I agree, my darling little brother, but there is something even more important than the Party.'

'What is that?' asked Albrecht, wondering if he had missed something and hating the prospect of his sister pointing it out.

'Another piece of strudel with lots of that heavenly cream. This is where my immediate future lies,' she said, laughing and patting her already swollen stomach.

Her mother, Lottie, who had been sitting darning socks, busied herself cutting another piece of strudel and ladling a generous quantity of thick cream onto it. She smiled proudly at her daughter as she handed her the plate. Bauer, too, had beamed and gone over to hug his wife; only Albrecht had remained stern faced throughout. What a humourless prig.

Henni's attempt to change the subject proved unsuccessful and Albrecht droned on about the Party and Hitler's plans for Germany and the great future that lay just ahead of them. The longer he spoke, the more strident his tone became and the more disturbing the ambitious plans he outlined.

A rant not dissimilar to one of Hitler's. Would he ever shut up? Albrecht only halted when he needed to attend his local Party meeting; he stood to attention, clicked his heels and gave a Heil Hitler salute before kissing his sister goodbye and shaking Bauer's hand with a powerful grip.

'Don't forget what I said, will you?'

'No, Albrecht, I won't forget,' replied Bauer, fighting a sudden desire to punch his bumptious brother-in-law in the mouth.

With Albrecht gone, the atmosphere in the room lightened, and Lottie chatted about domestic matters and asked about their plans. When Henni's father, Gunter, came in from milking, the women disappeared to prepare the meal, chatting and laughing together. The evening passed with good solid food and plentiful beer for Heinz and Gunter and several games of rummy before they all retired to bed.

Early next morning, with Albrecht nowhere to be seen, the couple said their goodbyes and headed back to Berlin.

'You don't like Albrecht, do you?'

'Oh Henni, he's just young and full of himself. What is he now? Eighteen? Nineteen?'

'Nineteen, nearly twenty.'

'I'm sure I was the same at his age.'

'But he's right, don't you think, about Hitler and Germany's future?'

'No, I'm not sure he is. We have all been through hard times. The war was a terrible time and we're still suffering the effects. Look at your parents – they lost three sons which must have been heart-breaking for all of you. Gunter struggles to manage the farm and Albrecht doesn't seem keen to help.'

'No, he's set on a career in the Party. What will Papa do without him?'

They drove in silence for a while.

'What was it like here during the twenties?'

'We were very lucky. The farm has belonged to my father's family for generations so we had that financial stability and Papa never wastes money on new equipment so we had no loans to pay off. When inflation soared, we avoided buying anything. We didn't eat a loaf of bread for a long time but we never went hungry. We had our own vegetables and eggs and milk and we ate an awful lot of rabbit stew.

'Theft was a terrible problem, though. We had always had one or two dogs on the farm to keep the rats down but my father decided we needed two proper guard dogs. He trained them himself and he wouldn't allow us to treat them as pets. I found them frightening, actually, but they kept strangers off the land.'

'I remember those times so clearly. Money ceased to have all meaning. How can you take a banknote seriously when you need a suitcase to take home your weekly pay and you can't even buy a loaf of bread with it? And I was one of the lucky ones because I kept my job. Millions didn't, and they went through hell.'

'That's why I think Hitler is right because he wants to make sure we never suffer like that again. We need to be self-sufficient; we need to get unemployment right down and we need to have a strong army to protect ourselves.'

'Well, I don't disagree with any of that but when you hear Albrecht go on and on about the Jews being to blame for everything it strikes me as simplistic.'

'And yet they don't seem to have suffered as much as the rest of Germany. Look at all the businesses they own and the big houses they live in.'

'Oh, Henni, of course they suffered. Jews lost their jobs in the Depression like everybody else. Inflation hit them as badly as the next man and they fought in the war just like all Germans did and their families had as many losses as anyone else. And…'

Bauer hesitated; he wanted her to understand, but this wasn't a tale to tell in anger; so he said nothing and gripped the steering wheel with white knuckles.

'Anyway, they killed Jesus.'

'What?'

'The Jews killed Jesus. That's what our Pastor says, anyway.'

'Technically, I think the Romans crucified Jesus.'

'Oh, now you're making me angry.' She remembered more of the Pastor's sermonising.

'The Jewish High Priests handed him over to Pontius Pilate and then the crowds, who were Jews, called for them to crucify him.'

'If so, they killed one of their own.'

'What?'

'Jesus was a Jew.'

'A Jew? No, no, no. Jesus was Christ, the Son of God, the very first Christian.'

'Born into a Jewish family; circumcised; an expert on Jewish law; a worshipper at the Temple. What more evidence do you need?'

'Well, that's like a Christian baby being adopted by a Jewish family. He would have to follow their customs but it doesn't make him a Jew.'

They drove on in silence. Bauer hated this animosity between them. He didn't care for politics and even less for religion. Now both were causing this unnecessary friction. Although he listened to the news on the radio, he seldom picked up a newspaper, having more than enough to read with case notes and police reviews. If he had a philosophy outside work, then it was to live and let live; after the brutality of trench warfare it seemed a worthy aspiration.

When he returned to his police studies after the war, he knew his colleagues regarded him as a loner. Perhaps it was true; he didn't initiate social gatherings although he always responded to invitations and played his part as a guest with genuine warmth. He remembered the things people told him and was never at a loss to ask questions and listen to the replies.

In his spare time, he enjoyed walking and when forced on annual leave, always headed for the mountains of Bavaria. On one of these holidays he stopped in Munich; two young men waving swastika flags and distributing leaflets accosted him as he headed out for a beer.

'Join us and listen to our great leader Adolf Hitler. He will address us in the beer hall across the road there in just a few minutes.'

Well, why not? He would have a beer and see why people made all this fuss about him.

The meeting proved a revelation; supporters packed the hall and there was standing room only. Bauer positioned himself near the side exit and looked over the crowd which bubbled and frothed like the beer he had anticipated. When Hitler walked onto the makeshift stage, thunderous applause and the stamping of feet vibrated through the air for several minutes. A signal silenced the crowd and Hitler spoke, at first so quietly that everyone, including Bauer, leaned forward to catch the words.

The speech began, in a thoughtful tone, as Hitler remembered his days as a soldier fighting for Germany. He involved the audience as he spoke of the sacrifices they had made, men, women and children, for Germany; how shocked he had been by the country's capitulation in 1918 and the realisation, his voice now rising to fever pitch, that their civilian leaders had stabbed them all in the back. Hitler interweaved economic, social and political conditions in Germany with the conspiracy of Marxists and Jews and he swept from the Treaty of Versailles to the present day. A spellbinding performance, it trapped Bauer in a storm of emotions until he lost all measure of time and place.

When the meeting ended, he made his way to a local hostelry and sat drinking, still in a state of shock. A filling meal of noodles and ham and he was ready for his bed.

The next day, a haversack on his back, he took the early bus to Wallgau and set off for Krottenkopf. In the coolness of the morning air he walked with a steady pace and soon warmed up. As always in the mountains, he sensed his mind clearing; yet something still nagged at the edges of his brain. He didn't try to analyse it; walking often produced unexpected thoughts or solutions to problems that had been troubling him. Perhaps a new avenue of enquiry would suggest itself to him or a decision would become so obvious he would wonder why he had ever delayed making it.

He passed the occasional hiker and exchanged friendly greetings, but soon he reached the higher slopes and found himself alone. Resting for a moment he watched two buzzards soaring in the distance, catching the thermals until they became almost invisible. He had always experienced spiritual joy in the mountains; they were his cathedrals and left him calm and authenticated.

This time it was different and he couldn't understand why. He took a path leading round the side of the mountain and his feet picked up a marching rhythm until the thud of his boots and the sound of the Nazi victory salute "Sieg Heil, Sieg Heil" rang in his ears. He slowed to a hesitant walk remembering the tumultuous ending of yesterday's meeting and the effect it had on him. Slowly it dawned on him that what he felt right now was cheated: in an atmosphere of evangelical fervour, he had been offered salvation through faith in Hitler, only to wake up to find the world unchanged and its men and women, so to speak, merely sinners.

The tirade he witnessed had been nothing more than hypnotic propaganda; the reactions of the audience nothing more than mass hysteria.

How on earth did he fall for that? He had been ready to pledge allegiance to the Party then and there. Only the Kripo's rule of political neutrality and the thought of a thirst quenching beer propelled him out the door. How had Hitler done it?

Bauer had nodded in agreement with him several times: on the sacrifices ordinary people had made during and after the war; on the bravery of German soldiers; on the humiliation meted out by the Treaty of Versailles; on the lack of political direction; on the need for a better deal for war veterans; on the terrible waste of unemployment. Perhaps that was it: Hitler took a small truth that bound the audience to him and then expanded on it until he had something so wide ranging and impossible to disprove that everyone accepted it willingly? After all, what did even reasonably well-educated people understand about Jewish conspirators and the links of international finance to Bolshevism?

After his beer hall experience he remained wary of Hitler and bemused to learn of his arrest for treason following a failed coup. That would be the last they heard of him. How wrong he had been. And here he loomed responsible, indirectly, for their first marital discord.

'Oh Henni, I'm sorry.'

Bauer glanced at his wife, but her eyes remained closed and a purring sound filled the car. Hours passed until he turned into a roadside restaurant and filling station. Henni stirred in her seat.

'Are we home already?'

'No, my love, we'll be on the road for hours yet, but this is a good place for lunch.'

'Oh, that is a good idea and I can go to the toilet which I suddenly need very badly.'

Although she seemed to have forgotten about their row Bauer wanted to clear the air properly.

After they ordered their meal, he took hold of her hands and apologised.

'I'm sorry we argued, Henni, and sorry for my brusque tone.'

'Thank you, Heinz, and I am sorry too.'

'Shall we agree on something once and for all time?'

'That depends on what it is' she replied, leaning towards him, a smile playing on her lips.

'Can we please make our home a place where we never discuss politics or religion or anything else that is likely to cause arguments between us?'

'Oh yes, let's do that.' She squeezed his hands.

'It might mean we have to ban Albrecht from our apartment.'

He grinned, back on the same wavelength as his wife.

'I would never ban someone who means so much to you.'

A lunch of ham and eggs consolidated their good humour, and they set off for home chatting about baby names and colour schemes for the nursery and all the usual preoccupations of parents-to-be.

Bauer dismissed Hitler as a charismatic politician who, with rather more ranting and raving than normal, would get on with running the country and leave people like him to get on with their lives. He was at a loss to describe when or how, but suddenly, and with exponential speed, everything became political: the Party encroached on every single area of their lives; it issued rules and regulations with monotonous regularity; every day startled them with rumours and whispers, denunciations and disappearances, marches and declamations. They feared their neighbours and said nothing and did nothing the Party might interpret as a lack of enthusiasm for Hitler and his glorious Third Reich.

One evening, not long after their return to Berlin, Henni asked her husband to accompany her on an evening walk.

'No need to comment. Albrecht has joined the SS.'

They tried to walk out most evenings, at first on their own, and later with a pram. They didn't always have anything important to say but when they did the simple sentences took on the flavour of a secret code between them, initially prefaced with a 'No need to comment' and then simply spoken with just the squeeze of a hand registering the import of what they said and what they left unsaid.

In this way Heinz told her about joining the Party and later his transfer to the Gestapo. Henni kept him abreast of Albrecht's career and told him local news such as when neighbours disappeared in the night. From time to time, they talked more freely as they visited parks away from nosy neighbours and listening devices but the feeling of being watched never left them.

Once back inside their apartment, they always talked of innocent things: schooldays and holidays, families and friends. They listened to music on their gramophone and they played card games. When the children arrived, they had a new focus in their lives and delighted in watching them grow up.

Thanks to his Party membership and transfer to the Gestapo, they moved to a much larger apartment in a tree-lined street in a better part of the city. On one of their last walks together before the move, Heinz warned his wife that colleagues had probably bugged the apartment, and they needed to be just as careful as ever. She nodded sadly in response.

Then, in 1943, when they had been married for ten years and little Tomas was four years old, Henni announced she was expecting once more.

The pregnancy did not progress well. Henni complained of exhaustion almost from the start and grew uneasy about staying in Berlin. Heinz welcomed her decision to take the children and stay with her parents.

His daughter Lisle came into the world on the 15th February 1944 and lived for less than 24 hours. Henni's despair frightened him. Released from hospital she returned to her parents' farm to convalesce and refused point blank to return to Berlin.

'And so here we are, Henni, here we are.'

The knock at the door sounded like the lightest tap.

'Come in.'

'I'm sorry, Sir, I thought you had somebody with you.'

'No, no, just talking to myself again. People tell me I'm a great listener.'

Brigitta flushed and handed him some files.

'Criminal Director Fuchs would like you to go through these cases and he's booked you an appointment to see him at 4pm.'

'Thank you.'

'My pleasure, Sir.'

14

Dear Diary,

I am so thrilled I found you! As soon as I spied you, tucked in among my childhood treasures, I knew you were the answer. I've been going mad without someone to talk to. Now I'll be able to unburden myself to you.

I don't dare talk to Mama and Papa or ask them what their views are. There's a Nazi flag at the entrance to the farm but nothing inside the house except for a photo of Albrecht in his SS uniform. I'm guessing what that means, but it doesn't do to make assumptions. Heinz taught me that.

The atmosphere is different here. I can breathe and I've noticed a change in Monika too. Away from school she's not as obsessed with Hitler. Oh, how I wish I could keep her here forever.

So what are my views? They've changed for certain. With Mama and Papa looking after the children and insisting I do as little as possible, I've had plenty of time to examine my life. When I recall the early years of our marriage, it was like I was living two lives. One of them belonged to Heinz and my family. The other belonged to Hitler and the Party. Does that make any kind of sense?

I think perhaps if we hadn't made a pledge to each other never to talk politics, if we'd always talked freely at home, I would have come to my senses a lot sooner, but then I knew exactly why we didn't talk. It wasn't just our promise to each other; it was the way you could never be sure who was listening, even inside your own home.

I wonder if things would have been different if we had been able to stay on the farm. I was happy to be with Heinz so I didn't mind moving to Berlin but now I think maybe I missed the open countryside and the freedom of the mountains more than I realised at the time. I know one thing for certain – I didn't like the way we had to conform, all of us, all of the time.

At the flat in Kurze Strasse, there was a block warden who got up my nose. A stupid, petty, vindictive little man, keen to flaunt his authority. Have you put out the flags Frau Bauer? Have you done this Frau Bauer? Have you done that? This is the new regulation for this. This is the new regulation for that. It drove me mad.

When we moved to Schulstrasse life improved, but by then news had spread about Heinz being in the Gestapo, so nobody dared to be unpleasant. Although I can't pretend I didn't enjoy the protection, it also alienated me from the others in the block.

As long as I stayed at home I felt quite happy. It was a different matter when I had to go out shopping. It worried me when I used to come across the brownshirts patrolling the streets. They were always polite to me, I can't say they weren't, but there was something menacing about them like a field full of bullocks. You were never quite sure what they were going to do with all that energy.

One day a group of them beat a man up in front of me. One came over and said: 'Let me help you with your shopping.'

'But what are you doing?'

'Keeping Germany clean and safe for you and your children.'

I did wonder then if Albrecht was keeping Germany clean and safe in the same way. When I told Heinz that night, he went very quiet and then reassured me that I was quite safe.

'But who were they beating like that?'

'A Jew or maybe a communist. Both seem to be priority targets.'

I remember thinking he must have done something terrible.

When we moved to the larger flat, I still kept in touch with Frau Rose who had been so nice and welcoming when I first moved to Berlin. By then I had little Monika who was born on Tuesday, 8th February 1934.

You should have seen Heinz's face when he held our little girl for the first time. I thought he would burst with pride and joy and it made me cry with love, love for him and Monika. I could not have been happier.

And she was such a good little girl. She hardly ever cried and before long she was smiling and laughing and bringing us joy every single day. She was a bright little girl too, picked up on things so quickly. She was reading at three which was amazing and I didn't push her into it at all. I just used to read to her and she would sit on my lap and before we knew it she was pointing to words and saying them.

***

Dear Diary,

One day, not long after the storm troopers incident, Heinz brought home a poster of a horrid-looking person. Hairy like an ape, a huge pock marked nose, tiny pig-like eyes with an evil expression in them. A grotesque image which made me shiver.

Heinz said: 'This is what a Jew looks like. If you come across one like this, you must inform me straightaway. Have you?'

He often asked me and I didn't understand why. But even when I walked past Jewish shops and customers, I never met a Jew like the one on the poster. And slowly, slowly, I realised what he had been trying to tell me. Jews don't look like that or like the other horrible posters you used to get around the city. And if they don't look like that why believe anything else they say about them?

When Hitler told us about Jewish conspiracies, I believed him. I couldn't explain it to you but I didn't feel I needed to. It was enough that I trusted him to know how it worked and what he needed to do about it. Now I'm not so sure.

I continued to visit Frau Rose but one day, much later, I knocked on the door and another woman said she lived there now. Frau Weber told me she was Jewish, so the Party ordered her to leave and a local official and his family took her home. What a sour face she had when she told me, saying she wanted the building disinfected to get rid of any traces of vermin. That was the word she used, vermin. Like the rats on Papa's farm.

Sometimes I wish Heinz had been a farmer, a son of the soil bringing home the harvest for the good of his family and all of Germany. I know he's not as happy in the Gestapo as he used to be in the Kripo but that's not surprising when you see how people react to him. They're either scared witless or keen to give him information about somebody they know or more likely don't like.

I'm not really sure what it is he does in the Gestapo. He told me their work was to protect the state against its enemies, but he wasn't allowed to talk about it in any detail. I asked him once why he had transferred across. He told me he had been invited to join and that he didn't feel it was wise to refuse. It was the same when he joined the Party. Then, no sooner had he joined both, we were being offered a much larger apartment in a very nice, respectable street. So I think he made the right decision.

On Sunday, 2nd August 1936, my labour pains started a month early. Little Carola seemed in such a hurry to come into the world and so disappointed once she got here. She was a tiny little mite, and all she seemed capable of doing was crying.

Heinz and I worried. The doctor said we needn't, that some babies cry a lot, and that she would be fine, but a mother knows and I said to him 'But she's too busy crying to eat' and he said 'Oh babies don't starve themselves.' Well, she seemed to be the exception. After one awful night, when I paced up and down with her, something compelled me to visit Frau Rose.

She hugged me and sat me down. After my tale of woe, she asked if I would be prepared to see a Jewish paediatrician. I said I would be prepared to see the Devil himself if it would help Carola. She laughed and said some people say they are one and the same. Perhaps that's when I should have guessed, but I didn't.

Dr Kessler let me have an emergency appointment that same afternoon and he performed a miracle. He asked me various questions about the labour and told me about being a chiropracter. He held Carola in front of him, head in one hand and the rest of her body in the other. She was still crying when he sort of twisted her head and pulled on her body and the screaming stopped.

Well, my mouth fell open. He explained the manipulation had sorted out the problems caused at birth and would no longer trouble her. In fact, she slept in the pram all the way home and didn't stir when I put her in her cot. I didn't wake her for her evening feed and she slept right through until dawn when she had a good feed and fell asleep again.

To this day, I don't understand why I turned to Frau Rose, but I have never regretted doing so and Dr Kessler was right – Carola had no problems after that. In fact, she thrived.

I hope that Frau Rose and Dr Kessler are both safe and somewhere nice even if they are Jewish. They saved my baby's life and I will not deny it or pretend otherwise.

***

Dear Diary,

The years flew past with two little ones. Carola grew into a placid child but took her time talking, and she didn't pick up reading quickly either, but she was happy and healthy. How we used to love spending time with the girls, playing games, taking them to the local park. Life seemed idyllic, and I continued to ignore the world around us.

Then, on Sunday, the 18 September 1938, I gave birth to Tomas. Oh God, what a long birth. If Carola arrived in too much of a hurry, Tomas had all the time in the world. He would not rush for anybody. I was exhausted by the end, but so delighted to have given Heinz a son, even though he always said it didn't matter.

Boys are so different. He was much bigger at birth than the girls and he didn't talk until past his fourth birthday and never showed the slightest interest in reading a book. Instead, he raced round the flat on his bottom and poked his nose into everything.

***

Dear Diary,

I never understood why people kept diaries. It seemed such a waste of time to write about things instead of living them, but now I understand how liberating it is to put your thoughts down on paper and it's something to do when I'm so big it's hard to do anything else.

On Hitler's 50th birthday, they organised huge celebrations in Berlin. I put flags out on the balcony, like everyone, but even though Heinz had got the day off work, we decided not to go into the centre and listened on the radio instead.

When I heard the descriptions of all the pomp and ceremony, my spine tingled. The cheering and applause of all the crowds filled our little home. What a difference to the depression and the poor state of Germany before Hitler came to power. Heinz bought me a book of photographs they published after the event and I enjoyed having it on display and looking through the pages.

Then, suddenly, we were at war. That came as a complete shock. I was only ten when the Great War started but I loved my three older brothers and cried as much as Mama did when the news came of their deaths. Nobody who lived through that terrible time wanted another war, I am sure of that, and I trusted Hitler to use all those troops to keep the peace.

I know it was selfish of me, but I was so glad Heinz was older and in the Gestapo, so there was very little chance of him going to war. I wasn't sure how Albrecht would be affected in the SS, but at least he wasn't in the army.

Although we had rationing and things became difficult, I didn't worry about the war that much, once it started. With three children to bring up I was busy and before long we were getting ready for Christmas. We tried to make it special with a large tree and all the decorations I'd kept from previous years. There were few presents but plenty of love and laughter and we played games and sang carols and had a wonderful time.

The memory of that Christmas kept us going through the following months when it turned so bitterly cold. All the canals and lakes and even the larger rivers froze. Snow is great fun at first, especially when you can take the children sledding and come home to a cosy apartment. But it didn't take long for the city to grind to a halt. The coal supplies ran out, and they only allowed us to have hot water at the weekends. Thank goodness we had an old electric heater, but we still ended up sleeping in one room to keep warm. 'We're camping indoors' we told the children, and they loved it.

More than the cold, I worried about the lack of food. There was no milk, no potatoes, nothing unless you knew somebody who knew somebody. And it turned out Heinz knew a lot of somebodies.

Every few days there would be a knock at the door and I would find a sack left on the mat. Sometimes there would be a few potatoes, sometimes a cauliflower, usually a container of milk, sometimes coal. I didn't ask him about the supplies, but when I looked at him at the dinner table, he said 'People are very kind.'

Much later he told me several people owed him their lives and responded generously to his requests for help. I didn't ask him for details because I didn't want to know. I had milk to give the children and food for the table, nothing else mattered.

***

Dear Diary,

I realised today I haven't had my nightmare once since coming here. I never told anyone about it because it seemed so silly dreaming about a huge and threatening teddy bear. It belonged to Monika and had swastikas for eyes and kept telling me to watch out. I used to wake up in a terrible sweat wondering if I'd said or done something wrong.

Once Monika started school in 1940, life became a minefield. She was so proud of school and wanted to bring home the things she learnt there.

'Mama, our teacher says we should begin the day the German way.'

'Don't you want to say Good Morning and give Mama and Papa a kiss first?'

Poor little Monika looked so confused.

'Yes, I suppose so, but then we should all have the German greeting.'

'Well, that sounds a great way to start the day. That's what we'll do.'

Monika looked pleased, but the idea appalled me. I'd tried for so long to keep politics out of our little home and now it would not be possible. Imagine having to chant Heil Hitler round the breakfast table.

When I looked at her reading book, my heart sank. It contained pictures of evil looking Jews, nothing as bad as the poster, but still not pleasant. But I didn't dare say anything. Heinz told me about the denunciations made by school children about their parents. He always gave the parents stern warnings in the cases he investigated, but in others they sent the parents to prison. I would not risk that happening with Monika. I love her with all my heart, but I don't think it's a coincidence the nightmare teddy bear belongs to her.

Heinz didn't bat an eyelid when Monika kissed him, said good morning and then gave a Heil Hitler salute.

'Heil Hitler' he replied and then added 'I don't think we need the salute at home, do you? Just Heil Hitler will do inside the house.' His tone was very pleasant, but it didn't broach any argument and Monika agreed straightaway.

That Sunday we took the children to Muggelsee and while they splashed about in the water we talked. Heinz agreed it wasn't fair on Monika to have to deal with a different set of values at home and we would have to pretend that teacher knew best. Oh, but it was difficult.

'My teacher says this, my teacher says that.' My only response was 'I'm sure your teacher is right.' Then I changed the subject or asked her to help me with something. Once or twice she gave me a funny look, but I smiled and told her Hitler would be proud of her. That satisfied her.

Needless to say, I dreaded Carola starting school, but she took all the Hitler business in her stride. Back home she played with her dolls and practised the piano.

Tomas will start school this September. And this year Monika will have to join the League of Young Girls and get a double dose of Hitler this and Hitler that. Where will it all end?

Yet I still keep the portrait of Hitler at home. Mind you, I wouldn't dare get rid of it now. What would Monika say? At first I displayed it because I was proud of what he was doing for our country, then it became useful as a sign of our allegiance. Now I hate it as much as I hate the red, white and black you see everywhere. Even when you brush your teeth, there's a swastika on the toothpaste.

That is why I love being back here on the farm, seeing all the natural colours even in winter.

I can't tell you when I started to doubt Hitler. Lots of things niggled at me, but I didn't add them up at first.

I didn't like the way we kept hearing about executions and prison sentences for people found guilty of crimes as silly as malicious gossip or telling a joke that made fun of the Third Reich. Heinz used to say there was more to it than they published but still are we not allowed to laugh anymore?

Perhaps I am making excuses for myself now, but whatever happens in the wider world, home life still carries on when you have small children. I know there was a constant fear of saying the wrong thing to the wrong person or doing the wrong thing, whatever that might be, but there were still plenty of good things to cheer you up and make you feel life wasn't so bad.

For example, my sadness about the war didn't stop me enjoying our victories, and I gave a little cheer when Paris fell because it seemed right after everything Germany had suffered because of the Treaty of Versailles. Plus, we had three days' holiday to celebrate, with crowds cheering and church bells ringing.

Then again, I remember when Hitler returned to Berlin, after visiting the troops in France, a huge carpet of flowers covered the road as he drove to the Reich Chancellery. The radio report described it as a perfumed avenue of greens, reds, blues and yellows. Heinz told me there had been an order not to throw any flowers because of the security risk, but everyone ignored it. That mood of optimism affected everybody.

I think it was not long after England's air force started their bombing raids on Berlin that I lost faith in the Third Reich. Night after night the air raid alarms sounded and we had to traipse down to the cellar, keeping the children calm and pretending to enjoy the big adventure.

The government told us bombing raids like these were impossible. Goring even claimed if a single bomber reached Berlin, then his name was Meyer. Well, they lied. The damage affected all parts of the city. Fires burning in the night. Families made homeless. People killed.

They lied about the Jews with their posters and suchlike but they always made it clear they didn't want them living in Germany. This was different, this was lying to the German people and once you know you've been lied to, you never trust the same way again.

Because of the bombing they put pressure on families to evacuate their children. Someone from the welfare association interviewed me, but I put them off by telling them I had family in Bavaria and they assumed I would go.

Funny how you can get used to anything, war included. Rationing, air raids, the lack of any new clothes, they all became normal to us. And yet we still had fun and enjoyed ordinary family life.

We'd taken the tram to the Tiergarten the day Hitler invaded the Soviet Union. It was such a beautiful day I couldn't be downhearted, even though it would mean more losses on the battlefield, but the news upset Heinz.

'This won't end well,' he said.

Later that same year Heinz helped evacuate Jews from the city. It wasn't his department but everyone had to get involved. I have never seen him so quiet. Each night he put on his favourite record and sat listening to music with his eyes closed. One night he even poured a large glass of schnapps and downed it in one gulp which he never normally did.

When I asked him where they were being evacuated to he said to various places like Litzmannstadt or Warsaw where they had set up camps. When we had the chance to talk, I wanted to ask him more but all he said was 'The poster worked.'

The next week he was back at the Alex working on a new case and seemed more himself. Not long afterwards, I visited Frau Rose, but she had already gone. When we next talked, I told him how sad I was to lose a friend and I asked if she would be all right.

'I don't know, Henni. You're not encouraged to ask questions and find out.'

Then he told me how a Jew had saved his life in the Great War. Heinz was part of an attack on the enemy when a shell landed near him and blew him off his feet. He lost consciousness in no-man's-land. When he came to, he saw the danger of his position and so did Isaac Bernstein, another member of his platoon. Despite heavy shelling and snipers and goodness knows what else, Isaac inched his way over and pulled him back down into the safety of their trench. They awarded him the Iron Cross for his bravery under fire.

Then I understood why Heinz had been so upset, not just about the expulsion of the Jews, but about all the propaganda and all the attacks on them. He took every attack personally.

***

Dear Diary,

The problem with writing a diary is that you get carried away. Your thoughts go this way and that and all over the place, but I hope you will forgive me because I am unburdening myself of all these long years of war.

The year 1942 came and went quietly. Carola started school in September, which gave me more time to keep up with Tomas, who always had so much energy.

In February 1943 we found out about our defeat at Stalingrad. As Heinz had predicted it was all ending badly. We had lots of bad news that year but the worst from our point of view was the bombing of Berlin which resulted in huge swathes of the city being turned into rubble.

In June I told Heinz about our fourth Bauer baby. The pregnancy thrilled me because it meant we would be a proper family according to Hitler's rules, but from the start I didn't feel right. Tiredness overwhelmed me, I had morning sickness for the first time and my legs swelled up like balloons. At first, I put it down to being older, but *something gnawed at me, some instinct that things weren't going right, not with the pregnancy particularly, but with life in general.*

In July we heard about the terrible bombing of Hamburg. That is when my gut instinct of being safe disappeared. I didn't want to leave Heinz, but a few days later we travelled by train to Munich where Papa picked us up.

Mama spoiled me (still does) and insisted I rest and put my feet up. I used to write to Heinz every week (I had a few letters back but not as many as I wrote him!) and he got away a few times to visit us. At Christmas he came to stay for a whole week and I cried when he told me what had happened to Berlin. In November, hundreds upon hundreds of bombers came over the city night after night and they turned it into a mound of rubble. All the magnificent buildings, all the beautiful streets, all destroyed. Thousands lost their homes and their lives.

Even the zoo, with all those poor animals who couldn't understand what was going on and must have been absolutely terrified, was bombed to destruction.

I don't want the children to witness all that destruction, and I don't want to myself. When Heinz went back to Berlin, I wrote to Albrecht explaining how I felt and asking for his help. Every day I wait for a response but so far nothing.

***

Dear Diary,

By the middle of February my enormous tummy made me waddle and kept me from sleeping. When I had my routine check-up at the doctor's, he wanted me to go to the hospital. His calm and matter-of-fact manner lulled me into a false sense of security.

That changed as soon as the obstetrician examined me. He listened to the baby's heart, called in another colleague, then a third, so that I was frantic by the time they finished and kept asking if the baby was all right. The baby's heartbeat worried them and they wanted me to have a caesarean. I was in a complete panic, but what could I do? Minutes later they wheeled me into surgery.

When I came round, Mama sat by my bed.

'What's happened? Where's the baby? Is it all right?'

Mama told me it was a girl, and she was being well looked after by the nurses.

'I want to see her, Mama.'

'Now, Henni, you've had a big operation, maybe now isn't the best time.'

'Not the best time? What are you talking about? I need to see my baby.'

I became hysterical. The first thing any mother wants is to see her baby. Surely my mother, of all people, understood that? Why were they stopping me? The obstetrician came in at that point and I begged him to let me see my baby. He said that wouldn't be wise, but when I started to get out of bed to go in search of her, he changed his mind and said he would agree on condition I stayed in bed.

'Perhaps I should warn you...'

'What?'

'That things are not as they should be.'

'What do you mean?'

Mama answered for the doctor. 'He means she's mongoloid, Henni.'

'I don't care. I still want to see her and hold her.'

They brought her then, and she was beautiful. Lots of dark hair and a cute little nose and when she opened her eyes, I fell completely in love with her.

The doctor explained his concerns for her heart, but I couldn't take it in. She seemed fine lying in my arms content. They kept trying to reassure me she wasn't in any pain. Well, I could see that for myself. Why were they making such a fuss?

Mama suggested calling the Pastor, and I agreed to make her happy.

In the early evening he came and baptised Lisle. Heinz and I had already discussed names: Lisle for a girl and Otto for a boy. I was still vaguely irritated by the whole thing.

I insisted they brought me her cot, so that Lisle slept beside me and they thought better of opposing my wishes.

Mama assured me they had sent a telegram to Heinz and that he would be at my side as soon as humanly possible.

The doctor gave me an injection to assist with something or other, but everything went hazy so quickly that I'm sure he gave me something to knock me out.

When I woke the next day I was so groggy I could hardly work out where I was or what had happened. A nurse sat knitting.

'Are you knitting clothes for my baby?' I said and then I remembered.

'Where is Lisle? Where is my baby?'

'With the doctor, I'll get her.'

A few minutes later the doctor walked in.

'I'm sorry, Mrs Bauer, your daughter didn't survive. The heart disease was more serious than we thought and she died this morning at 9.35am.'

I screamed long and loud. The expression on the nurse's face made me scream all the more. The doctor called her over and she held me down while they gave me another injection.

When I woke up again, Heinz was by my side. I cried and cried while he held me. Eventually the tears dried up, and I asked Heinz if he had seen her and he said, yes, and that she looked very peaceful and very beautiful. I'm so glad he said that because I needed to know she was beautiful in his eyes and mine.

Heinz made all the arrangements for her funeral while I lay in hospital so grief stricken I barely spoke. Even when they stopped giving me sedatives, my limbs weighed so heavy I thought I would never walk again.

I only began to get better when Heinz brought the children in. Monika was so serious and held my hand, Carola got straight on the bed and hugged me, while Tomas stood hand in hand with Heinz, his eyes full of tears, biting his lower lip.

The children gave me the strength to move forward. Lisle is always in my heart, but I realised they needed me and I had to try for their sake. When Heinz returned that night without them, I walked to the bathroom with his help and slowly I regained my strength.

***

Dear Diary,

I still don't know what to think about all this. Are they telling me the truth or am I just believing what I want to believe? When I returned to the hospital to have my stitches taken out, I saw a different doctor, but the same nurse assisted him. I recognised her straightaway. She was a hard-looking woman, and I remembered her expression when they told me Lisle was dead. Triumphant. There is no other word for it. How can you look triumphant when a baby has died, and a mother is in despair?

When the doctor left the room, I confronted her.

'You were glad when my baby died?'

'Yes.' Her manner was not the least bit ashamed or sympathetic.

'But why?' Her attitude seemed so strange.

'We don't need children like that in Hitler's Germany.' She almost spat out the words 'children like that.'

'How dare you? She was my daughter, and she was beautiful and I loved her as much as any of our other children and so did my husband. She was special from the moment she came into this world to the moment she left.'

The nurse snorted.

'Special? Yes, she was special and there is only one thing to do with special babies, special children and special adults and that's get rid of them the way Hitler commands us to.' And with that she drew her hand across her throat.

I felt sick and a terrible thought struck me.

'Is that what you did to Lisle? Murder her?'

She laughed, can you believe it, laughed and her face took on that triumphant look again.

'Well, did you?'

She hesitated a moment, her eyes narrowed, and then she tossed her head back and said:

'She had heart problems, Mrs Bauer, just like the doctor told you.'

And with that she walked out of the room.

I had to sit down. What did she mean 'The way Hitler commands us to'?

When did we start killing disabled people?

Papa drove me straight to my own doctor who's known me from a child. I trust him and he explained the Hippocratic

Oath and said the doctors at the hospital would have done everything they could for Lisle which reassured me.

Then I spoke to the Pastor but he kept talking about God's mysterious ways and how one day we would be reunited with Lisle in heaven. When I tried to pin him down about Hitler's policies he kept looking away and quoting the Bible. In the end I was glad to get away.

Mama wrote to Albrecht to let him know what happened but I warned her not to say anything about Lisle's condition. This time, he responded straightaway and wrote a lovely letter sympathising with my loss and promising to help.

***

Dear Diary,

We'll be leaving soon and I shall have to hide you away. Writing all this down has done me so much good. There is so much that is wrong with all our lives, but there is nothing I can do about it. Somehow, I have to keep going, living my two lives, bringing up the children as best I can, and hoping, hoping that all this madness ends soon.

15

TIME DRAGGED IN CELL 14 as surely as it had in Marta's brief solitary confinement, but without the psychological damage, the desolation and despair. Sometimes she felt alone, and she was sure the same was true of all the prisoners, but this stemmed from their individual circumstances, their stories, which they could only share up to a point and then had to deal with in their own way.

As the days passed, the friendship between Marta and Danuta deepened. They made a strange pair physically: Danuta tall and blond; Marta short and dark. The other prisoners called them Don Quixote and Sancho Panza.

'Don't you mind?' said Danuta, when they heard the nicknames.

'Not at all. At least I'm not the donkey. Besides you're the one tilting at windmills.'

'If only it was windmills.'

Marta squeezed her hand. Danuta had told of her arrest for distributing underground leaflets and the interrogations which followed when they had beaten her repeatedly. Although by nature a friendly, outgoing individual, the experience had marked her soul as much as her body and there were long episodes when her grey, almond-shaped eyes darkened and glazed over and nobody could reach her.

The day the parcels came was the highlight of Marta's imprisonment. She smiled at the excitement the other women showed like children at Christmas or at a party. Almost as soon as the parcels came through the door, they rushed forward, searched for their names on the packets and carried off their prize.

'Aren't you going to get yours?'

'I have a parcel?' She whooped and picked up the remaining packet.

The handwriting was Ludek's; nobody else she knew used the Greek alpha for the letter A. She held the parcel and stared at her name; then hugged it to herself and danced around the room.

Helena watched and hissed, 'Stupid cow.'

Marta heard but nothing dampened her elation. All that mattered was that he was safe.

Inside she found food, including an onion, which she threw in the air and caught with a squeal; there were cigarettes, matches, a pencil and one blank sheet of paper lining the bottom of the cardboard box. Neatly folded was a pretty scarf in vibrant colours which she recognised as one of Wanda's she had always admired. She could not have been more thrilled with the humble contents of her little parcel than Aladdin opening his cave of treasures.

She had half-hoped to find a letter inside, but that was being silly; Ludek would risk nothing personal which might lead them to him. Yet how she longed to read something from him: words of encouragement, words of courage, words of love. She lit a cigarette and stared at the beautiful scarf, absorbing its colours and thanking both Wanda and Ludek.

After the initial excitement died down, the women offered to exchange cigarettes for food and vice versa. One of Zofia's friends admired the scarf and asked if Marta would swap it for a small jar of blueberry jam.

'The colours would give Zofia so much pleasure.'

Marta understood. Captivity deprived the women of pretty things and vibrant colours; in the greyness of prison life a scarf like this could boost their mood.

'Please don't think I'm being selfish, but I need that scarf for my next interrogation.'

The woman looked puzzled.

'Oh dear, it's a long story but I'll happily lend the scarf to Zofia in the meantime.'

She knelt next to the sick woman.

'Your friend offered to swap her jam for this scarf as a present for you. Unfortunately, the scarf is the one I described in my interrogation. I don't suppose it'll make any difference, but I'd like to have it with me. Until they send for me again, please enjoy its colours.'

Zofia smiled and thanked her quietly, taking the scarf and laying it across her body, where it delighted everyone who passed by.

The very next morning guards escorted Zofia to hospital and Marta, retrieving the scarf, saw it as a talisman for all of them. That night the prisoners gathered to pray for Zofia's recovery and an air of hopeful expectation pervaded the cell.

Marta's turn for interrogation came the next morning. She winked at Danuta and sauntered out the room with her chin up; this time she had something concrete to show Inspector Bauer, instead of all the lies and dead people she kept summoning up, like a conjuror trying to win over a sceptical audience. It never occurred to her that she would be endangering Wanda and possibly Ludek as well. At Pomorska Street she headed up to his office, but the guard pulled her away and marched her to the interrogation room, her legs growing more feeble by the step.

Assistant Inspector Friedman walked in alone and her stomach turned to lead. She looked all around her as he sat down and crossed his arms, spreading his legs out wide. Where was Inspector Bauer? He had no paperwork and stared at her with ill-concealed contempt; no, it was worse than that; it was hatred, all-consuming, merciless. She smelt it as surely as a rotten egg suffocating her throat.

'Sit down. You make me sick standing there.

'Tell me once again about your work for the resistance. And don't bother with any of your stupid lies.'

She couldn't catch her breath and stuttered her first words. The crack of his knuckles made her flinch. Any display of what he would term arrogance would send him over the edge. She lowered her voice and repeated her story slowly, avoiding eye contact.

As he towered over her, he screamed into her ear:

'LIAR. LIAR. LIAR.'

Instinctively she cowered from the noise and knew she'd made a mistake. Questions shot around her brain like a bagatelle ball. Why had she shown weakness? Would she survive the interrogation? Where did that pain come from? Had he burst her eardrum?

Now he laid into her slapping, punching, karate chopping, until both she and the chair went flying. Rolled into a foetal position, she covered her head. He kicked her and picked up the chair to beat her. His fury seemed to increase with every blow.

Then he flung the chair away and grabbed her by the hair raising her up from the ground and thrusting her head against the wall with a sickening thud. And now a smouldering anger rose inside her and she glared at him through narrowed eyes, even as every fibre of her body ached and her brain throbbed.

'Would your mother be proud of you now?'

'My mother? My mother's a whore like you, pleasuring a man while my father fights for us at the front.'

His face shrivelled into a gargoyle of hatred.

'Only her German blood stays my hand... for the moment. But you, you're a filthy whore, a disgusting Slav prostitute, with nothing, nothing at all to save you.'

Envenomed with propaganda, he shouted and screamed obscenities at her and thrust his forearm against her throat, choking her; he punched her repeatedly in the stomach, his face contorted with rage. Then, in a change of mood that was as quick as it was unexpected, he brought his face close to hers and whispered.

'Mark my words, bitch, your time will come. When we've killed off every Jew in Europe, then we'll come for you, you and every other worthless Pole.'

He spat in her face and dropped her to the ground. Marta wiped away the spit and swallowed hard to keep the nausea from reaching her mouth, but despite her efforts she vomited again and again, shaking uncontrollably.

'Stand up.'

He spoke in a normal tone of voice, his anger apparently spent, but wary of him she edged herself upright until she was leaning against the wall. He seemed to wait for something from her and she didn't know what it was. Then the words came to her.

'What a fool I was. A man I care nothing for duped me and now I've lost my freedom and maybe even my life.'

'Ha. Well, we don't expect any intelligent thinking from Poles. Not now, not ever.'

He took several deep breaths, savouring his victory over her.

'Guard... take her back to Montelupich.'

'Yes, Sir.'

Marta was turning when Friedman grabbed her elbow, spun her round and punched her in the face with such force she hit the edge of the open door before blacking out.

She had no recollection of the journey back to prison and did not regain consciousness until the early evening. The women were kindness itself. One prisoner who always complained of cold hands placed them on her throbbing forehead and her swollen eyes; Danuta held her hand and spoke soothingly to her; one woman, who was a nurse, checked her over.

At mealtime she didn't want to eat, but swallowed a few sips of the brown liquid and dunked her bread to soften it. When evening roll call came, they tried to persuade her to stay lying down, but Marta didn't want to cause trouble and thought only Zofia had earned that privilege. She stood and stared at the floor, glad the inspection passed quickly.

She lay back down on her mattress and closed her eyes, tears of pain and humiliation seeping from them. There were no bones broken, but she felt broken inside; her spirit crushed; her self-respect battered with every blow remembered. To beat people senseless, people who had no means of defending themselves, seemed at that moment more reprehensible than killing them outright.

'And yet you survive.'

'And yet we survive.'

The remembered exchange brought her a modicum of comfort and helped her rebuild, however falteringly, her sense of self, her belief in her dignity as a human being.

Her head still throbbed the next morning when the guard called her out for interrogation. The other prisoners gave her sympathetic looks and encouraging words.

'We will pray for you,' said Danuta, eyes full of concern.

'Have courage,' said another.

Only Helena stayed silent.

Courage, yes she would need that if she had to face another beating. Yet he never sought information from her; she was never in danger of betraying Ludek and for that she thanked God. No, that wasn't an interrogation: it was an orgy of hatred directed at her because she was Polish. Please God the war would end before they succeeded in destroying her nation.

16

Seated in his office, Inspector Bauer questioned his assistant.

'I have a list of ten names with the initials SJ or FJ, all officers of the rank of Oberlieutenant or above. I've allowed for the possibility of promotion.'

'Yes, good, that's sound thinking.'

'They are all based in Warsaw so we can hand the investigation over to our colleagues there, unless you want me to pursue the matter myself?'

'No, not unless you are keen to do so. There are plenty of cases to keep us busy here and you have your examination for promotion coming up, so I expect you would prefer to remain here.'

'Yes, Sir.'

'That's settled then. Let me know of any progress by our colleagues in Warsaw. I'm interested in getting a satisfactory outcome to this enquiry.'

Bauer smiled at Friedman, thinking he would buy the man a drink if this wild goose chase produced anything approaching a result.

'Now, according to the diary, you interviewed Miss Paciorkowska yesterday while I was at the police conference.'

'Yes, Sir.'

'Did anything come of the interview?'

'No, Sir. I don't believe she knows anything of interest to us.'

'No, Friedman, again I applaud your intuition. That is very much the conclusion I have come to. It bodes well for your chances of promotion.'

There was a knock at the door.

A guard stepped into the office followed by Marta. Pain was making her take small, hesitant steps, but she held her head high and her voice was strong as she said 'Good morning, Inspector Bauer.'

'Good morning, Miss Paciorkowska. Please sit down.'

The state of her bruised and battered body shocked Bauer. One swollen, blackened eye was closed; the other showed multi-coloured bruising; there was a long bruise down one side of her face; her arms, as she steadied herself against his desk before sitting down, were black and blue.

'Is this your handiwork, Friedman?'

'Yes, Sir.' His eyes bored into his boss and he sported a thin smile.

Bauer could not complain: this was what he had signed up to when joining the Gestapo. How his colleagues could go home to their loved ones after inflicting pain on a fellow human being was beyond him. But was he any better than them, knowing the pain was going on in a different room, a different building? If he did nothing to stop the torture, wherever it was happening, then wasn't he as guilty as the men striking the blows or worse? After all, he too forgot its existence when he returned home.

He didn't view himself as a monster, but as a man caught up in a pernicious world. He couldn't influence or fight against this madness. To do so would be to endanger himself, but more importantly his precious wife and children. Did that make him a coward? No, he didn't believe so; he had faced danger in the last war and never faltered in an attack on the enemy, not even as bullets whistled close by or his comrades fell alongside him in agony or in silent death. To fight Nazism did not strike him as bravery, but as complete foolhardiness. This was a sickness, a disease that had to run its course and the only thing its victims could do was lie low and wait for the fever to break. How happy he would be when that day came.

'In view of our previous conversation I need not detain you any longer, Friedman. Please continue with your other assignments.'

'Yes, Sir. Heil Hitler.'

'Heil Hitler.'

Prisoner and interrogator faced each other. He wanted to apologise for the beating she had undergone, but recognised how lame that would sound to his ears, let alone hers. Instead, he offered her some information to buoy her up as her wounds healed.

'Brutality is always to be regretted, particularly now, when the Allied forces have landed in France and we face more important battles, ones which may yet finish this tiresome war.'

Marta said nothing. Did this signify the beginning of the end? She hardly dared hope for something so wonderful, so miraculous, the answer to all their prayers.

'In the meantime we have paperwork to complete before you return to Montelupich. My secretary has prepared the following statement for your file. Read it, make any adjustments and sign it.'

Marta examined her confession; her eye troubled her and an aching head made it difficult to concentrate. She baulked at the word prostitute; it looked so much worse typed in black; the thought of signing her name to it, dishonouring her family, nauseated her.

Stop it. Have you forgotten why you are here? Have you forgotten Ludek? You have done what you needed to do to protect him. There is no dishonour in what you have done for love. She reached for the pen.

'What happens now?' she asked.

'That is outside my control. The authorities will make their decision in due course.'

'How long will that take?'

'It's difficult to say.'

Marta nodded slightly in acceptance of her fate.

'Will there be any more interrogations?'

'No, I will mark the case closed and I will keep Assistant Inspector Friedman so busy that he won't have the energy to brush his teeth let alone raise a hand to you.'

'Thank you.'

Bauer gave her a nod of sympathy and called the guard.

Three weeks later, he sat in his boss's office alongside the newly promoted Friedman, as they discussed their case load with Fuchs. Eventually, they reached the closed cases and the one that Bauer was dreading: Paciorkowska, Marta Antonina.

Discussion was brief and centred on investigations in Warsaw where there was no discernible progress.

'Perhaps our colleagues are not as diligent as we are here in the Central Government,' said Fuchs, as Friedman preened himself.

'No,' said Bauer, wondering if he dared suggest Friedman pursue the investigation himself, but Fuchs pre-empted him declaring they had more than enough to keep them busy here.

'And the prisoner?'

'Send her to Ravensbrück.'

'Yes, I'm sure the SS guards will appreciate some new pussy,' said Friedman and laughed with as much enjoyment as Fuchs.

'You're not laughing, Inspector Bauer. Perhaps you don't share our sense of humour?'

Friedman's tone was pleasant enough, but he didn't fool Bauer. The man resented his recent, strenuous workload and with his promotion confirmed regarded himself as an equal.

'No, not at all. I was just wondering how my brother-in-law would react to the joke.'

Both men stopped laughing. Obersturmbannfuehrer Hoffmann had a fearsome reputation and was a figure of considerable importance in the Central Government and the instrument of Bauer's transfer from Berlin to Krakow. He wasn't a man you messed with.

'But on balance, I'm sure he would find it hilarious,' said Bauer, laughing and giving Friedman a friendly pat on the shoulder. All three men laughed together, but a point had been made and they all knew it.

'Well, that's enough business for one day. Now why don't we all celebrate your promotion Friedman and the first drink is on me.'

'And the second on me. Where do you propose? There are a few things I need to clear up and then I'll go straight there.'

With the location agreed, he headed for his office where he locked the closed cases files in his desk and pocketed the key.

At the Luxus Bar on Burg-Strasse, the drinking continued for most of the night with Bauer matching them drink for drink but always losing the contents of his glass so that by the end of the evening his drunkenness was pure show. With a display of brotherly love for his colleagues, for Hitler, for the whole German race, Bauer extricated himself from his fellow drinkers and headed home.

The next morning he was at the office bright and early. He requested plenty of coffee and made much of the headache that followed such a marvellous evening's drinking and then asked Brigitta not to let anyone disturb him.

Unlocking his desk drawer, he pulled out the files and placed Marta's on top. He took the transfer order form and filled it in. To avoid arousing suspicion, he continued with all the closed cases files, filling in the forms as appropriate.

'Remind me, Brigitta, does Criminal Director Fuchs need to countersign these?'

'Inspector Bauer, that drinking session really didn't do you any good. Leave them with me. They do require a countersignature, but as it happens Criminal Director Fuchs was rather late in today so I will sort these out with his secretary and get them signed and stamped.'

'Thank you, Brigitta, you are a Godsend, and if you organise some more coffee, I shall declare you a veritable angel.'

Friedman didn't appear in the office at all which pleased Bauer. He saw Fuchs as the man was heading home.

'You must have hollow legs, Bauer. How on earth did you get into work so early?'

'I don't know about hollow legs, but my head has been pounding like a big bass drum for most of the day.'

'Mine too. I'm going home to sleep it off and I suggest you do the same.'

'Yes, Sir.'

The next morning Brigitta brought all the files, countersigned and stamped and placed them in front of Bauer who produced a small box of chocolates from his desk drawer and presented them to his secretary with a flourish.

'These are for you for being so solicitous yesterday when I wasn't quite myself.'

'Och, you shouldn't have, Inspector Bauer.'

But his gesture filled her body with pleasure and she blushed as she left clutching her gift.

He flicked through the files, found Marta's and checked the transfer document. All was in order.

'These can go now.'

'Yes, Sir. I'll send them straightaway.'

'Thank you, Brigitta.'

RAVENSBRÜCK
1944

17

THE CONVOY RUMBLED ON. Inside the prisoners huddled together. Marta made her peace with the prickly Rachel. She sensed the woman didn't like her but didn't understand why or what she could do to change her opinion. It was the same wherever she went; there was always someone who took exception to her and the unfairness bewildered her. What had she said? What had she done? She never had this trouble with male companions. It was a mystery when she made friends easily and inspired loyalty to match her own.

They stopped for hours at a time, but couldn't see out. Where were they? How long would they have to wait? The guards had distributed chunks of bread before they left Krakow, but how long was it meant to last? Marta took a bite and chewed it into a mushy pulp.

There was no water; the sun heated the carriage and sapped their energy; some fainted and others moaned until the guards told them to shut up or they would close their mouths for ever. The thirst never left them.

Her tongue was a riverbed in a drought: fissured, pitted, cracked. Her skull tightened like a vice, and she hallucinated: Ludek appeared before her and she smiled in surprise; he morphed into her mother and she whispered 'Mamusiu' and reached out, but as her hand touched the wire, she disappeared and the disappointment overwhelmed her and she sank into blackness.

How long had they been travelling when the train screeched to a final halt? They heard dogs barking and women's shrill voices shouting and cursing.

She saw the white fangs of snarling dogs and the dark uniforms of women guards armed with thick sticks and rubber clubs which they used with grim determination on anyone too slow or too hesitant. There were several rows of five women ahead and she joined a new row. Shouts, curses and blows continued nonstop until they gave the order to move.

Bedraggled and stiff, they marched at the double through the outskirts of the town of Fürstenberg. It was early in the morning and most of the inhabitants were in their beds. Marta's eyes darted from side to side as she looked at the pretty houses and saw a church in the distance. The momentum of the march and fear of the consequences of falling behind kept them going step after step until they reached their destination. They had arrived at Ravensbrück concentration camp.

Iron barred gates opened onto a sandy arena, the Appell-platz. Vast grey walls surrounded the whole camp; electric fencing trimmed the perimeter walls; skull and crossbones placards vibrated in the breeze creating an eerie wail. Wooden, single-storey barracks formed a grid alongside the main street, the Lagerstrasse. A tannoy system hung on poles.

They lined up again. The air warmed under the sun's rays. A woman in the front row fainted, then another.

A prisoner stepped forward from the ranks and called out 'Permission to speak, Frau Oberaufseherin.' The chief woman guard stopped mid-stride, jerked her head back and played with the whip in her hand. The silence was palpable. Marta held her breath and waited for the thrashing to begin.

'Permission granted' issued from the black crow's mouth.

'The women have been without water for four days and nights. Water will stop them fainting and make them more useful to the glorious Third Reich. Thank you, Frau Oberaufseherin.'

The prisoner spoke in cultured High German, bowed and stepped back into line.

Inspired by her courage, other voices whispered 'water, water', but the head guard shouted 'silence pigs' and hit out at anyone who stood near her. She kicked those who had fainted to get up and back in line.

With order restored, she issued instructions. A runner, dressed in prison stripes and wearing an armband, ran off. Minutes later the prisoners watched precious water slop out of buckets onto the ground. An order given, they crowded round, some dipped their hands straight into the water, others waited for the ladle; all drank greedily as the water revived their bodies and spirits.

The camp stood in the middle of pine forests and lakes, a place of recreation for German families, and Marta breathed in the scented air. Then she noticed more of the camp's inmates: some waited outside a building; others pushed a handcart loaded with, Mother of God, they looked like corpses; no, she must have hallucinated that; others dragged a strange contraption with a long hose. They were the living dead: grey drawn faces without colour or expression; heads bent down; dirty grey striped dresses hanging off them; skeletal arms and legs; strange bulges where you would expect stomachs or chests.

The blood drained from her face and her scalp prickled with a new fear: she wouldn't survive this.

A commotion to the rear of the new arrivals distracted her. An SS officer dragged a woman by the hair and flayed her with his whip. All around the dogs launched themselves on their leashes in a frenzy of snarling, growling, and barking.

Nobody moved until the woman lay bloodied in the sand. He held aloft a packet of cigarettes and observed his audience.

'I forbid you to smoke. Anyone caught with cigarettes knows what to expect.'

A woman moved to help her friend up.

'Leave her there.'

Marta drifted to the edge of a barrack. She scanned her surroundings, bent down to rub her ankle moving it forward to form a barrier with her other leg while she buried her own packet in the dirty coloured sand behind her.

She would follow the rules; she would not give them an excuse to punish her.

They ordered the prisoners into a building to the right of the iron gates. 'Quickly, quickly' rang in her ears as the guards ordered them to strip, leave their clothes in piles, run to the showers. There was shouting and cursing, shoves and slaps to keep them moving, disorientated and compliant.

Vile men, SS Officers with no sense of shame, wandered up and down, assessing the women's attributes, laughing and mocking. One of them used his riding crop to caress a young prisoner's breast then drew it down over her stomach to part her labia. Her face bright red, she stared into the middle distance; the officer slapped his thighs and roared with laughter. Another prisoner shaved her head and removed her pubic hair with speed and haphazard scissoring. She looked like a skinned rabbit. He lost interest and looked for another victim.

Marta hurried through every foul, debasing action with jaw-clenching anger. How dare they treat women like this? Didn't they have mothers, sisters, girlfriends, wives? The stripping, the searching, the showers and every humiliation put her senses on alert. Now her mind was resolute: she would survive this and she would remember every detail of what they had done to her and to all the others.

Someone handed out uniforms: grey drawers; grey shirt style jackets; striped cotton dresses; headscarves or head bonnets; clogs. They did not bother matching the clothing with the prisoners. Some wore dresses too large, others too small. They set about swapping their mismatched clogs but there was so little time.

They dressed and lined up to collect their triangles and numbers. No longer naked, Marta took control of her emotions, and listened. Each person gave their name to a camp administrator, a fellow prisoner who found it on her list.

There was a pile of different triangles, but most received a black or red one, according to their crime of being an asocial or a political prisoner. Marta dreaded facing the other women with her back triangle. She had told no one her cover story, not even Danuta, and wondered how they would react. Her heart hammered away and her mouth dried up. Would there be other consequences of being marked out as a prostitute? Was this where Lady Fortune abandoned her?

She wanted to survive, to return home to Ludek, but there were things she could not do and would end her life on the electric fence sooner than comply. Tears stung her eyes, and she swallowed hard. Don't let them see you cry; be strong and ready for anything.

She stepped forward.

'Name?'

'Marta Paciorkowska.'

'Polish. Red triangle. Number 44911.'

A rush of energy surged through her body as she joined the other women. She could not believe her luck. She touched the P in the centre of her triangle and brought it to her lips before sewing the two pieces of fabric onto the arm of her jacket.

A siren screamed across the tannoy system. The women lined up on the Appell-platz in rows of ten, hands by their sides, eyes to the front and experienced their first roll call. The counting restarted several times; it was a taste of things to come.

At the end of roll call they had to pick up a wooden bowl, a drinking cup and spoon and head into the barracks designated for quarantine. Already traumatised by their reception into the camp, the women gasped and reached for each other's hands as the guards pushed and shoved them into a stinking space already occupied by hundreds of women from previous transports.

How could they call this quarantine when the overcrowding alone would cause diseases to spread rapidly?

Wooden tiered bunks from floor to ceiling, jammed so close together you couldn't walk between them. They could have relieved the crush of bodies but nobody sat or lay on them. As they edged their way along, they tried to orientate themselves within the barrack. They could see a central wash area with several basins and latrines; next to it was an area containing a few tables and stools, already occupied, and two sleeping quarters.

Everywhere the women stood or sat or slumped in every attitude of weariness, resignation, hopelessness. Marta sighed. Fate had sucked them into a maelstrom of madness: a place where words were punctuated with slaps and punches; where piteous images, one after the other, seared their eyes; where rules were issued after they had already been punished for disobeying them; where prisoners were guards and guards were there to destroy them. Nothing here was normal.

Someone tugged on her sleeve. She turned, and a smile beamed across her face.

'Danuta! You're here, how wonderful, I knew you were on the same transport, but I never saw you after we left. Mind you, I was crying so hard I'm surprised I saw anything at all.'

'I know. I was the same, wondering all the while if I would ever see my friends again, if I would ever walk through Krakow again. I'll never forget the way people called out to us to have courage and saying they would pray for us. They were so kind and brave, really; you could see the guards didn't like it. Remembering their words kept me going on that dreadful journey. And now we are here, in this hellhole, and the journey feels like some luxury trip we were lucky to have. This dump is beyond my wildest imagination. I don't know what I was expecting, but it wasn't this.'

'No, you're right, it's beyond imagination. How did you get away without having your head shorn?'

'I have no idea. Perhaps it was short enough already. I don't understand the system here at all except it involves a lot of slaps and worse.'

There was a shout for silence as a tall, robust woman wearing a green triangle, pushed a prisoner off her stool and stood on it. Two fierce looking prisoners, also wearing green triangles and carrying stool legs accompanied her.

'Welcome to paradise,' she called out in German and laughed manically, the helpers joining in.

Then her face turned serious and threatening.

'Learn the rules, my friends, and learn them fast. I am your block senior and these are my room seniors. We maintain discipline in this block and you will obey us or you will be sorry.'

The room seniors banged the stool legs against the nearest table and made threatening gestures to the nearest inmates who stepped back in alarm.

'The siren will go off at 4am, that's when you will get up and you'd better be quick about it. Wash, use the toilets, make your beds military style. You will not use the beds again until night-time.

'My room seniors will choose someone to assist them collecting bread and coffee for breakfast. You have one hour before the 5am siren sounds for roll call.

'As you are in the quarantine block, you will not go out to work but you will work inside, keeping the block clean, keeping the washroom clean and anything else we tell you to do.'

Thoughts were spinning in Marta's head: hundreds of women using one tiny wash area, how would they manage? How long would their quarantine last? What work would they have to do when it ended?

'There will be another siren for lunch when you will get our delicious soup.'

The manic laugh reverberated round the barrack.

'You will line up and hold out your bowls. You will clean your utensils after every meal. There will be more soup and bread for supper.'

'Nobody is to leave the quarantine barrack except for roll call and nobody may come in except those on official business. You can identify them by their armbands.

'Thank you, ladies, for your kind attention and now go about your business.'

With the welcome speech over, the block senior stepped off the stool and headed for her separate quarters together with her room seniors; the two women swiped their clubs left and right but most of the inmates were quick to step right back.

'What was that all about?' asked Danuta, who only understood a little German. Others were asking their compatriots the same question and Marta translated.

The lunchtime siren brought a new shock as they found out how meagre their portion of soup was.

'Ah so this is our delicious soup – a consommé that's never seen a piece of meat in its life. Well, who would have thought?' said Marta, raising her eyebrows.

'Oh God, it's inedible.'

'All the same eat it. There may be some nourishment in it and we need to keep our strength up.'

'I can't, Marta; it is beyond disgusting.'

The doors to the barracks opened and ghosts – for what else could you call these Godforsaken creatures? – wandered in, holding out their bowls and mumbling. Festering sores on their arms and legs, eyes wild like a trapped animal, they had the effect of lepers on the other prisoners, who drew back from them in horror.

So much for the strict quarantine, thought Marta, as she too stared at the wraiths. Danuta poured her soup into the nearest bowl; others followed and even Marta who had swallowed several spoonfuls gave up and donated the rest to these repulsive creatures who drank the soup and looked for more.

'Get out you miserable, stinking pigs,' shouted the room senior heading for the nearest trespassers with her club raised high and they half-ran in front of her and out the doors.

'I see you've met our little pieces of jewellery, our schmuckstücke. Don't bother feeding them, ladies, they're already dead.'

'I cannot believe what I have just seen.'

'No. That was Dante's Inferno staged in front of us.'

Her words triggered the memory of Ludek describing the Grand Guinol, the Parisian theatre of horrors where realistic portrayals of rapes, murder and savagery of every kind made audiences faint or vomit.

Only they weren't the audience; they were the players; the extras.

'What else is waiting for us out there? That's what keeps bothering me. What's yet to come?'

'Come on, let's get these bowls washed, although I'm not sure it's worth the effort.'

The wood of the bowls had furred up over time, but they went to the washroom to follow the rules. While they stood there, Irenka, a fellow inmate from Montelupich joined them and shared information that would save their lives.

They learnt never to leave any of their utensils lying around because someone would steal them and without a soup bowl or drinking cup they would starve. In fact, they needed to keep all their possessions with them at all times and until they sewed themselves some bags, they would need to insert them inside their clothing.

Now Marta understood the strange shapes she had seen.

'How do you know all this?'

'I'm a communist. We look after our own so we've already had a visit from one of our group who arrived here last year. We're helpless on our own, but if we stand together than we have a chance against these Fascist bastards.'

She told them how to address the SS auxiliaries or women guards as Frau Aufseherin and the head guard, if they were unlucky enough to merit her attention, as Frau Oberaufseherin. Then she told them the camp jargon: blokova for a block senior; stubova for a room senior; kolonkova for a work detail senior. A good blokova could make life a great deal more comfortable, but some blokovas were dictators and when they weren't beating you up themselves, were all too quick to report you for punishment by their aufseherin.

She described the different categories explaining that their current blokova was a criminal; she earned her green triangle by murdering her husband while he lay asleep in bed. Marta and Danuta exchanged glances. Besides the asocials and politicals there were also Jehovah Witnesses who wore a lilac triangle and Jews who wore yellow triangles sometimes with another, red one, superimposed on it.

'Don't let them see you helping another prisoner. It's against camp rules. If someone collapses at roll call, leave them there. The overseers excuse no one from roll call. If you need the toilet, you must hold it in and if you can't you'll just have to let nature take its course.'

'No wonder it stinks around here,' said Danuta. Irenka shrugged her shoulders.

'The smell will be the least of your worries. When you've been here for a while you should be able to organise things for yourself, barter food for extra clothing, that kind of thing. That is forbidden too, but everyone does it, so if you're careful it must be possible. If you put the word out you need something, you'll find someone will approach you with a price for it. The price will be so many rations of bread unless you have something useful they want in exchange.'

Marta thought of the packet of cigarettes she had hidden and wondered if she could still get it back, but then remembered they were being quarantined. Maybe it was for the best; it was one thing to hide something, quite another to go searching for it later and risk a beating.

'Try not to get ill, though I realise that's not under your control. If you do, then avoid going to the Revier or camp infirmary. There are no medicines and you could end up worse off than if you'd just kept going.'

With those ominous words, she wished them luck and left them reeling with all this new information.

Roll call that night took several hours to complete. Tempers frayed as the blokovas organised their prisoners into ranks with shouts and blows; eventually all were standing correctly, and the counting started. The blokova checked and rechecked her numbers; when she was satisfied they were correct, she stood on the right flank of the block and waited for her overseer.

'Attention,' she called out as her particular Frau Aufseherin appeared and the prisoners tried to stand up a little straighter to bring the whole tedious experience to an end. All the blocks had to be counted correctly, so the waiting continued. Marta observed the row of black crows, whose adamantine faces looked them over, as if they were so much vermin.

Disgusted by the sight, she turned her gaze to the beautiful sunset; awed by the radiant colours she remembered the scarf she had left behind for others to enjoy. It had been the right decision: none of their clothes or possessions survived the registration process, not even her special prayer, Our Lady's Dream, which she had written out and placed in her pocket.

Roll call ended, and they trudged back to their barracks for their final meal of soup and bread. The soup was still disgusting, but Marta dunked her bread, ate it and spooned up the liquid methodically.

‘To think I complained about the prison soup,’ said Danuta. ‘This is my punishment: for complaining then I have to eat this watery pigs’ swill now.’

They made their way to the washroom together; they rinsed their bowls and spoons and then held each other’s things as they went to the toilet.

Danuta scowled as she returned from the latrines and did her best to wash her hands.

‘This is so disgusting. How are we supposed to wash when there is no soap? How are we supposed to dry ourselves when there are no towels? How are we supposed to maintain basic hygiene when there is no paper to wipe our derrières?’

‘So long as we can use posh words like derrières we’ll be fine.’

‘I would happily say bum if only someone would give me some paper for it.’

It was a welcome moment of levity and both grinned as they headed for the sleeping quarters where a new challenge faced them: bodies occupied all the bunks and none of them looked willing to give up the little space they had.

‘Oh, my God. We will have to organise ourselves better tomorrow.’

‘Never mind tomorrow, where are we going to sleep tonight?’

Their stubova walked past and seeing their hesitation banged her club against the tiered bunks; rather than risk a blow to the head, everyone shuffled along and both women found bunks to get into even if their inhabitants grumbled and poked elbows and knees into them.

She longed for sleep, but all the different scenes of the day refused to leave her mind.

Soon the sounds of snoring and moaning, of quiet weeping and helpless cries pervaded the barrack and made sleep even more distant. She put her arms around herself and tried to sense Ludek's presence as she had done so many times in prison, but the magic no longer worked. Even his face seemed less defined as she brought his features to mind. She feared she would never see him again.

A hand groped its way towards her bowl and she lashed out with a violence she didn't know she possessed. No thief would make her starve; she curled up and cuddled her utensils.

Shouts of 'Get up, Get up' startled her awake. Her first action was to pat her stomach and check she had everything. She staggered out of the bunk and waited for Danuta to emerge.

'Sleep well?'

'Like a baby.'

Grimacing, they both headed for the washroom. They stripped and washed in the cold water before wiping off the water with their hands and dressing.

By the time they finished, coffee and bread was being handed out in the dining area and they lined up for their share.

'Before the war I used to love a milky coffee first thing in the morning,' said Danuta. 'I used to dunk my pastries in it. It was heaven in a mouthful.'

Marta nursed her mug of watery brown liquid and doubted whether remembering such delicacies would make their breakfast more palatable, but said nothing and chewed on her bread. Encountering a hard lump she suspected it had more than its fair share of sawdust.

They made their beds and had just enough time to wash their cups before the siren sounded and they headed out for roll call. Their blokova was in a foul mood and yelled at her charges and punched several hard in the mouth and boxed their ears before she calmed down and was ready to start the count. Their aufseherin witnessed the aggression with glowing eyes: violence preceded order, as it should.

The morning roll call ended without incident and as the work crews were being assembled, Marta's convoy headed back to the quarantine barrack. With nothing to do, they found places to sit and shared their thoughts.

'Do you remember that woman who asked for water?'

'Yes, I wonder what happened to her. I don't think she's in the barrack; at least I haven't seen her.'

'No, me neither.'

Irenka enlightened them later that day when she came to find them sporting a cotton bag containing her possessions.

'You haven't wasted any time,' said Danuta, as she shifted her own things inside her dress.

'I told you, we look after our own.'

'Bully for you.'

'We'll sort out bags in due course,' said Marta and asked Irenka if she knew what had happened to their water heroine.

'The Oberaufseherin took a shine to her, and she's now working in the administration offices.'

'So no quarantine?'

'No, she won't need it where she's gone. She'll be in one of the elite barracks where they get a daily bath and extra rations and new uniforms when the old ones wear out. The SS don't want their offices filled with smelly inmates who keep scratching because of their fleas and lice.'

Marta stopped; she hadn't realised she was doing it, but now rolled up her sleeve and saw the telltale reddish brown spots.

'Oh great,' said Danuta, noting her own bites on her arms and legs.

'My advice to you is not to scratch them if you can help it. You don't want to get them infected.' Irenka nodded to the two women and left to find her communist companions.

'My advice to you… I know where I'd like to stick her advice and her fancy bag.'

'You're only jealous.'

'Yes, I am. Who wants to spend their nights with a cup sticking into your breasts and a spoon wedged into your ribs?'

'Well, put the word out and find out what they're charging for bags.'

'I will.'

After roll call that night a group of prisoners started to sing folk songs and the soothing sound gladdened their hearts. German songs only, ordered the blokova, but she didn't try to stop them and singing became a welcome feature of their lives.

18

THE DAYS AND WEEKS passed in a morale sapping routine of monotonous roll calls, disgusting soups and bread, petty fights and senseless bickering, often brought to an abrupt halt by the blokova yielding a stool leg or just her fists.

After nearly five years of rationing, none of the women had much fat to spare and most had lost even that during their recent stay in Montelupich; nevertheless, they all noticed how much thinner they had become since arriving at Ravensbrück.

'And that's without working,' said Danuta as they compared the size of their arms for the sake of something to do.

'I know and yet I think I would prefer to be doing something, anything, rather than sitting around here all day.'

'Well, maybe not anything.'

'No, you're right. I've been overhearing the blokova's conversations and I can't believe some of the things they've been talking about. Do you know they actually have a road building crew here and a general construction crew? Can you imagine it? Women as thin as sticks, surviving on soup rations, expected to build a road or office buildings or anything else for that matter. It just defies belief.

‘The first day we arrived here, I thought I was hallucinating when I saw some of the inmates pushing a handcart with what looked like bodies on it. I wasn’t hallucinating. Apparently they have a corpse crew which goes around all the barracks collecting the dead.’

‘Dear God, how do they get away with it? Do people on the outside know about all this? What about the Red Cross? Can’t they do something?’

‘I don’t know. I’m beginning to wonder if anybody cares.’

The next morning’s roll call was particularly tedious as the figures failed to add up hour after hour.

‘I thought the Germans were supposed to be good at this sort of thing,’ said Danuta tugging at her headscarf as they headed back inside.

‘They are, only it’s not called counting, it’s called sapping the will of anyone who wants to leave this place alive.’

‘Perhaps if I think of it that way I’ll stop getting so bloody annoyed about it.’

When everybody was back inside, the blokova called for silence and said she had an announcement to make: today marked the end of their quarantine and their convoy would be transferred to different barracks as soon as they had undergone their medicals.

Most people reacted to the news quietly and speculated what it might mean for them and, most importantly, what kind of blokova they would get in their new barracks. Shortly afterwards, they were ordered out onto the Appellplatz to strip naked, leave their clothes and possessions on the ground in front of them and head to the Revier where they stood in serried ranks.

The siren sounded for midday soup, but they were not allowed to move. Prisoners walked past them, heads cast down. Two doctors left the building and strolled to the SS dining quarters without casting them a glance.

'Why are they doing this to us?'

'Because they can, just because they can,' Marta whispered back, hatred mounting inside her.

She had visited the latrines earlier but somewhere behind her a woman could contain herself no longer and they all felt the shame.

Marta absented herself from the misery around her and remembered the niceties of Polish high society where rules dictated that your first visit to an acquaintance lasted only fifteen minutes and where you did not, under any circumstances, request a visit to the bathroom. Sublime politesse exchanged for sordid affliction.

The sun beat down on them; flies buzzed around them; an elderly woman fainted. Nobody dared help her and she lay in an awkward heap. Skins unused to the sun turned pink, then red.

The doctors returned belching and smelling of alcohol. When they deigned to come out, they looked the prisoners up and down, ordered them to open their mouths and gave their teeth a cursory glance, before declaring them fit and well. The elderly fainter never regained consciousness, and they never saw her again.

They redressed, already pained by the touch of fabric on sunburnt areas, and stood waiting for the next instruction. The blokova consulted with the aufseherin and Marta wondered, not for the first time, why everything involving the Germans took so long while everything involving the prisoners proceeded at the double.

They separated the convoy into two groups and marched them to different barracks. Marta hoped she and Danuta would still be lodged together but she knew better than to look around and check. What would be, would be.

The new blokova, another green triangle, spoke in a German dialect Marta found hard to follow. A short speech, it comprised one rule and one piece of advice: don't make trouble and don't forget you're the newcomers here.

She spied Danuta at the back of the room and they made their way towards each other.

'I'm not looking forward to roll call. Can you imagine the chaos? We have no idea where to stand or how we're supposed to fit in with the current inhabitants.'

'Do you think we should use the time we've got now to wash so that we can get ahead of the others?'

'I suppose we could ask.'

Marta made her way to the blokova's room; one of the stubovas blocked her way and asked what she wanted. Marta requested permission to wash while the other inmates were out at work. The stubova said nothing then shrugged her shoulders with supreme indifference and turned away.

'I don't know if we have permission or not but I suppose it's worth a try.'

Even with fewer people around, they guarded their things while they strip washed in the cold water; one or two others joined them.

'I feel better for that.'

'Yes, it was worth doing.'

'You've caught the sun.'

'Yes, I know. I wonder if we could get some soothing yoghurt around here.'

'Well, why ever not? That sounds an excellent idea.'

Before the evening siren, the original inhabitants came back. Marta heard Polish, Ukrainian, Russian and other languages. There was a lot of staring and ill-tempered muttering about 'more bloody inmates' and 'how many more do they think they can shove in here?' but nobody blamed them.

During roll call their blokova was efficient and stated all were present and correct.

'Anybody I need to place on Report?' asked the crow.

'No, Frau Aufseherin.'

But Frau Aufseherin was feeling deprived; she wanted to punish somebody and release her pent up aggression; anybody would do, and she walked up and down the ranks slapping someone here, kicking someone there, until satisfied she had stamped her authority on the Schweinehunde.

All of them learnt early on not to react to any punishment, no matter how unwarranted. To moan, or cry out, or remonstrate was to invite more of the same. So they stood, eyes to the front, and took the punches and the kicks and the blows with as little movement as possible and with mouths closed.

The blokova seemed a decent sort stirring the soup before she ladled it out giving everyone scraps of vegetables without favour. After washing their bowls they headed straight for the bunks where the stubova allocated them spaces.

Marta and Danuta found themselves on adjoining bottom tier bunks; both had one other occupant sharing with them.

Marta's companion was a Polish woman in her early twenties named Renata; she had been at the camp for seven weeks, six in quarantine and one in their shared barrack, and wore a red triangle. She was small and attractive, a black-haired gamine with a retroussé nose. Hair growing back in uneven tufts added to her elfin appearance.

They talked about their crimes: Renata said they'd arrested her, alongside her younger brother, for painting graffiti in their home town of Plonsk.

'Polska Walczy?' asked Marta, referring to the anchor symbol of a P with a W underneath, shorthand for 'Poland Fights'.

'Yes, we painted three before they caught us. It was only five in the morning and we thought no one would be around. Now I wish we'd just stayed at home. Jurek is only fifteen and I don't know where they've sent him or even if he's alive.'

'It was a brave thing to do.'

'Seems stupid now, landing up here for a bit of paint splashed on a few walls.'

'No, you mustn't think like that. People like you and your brother have kept us going. Do you know how inspirational it is to see one of your signs? It lifts your heart and makes you think we can win against these monsters.'

'Do you think so?' asked Renata, looking a little less forlorn.

'Yes, I do. We just have to keep going until the Allies bring this wretched war to an end.'

'But will they?'

'They've already landed in France. It can only be a matter of time.'

Renata's eyes widened, and she hid her face in her hands. The lights went out and one by one the different conversations tailed off.

The sound of Renata sobbing woke Marta in the early hours.

'What's the matter?' she whispered, conscious other inmates still slept.

'They've stolen my bread; the bastards have stolen my bread.'

Between sobs of rage and self-pity, Renata explained how she tried to save her evening bread for the morning when she needed more energy for work, but somebody kept stealing it from her.

'Oh Renata, maybe you shouldn't try to save it then. I can't fault your logic but better to have it at night then go without it altogether.'

'But how do they do it? It's so well hidden.'

'Get up, get up'. One of the stubovas came into their sleeping quarters, banging on the bunks with a wooden club, until everyone shifted. As they made their way to the washroom, Danuta introduced Agnieska to them; an Ukrainian of quiet demeanour and large soulful eyes whose abortion had merited her a green triangle.

'She's been here two years and works for a local farmer,' whispered Danuta.

As they drank their coffee, Marta tore at her portion of bread and gave half to Renata whose eyes softened as she mouthed a silent thank you.

'Eat it now. I want to see you doing it.'

After morning roll call, Agnieska joined her work crew while the others returned to the barracks; Renata explained they were now 'availables' and would fill in wherever there was a shortage of labour.

Marta spent the rest of the day digging sand and loading it onto a hopper car. It wasn't long before her arms and back ached with the unfamiliar physical work. She set her pace by another inmate who was a regular on the crew. She didn't want the kolonkova to lash out at her.

When the siren sounded for their midday meal Marta plodded back to the hut. To judge by their drawn faces and expressionless eyes Renata and Danuta had fared no better in the labour stakes. I suppose I must look the same, she thought, as she spooned soup into her mouth and tried to ignore her aching muscles.

The afternoon's work seemed to last forever. A relentless sun added to their misery and sweat poured off their faces and arms and inside their clothes.

A road building crew passed by and Marta glimpsed Rachel or thought she did. A bruised face and limping figure turned her stomach over and she tried to catch her eye but the woman kept her head down oblivious to her surroundings.

The tedium of roll call came as a blessed relief; she no longer had to dig or lift a spade or push a hopper along the rails and unload its contents somewhere else. Standing upright, eyes front, her mind was already asleep and her limbs, locked into position, at rest.

Irenka continued to update them on camp life.

'What are you chewing? I swear I can smell garlic.'

'A tiny sliver of dried sausage.'

'What? How? Where? Why?' Danuta spluttered in impotent rage.

'One of our group received a parcel and shared its contents.'

'A parcel?' said Marta, her mind racing back to Montelupich.

'Yes, they come through from time to time. As you would expect, the SS pilfer them, but if the senders are clever, they make any food as unappetising as possible and so bits get through. It helps if you've got contacts in the admin...'

'Which you have, no doubt,' said Danuta, cutting her off.

Irenka shrugged her shoulders and departed with a little wave of her hand.

'I'll swing for that woman.'

'But, Danuta, think, we could get parcels too.' She clutched her friend's arm. 'Imagine it: a parcel could save us, stop us feeling so hungry if nothing else.'

Marta's hope soared like an eagle carrying prey back to its eyrie. She dreamt up endless scenarios of Ludek finding out her destination, putting together the contents with ingenuity and love. But the parcel never materialised, and she puzzled over the situation. Had something happened to Ludek? And Wanda? They must have found out where she was, and they wouldn't have forgotten about her. Or maybe the parcels had never reached their intended recipient? Perhaps someone had stolen them, perhaps Ludek had been too generous with his contents? Yes, that must be it, he had just cared too much.

Summer turned to autumn turned to winter. They had survived six months at Ravensbrück. Their faces were as grey as the inmates they had seen on arrival; arms and legs as skeletal; eyes haunted by what they had seen and what they had done. Hunger consumed them and mocked their nights with vivid dreams of abundant food.

Marta's stomach shrivelled and shrunk into a tight, malevolent ball; her guts seeped in daily sabotage; her body had become a treacherous companion in the fight for life. Only her mind pared itself back to an essence, not so much of intelligence, but of instinct. With atavistic precision she knew when to act, when to melt into the background, how to look, when to speak, when to stay silent.

Hatred became her armour against the random violence and casual cruelty of their lives. Shielded from sight, she spat at the crows, blinded their pitiless eyes, silenced their screeching voices, paralysed their beating wings.

Small differences made the days more bearable: Danuta now had a hessian sack for her goods, a gift from Agnieska who wanted nothing in return except her continued kindness and friendship; Marta had picked up a thin rope on the construction crew and used it as a belt to which she tied her utensils; she also bartered her bread for some paper and a pencil and wrote out Our Lady's Dream which she kept hidden in a crack in the bunk; Renata found an old tin which someone could use as a cup or bowl and bartered it for a small bag.

The large Polish contingent in the camp organised lectures and educational programmes from language and literature to mathematics and astronomy.

'Shall we go? I fancy learning about the stars then we could stand at roll call and count the ones we recognise,' said Renata.

'You go, then come back and teach us.'

She didn't want to discourage her friend, but she couldn't see the point for herself. She had more than enough to think about.

She watched, amazed and humbled, at the gifts friends made for each other. Beautifully embroidered handkerchiefs, crucifixes carved out of sticks, little fabric dolls, cards illustrated with roses. Items stolen from their workplace or bartered for precious bread.

Food rations did not increase in the winter and there were regular fights over bread. When Marta found herself embroiled in a battle, she gave up her ration rather than fight for it; she didn't have the energy. From time to time she shared her bread with Renata whose instinct was still to hide her evening ration. Nobody fought over the soup.

Roll call now took place in freezing conditions but their dresses and jackets were the same they had worn all summer. As they stood shivering, the well-fed crows emerged in thick capes, warm hats and gloves and seemed to relish the fresh air on their faces; they didn't appear to be in any hurry to complete the counting and recounting. Roll calls could still last for hours.

'Have you heard?'

A prisoner from the neighbouring block burst into their hut one Sunday, their only day of rest.

'There's been an escape.'

The news galvanised them into whispering cohorts. Who was it? How did they do it? Would they get away with it? Scouts scuttled around the camp to find out whatever they could and by nightfall a dozen different stories were circulating among the prisoners.

The euphoria lasted until roll call. Guards dragged a cowering wreck in front of them and unleashed their dogs. Her bloodied and torn body tossed this way and that in a macabre dance to the music of her screams. Eyes front, hands at their side, nobody moved.

Overcrowding was now so bad they had erected a massive tent between two of the barracks. Inside there was no electricity or plumbing or heating; the women had to use the deep latrines dug outside, and it was a common sight to see one emaciated prisoner clinging onto another to prevent her falling into the pit.

Some prisoners spent a short time in the tent before being sent away to other camps, but the majority stayed and died in conditions which made the other barracks seem like the height of luxury. The tent blokova never stepped inside so there was nobody to organise the distribution of soup or bread. Only the fittest fought their way to the food.

They used the availables twice a day for corpse collection, dragging bodies out of the barracks and placing them on their hand carts; women who had never seen a body before now thought nothing of lifting stiff arms and legs into the cart, ignoring the pain and despair etched into the faces of the dead.

'What will people say afterwards when we will tell them about the camps?'

'They won't believe us.'

'You seem very sure about that.'

'Imagine a film crew recording everything we have seen since our arrival. Now imagine your friends and family watching it. They would say the director was mad, that nobody could survive such horrors.'

'And yet we do survive.'

'We do, indeed. I don't know how but we do.'

A new blokova arrived, took a dislike to Danuta and made her life hell. Her button was undone; her bed wasn't straight; she was looking defiant. The list of petty faults and lies resulted in beatings and then Reports.

Harsh punishments led to three days in the Bunker. They kept her there with no food, in almost total darkness, with no shoes and only a blanket to protect her from the cold. When she emerged, she was a broken woman. Agnieska held her hand and tried to persuade her to eat the bread ration she had saved for her, but Danuta just shook her head.

Marta and Renata were beside themselves with worry and gave her their soup when she refused to collect any for herself. She looked distracted and had a permanent frown; then it disappeared and a smile lit up her face as if she'd solved the problem troubling her.

'You've been the best of friends. I wouldn't have done any of this without you.'

Agnieska smiled back and embraced her when Danuta chewed on some bread, but Marta remained unconvinced. In the morning she was gone; the sack containing her utensils tucked in beside Agnieska. They found her when the siren screamed for roll call; she was hanging off the electrical fencing.

For days Marta plotted revenge on the green triangle; she was ready to murder her if she could only figure out how to get past the stubovas. Her imagination ran riot with ever more bizarre schemes until Renata, alarmed at her behaviour, touched her forehead.

'You're burning up. You must have a temperature of over 40.'

She went in search of the block nurse who came to look at her.

'Typhus. We should get you to the Revier and have a doctor examine you.'

'No, it's not that, nurse,' said Marta forcing herself to speak. 'I'm just distraught over the death of my friend so I've been tossing and turning all night and it's left me feverish.'

'Mm, I'll talk to the blokova and see what I can do.'

Marta expected nothing from this encounter but going to Revier risked her being placed in the Typhus Block to die with no treatment and even further rationing of food. What she didn't know was that the nurse was owed a favour by the blokova, and since she had known and liked Danuta, she decided now was the time to call it in.

'You're excused roll call and work for the next three days only. I'll try to get something to help with the symptoms.'

Marta closed her eyes and stretched her limbs. Just knowing she didn't have to face roll call or work crews, made her better.

Click clack. Click clack. The sound of boots on wooden floors woke her mid-morning. She sank back into the straw, willing herself to disappear. What was he doing here? The SS never entered the barracks leaving prisoner control to the aufseherinen and their chosen blokovas.

Her eyes met his and with one supreme effort she reached for the scrap of paper with Our Lady's Dream and held it tight in her hand. Minutes passed; there was no movement; there was no sound except her heart slamming against her ears; the officer turned on his heels and left.

She thanked God and slept again. Renata fed her soup at mealtimes and tried to bring down the fever with cold compresses using a clean rag the nurse had brought them, but it was Agnieska who saved the day; she bartered the surplus utensils for enough medicine to put Marta back on her unsteady feet and even got her extra bread.

After three days, the nurse insisted that she needed Marta's help in the Revier and she spent hours in the warmth rolling up bandages. The following day was a Sunday and there were no work crews which gave further time to recuperate. The nurse continued to provide her with additional jobs until by the end of the week she was fit enough by camp standards. Next day's roll call turned out to be their last at the camp.

19

IT WAS THE BLOKOVA who told them that two hundred women, including Marta and Renata, were being transferred to one of Ravensbrück's subcamps.

'Why? Where are we going?' The news alarmed them. Nobody had a good word to say for the camp, but they all feared change would mean a change for the worse.

The blokova shrugged her shoulders. She didn't know their destination and didn't care.

Guards marched them at the double to the station and loaded them into cattle trucks. Marta fell along the way, but Renata dragged her to her feet and although they both suffered blows and curses, they made it into the wagons.

Marta sat and continued to recover her strength. The next morning they found themselves at Finow, a small camp in the middle of woods surrounded by electric fencing. They saw a smaller Appell-platz, six barracks for the inmates, a kitchen and not much else.

'The crows look the same,' whispered Renata, as they stood for roll call.

An SS officer now made his way down the Lagerstrasse accompanied by a tall, grey-haired man in his fifties. They stopped in front of the assembled women and the SS man indicated them with an outstretched arm as if showing off his personal staff. The civilian asked any women who spoke German to step forward. Half a dozen did so, and he questioned their experience and educational achievements.

Marta embellished her qualifications claiming to have done secretarial work for a solicitor in the hope of procuring an office job. She need not have bothered as the man was looking for munition workers.

'What about these other women?'

Marta pulled Renata forward and said she used to work at a pram manufacturer's factory in Poland and she was teaching her German.

'Good,' said the civilian and walked away to confer with the SS Officer.

'A pram manufacturer's factory? What on earth do I know about prams?'

'It was the first thing that came into my head. They're not likely to check the information.'

'I suppose not. How are you feeling now?'

'Much better and more hopeful. Factory work would be almost as good as being in an office.'

The hope she experienced in her new environment lowered her guard. At roll call the Oberaufseherin announced that she needed more workers on the night-shift and called for volunteers to step forward. Marta was the only one who did.

Warmth enveloped her as she sat at a bench and a supervisor showed her what to do, stressing the need for concentration and nimble fingers. Red lamps lit the benches and black material covered the windows.

At six am they finished and headed back to the camp where they were latecomers to the roll call. Eyelids drooping, she yawned and waited to get into bed. She had no chance to speak to Renata who joined her work crew as soon as roll call was over.

'What the hell do you think you're doing?' The blokova was furious she'd disturbed a bed and boxed her ears.

'But I've been on night-shift.'

'You pile of shit. This isn't a night-shift barrack. You can't sleep during the day or you'll get me into trouble. Now find yourself a broom and sweep the floor and make that bunk up before you do.'

She scowled and muttered under her breath as she swept; her neck and shoulders tightened until her head ached.

She longed for nightfall. Hard planks, lumpy straw, a thin blanket: none of them mattered. Every muscle, every sinew, every bone craved sleep. At roll call she felt herself swaying and balled her fists to stay upright.

'Prisoner 44911 to join the night-shift crew.'

Where could she hide? What could she do? This was unbearable.

'Get a move on.'

She shuffled forward, giddy with the effort and trudged, five abreast, to the factory with no idea how she got there.

Sitting at her bench, she fantasised. Revenge on the crows would be sweet. They knew she hadn't slept for 24 hours, no 36 hours or was it… Her head dropped forward and hit the bench. Shouts and blows followed and the supervisor, incandescent with rage, ordered her back to the camp.

Inside the dark hut she crept into the nearest bunk and fell fast asleep. Renata found her in the washroom the next morning.

'What the hell did you do that for? Why did you volunteer for night-shift? The blokova couldn't believe it; the others said she talked about nothing else all evening.'

'I imagined I would come back and have a restful day, sleeping on my own, without all the noises you get at night.'

'So why are you here now?'

'I fell asleep at the factory.'

'Oh my God, Marta. What will happen now?'

'Nothing good, I shouldn't wonder.'

They ate their bread and coffee with heavy hearts.

After roll call they ordered Prisoner 44911 to stay behind on the Appell-platz. She stood alone, shivering for hours before two guards marched her out of the camp and up towards a series of bungalows. A neat garden filled with shrubs, lay either side of a path leading up to the first one.

She stepped into a warm and tastefully decorated room; impressionist prints hung on the walls creating calm and colour; classical music played in the background. It was a delightful environment that could have belonged to Marta or one of her friends.

Distracted by these pleasant thoughts, she never saw the first blow strike her to the ground.

'Get up.'

She staggered to her feet. A rubber truncheon hit her across the face. Knocked sideways she raised her hands up, desperate to protect her eyes, but the Ober kept snatching them away as she screamed at her for falling asleep. Blow after blow battered her into unconsciousness.

The guards threw her onto the first available bunk. The blokova left her alone. When she came round, bruised and sore, it was time for roll call. Renata pulled her up and stood alongside her; when they returned she helped her line up for her soup and bread never saying a word.

As they were eating, a Ukranian woman who worked in the kitchens slipped her two cooked potatoes. She clutched them to her chest and whispered her thanks before sharing them with Renata. After their meal and night-time wash, she went to sleep, never stirring until morning.

Refreshed and determined not to put a foot wrong, Marta worked diligently next day considering all the while how to sabotage the work. Every three hours there was a bell and the civilian workers left the factory for a fifteen minute break to rest their eyes from the red lights.

At midday they too had a break in which to consume their soup and some mashed potatoes inside the factory walls.

'Someone has salted these potatoes.'

'Yes, the soup seems thicker too.' Marta rooted around her mouth with her tongue.

'What's the matter?'

'My teeth are loose.'

'Is that where they hit you?'

'No, even my molars are loose. It must be the lack of proper food.'

Weeks turned into months and Finow became as familiar to them as Ravensbrück had been.

Marta eavesdropped the civilian workers talk about the progress of the war. She sensed they were getting anxious about the outcome although one or two continued to talk up their ultimate, glorious victory. Marta shared their fears about the advance of the Red Army; Irenka might want a communist future but not her. Nothing good came from the East and she wanted nothing to do with the Russians who had murdered her father and betrayed her country at the start of the war.

A scream ripped through the air like a lightening flash and thunder followed in the crash of equipment and the thud of boots running across the floor. Marta had whipped round and glimpsed the slap. She turned her body away, clutching her arms to her chest, rocking faintly.

Oh my God, Oh my God. What would happen next?

Her breath came in bursts and the sound of whimpering rose unbidden from her depths.

'Back to work.' The supervisor rushed from bench to bench but even the civilian workers struggled to control their feelings whether of pity or outrage.

'What's happened?' A tall woman, given to smiling at the prisoners, returned from the toilets.

'That woman over there slapped an SS officer in the face. Look they're taking her out.'

Battling against chaos, the supervisor announced a ten minutes break and Marta rushed to find Renata and hugged her tight.

'It's Ewa, isn't it? The poor thing. What happened? What made her snap?'

'I don't know.'

Ewa irritated her fellow prisoners with constant talk of her beloved little boy and her desperation to survive and return to him.

'As if we didn't all have loved ones we want to get back to' was a frequent comment muttered behind her back and sometimes to her face. She wasn't perturbed by such animosity. Her son was her hope and gave her the strength to continue. Until today.

Across the loudspeaker came the order: 'All prisoners out into the courtyard.'

The officer marched across to Ewa followed by the largest camp guards. He caught hold of her head and kept it in a vice-like grip, covering her mouth with his gloved hand. She looked like a bird caught in the jaws of a black panther. The others stood around, muscular and well-fed, breathing heavily and sweating with excitement.

He gave the order, and they set upon her, tearing her limb from limb.

Marta's lips moved in silent prayer. Distorted by tears, the scene fragmented before her: a spray of blood; a scrap of material floating to the ground; an arm held aloft in triumph then flung against a wall, sliding down to rest akimbo.

She had expected screams, but the air vibrated with the violence of snapped tendons, shattered bones and the sickening grunts and squeals of men playing tug of war.

Marta was shaking uncontrollably as she returned to her bench; all the women fumbled with their tasks and work slowed to a degree which infuriated the supervisor, but which he could do nothing about.

Back at the camp, evening roll call was mutinous as word spread of the savagery. Was it chance that the numbers tallied so quickly that night or did the aufseherinen sense the dangerous atmosphere and call an early halt to proceedings?

They returned to their barrack. Even the blokova was subdued. They consumed the soup and bread in mechanical fashion in silence. That night nobody fought over their rations. Washing in the cold water was vigorous as if they hoped to disinfect their minds and bodies of what they had witnessed. Nobody spoke but the sound of sobbing continued long into the night.

20

WORK FINISHED EARLY ON a Saturday and Sunday gave them the opportunity to visit friends in other barracks, walk around the grounds or gather their thoughts. Even the blokova relaxed and allowed them to sit or lie on their bunks.

Often they set about killing lice; they dug them out from under the seams of their clothes and squashed them thumbnail to thumbnail. Spots of blood stained their dirty uniforms, but they felt satisfaction in seeing another one dead.

The hut was quiet with just a murmur of voices in the background. For once nobody was arguing, nobody starting up a fight or seeking revenge for slights real or imagined. If you could ignore the stench and the discomfort, the unending hunger and the relentless anxiety that anything could go wrong, well if you could ignore all that, the atmosphere was almost pleasant. Marta leaned back and closed her eyes.

'I can't do this anymore.'

'No, I dare say it makes little difference; kill one and half a dozen take its place.'

'No, you don't understand, I can't do any of this anymore, any of it.'

‘Do we have a choice?’ Marta laughed sardonically.

When she opened her eyes her friend was slumped over.

She wasn’t sure how to react. Thoughts rushed through her head. Should she try sympathy or sternness? Encouragement or ridicule? Whichever way she needed to help her friend or risk watching her despair.

Danuta had only taken so much before succumbing to blackness; she had good reason to go under with her experiences, but there could just as easily be a slow burn towards extinction.

Leaning across she grabbed both of Renata’s hands: ‘What did you say when you killed that louse?’

‘What?’

‘What did you say when you killed that louse?’

‘I didn’t say anything.’

‘Well, that’s where you’re going wrong. Every time you kill one you have to say ‘Raus, raus, you filthy louse.’ It’s the only way, you can trust me on that. I’m something of an expert on the subject.’

‘Raus, raus, you filthy louse,’ she repeated and watched as Renata’s lips formed the words. Already, she saw a spark returning to dulled eyes. She held forth on the varieties of lice.

‘Now, the lice we find on each other, they’re German lice, no doubt about it. They can’t help themselves, they just have to invade Poland, so we get the German lice. If you had a magnifying glass, you would see their shiny black leather overcoats with little SS insignia on the collars and they carry miniature whips and dogs on chains. That’s why they’re so hard to kill: those chains get in the way of your fingernails.

'There are lice in Poland too, but they're too busy arguing among themselves to invade anyone, so you'll find no Polish lice here, no matter what the guards call us. The French louse is a different creature altogether. It wears a little black beret, and it has an air of je ne sais quoi, but it only wants to settle on the well fed so you don't see many of them around here.'

Marta carried on energetically until Renata's body relaxed and a smile twitched her lips.

'You are completely insane, you know that, don't you?'

'I would argue that insanity is the only sane reaction to this little world of ours.'

'Yes, Madam Professor, you always come back with a clever answer, but I would swap all your cleverness for the chance to get away from here.'

'Renata, we will I promise. Every Sunday we will sit here and talk our way out of here into a different world and we'll start right now.'

'Oh Marta, really?'

'Close your eyes. There. Guess what my favourite childhood treat was? Not cake or ice cream or chocolates or anything normal like that. No, it was a tomato and onion salad. Big red juicy tomatoes, cut into quarters and then into eighths, mixed with crisp, white crescents of onion, all salted to perfection and then the juice from a scented, bright yellow lemon squeezed over the top.'

Marta emphasized the colours and scents and textures. Renata needed to see and smell and taste her words.

'I used to love that. Gosposiu, dear housekeeper, I would say, please, can I have another helping and she would shake her head and say "All that sourness can't be good for you" but she'd get me another plate all the same.

'And she always gave me thick slices of bread and butter to go with it. She worried I would get tummy ache without something solid to soak up the juices, but I didn't care.'

Marta's mouth salivated. It would be a long time before they received their crust and watery soup. Better to change the subject.

'Did I tell you we used to live in a house on Hortensia Street in Warsaw? The garden there blossomed with every kind of flower. We had scented roses the colour of apricots growing up one wall and if you opened the windows in summer, the scent pervaded every room. I remember sunflowers against another wall, huge great heads turning towards the sun.

'My mother loved her garden. Her gentle soul must have despaired of me because I was always getting into trouble, especially with the nuns at school. They expelled me twice.'

'No!' Renata opened her eyes wide.

'Oh yes. One time I let loose white mice in the chapel. Oh my goodness, the pandemonium, the screams, the hysteria. Imagine the nuns running this way and that, except Mother Superior who tried to maintain control. They worked out who did it straightaway.' Marta laughed at the memory.

'Where did you get the mice?'

'I don't remember. I was only four or five.'

'What? Nobody goes to school in Poland at that age. You're just making this all up.'

Renata sounded sulky.

'If you're going to tell me fairy tales, stick to Hansel and Gretel or some such nonsense. I'm off to the latrines.'

Better anger than despair.

Renata harboured her indignation and spoke little. Marta watched to see she still washed, still made the effort to remain human. The week passed. After a record number of recounts on Saturday night, the Ober dismissed them.

Renata whispered: 'Escape tomorrow?'

A warm tingle spread through her body. It was going to be all right.

'Yes, escape tomorrow.'

Seated on their bunk they killed lice.

'Once upon a time…'

'Are you teasing me?'

'Well you deserve it after sulking all week. You reminded me of my little Daschund. A most wonderful dog, typical of the breed who was your best friend until you told him off for something and then he sulked for days.'

'Humph.'

'I didn't make anything up, Renata. Children normally start school at seven, but my parents sent me away early and to boarding school at that, because when they divorced they couldn't look after me.'

'Divorced! Oh my God, can you even get a divorce in Poland? That only happens in America, maybe even only in Hollywood. Honestly, I don't know of a single divorced couple in the whole of Poland.'

'And, of course, you know a lot of people in the whole of Poland?'

'Oh, don't tease me, it's not commonplace, is it?'

'No, though I expect there were others beside my parents.'

'What happened? Why did they divorce?'

'I'm not sure you'll believe me, Renata, because it is an incredible story, but it is the truth all the same.'

'Go on, I won't doubt you again.'

'Imagine a family of considerable social and professional standing. My grandfather Stanislaw Wilhelm Paciorkowski whose Coat of Arms was Gryf and his wife Konstancja Alina Tymowska whose Coat of Arms was Sas enjoyed high society. Trained as a lawyer, he became a judge of the Supreme Court. He also wrote at least one learned tome and numerous articles relating to the law and government.'

'Are they still alive?'

'My grandmother died a year after my birth, but my grandfather reached the age of 82 and only died two years ago in November 1942. Mind you, it was a miracle he survived that long, because he refused to accept the curfew imposed in Warsaw and would go out whenever he pleased, with his top hat and cane, his luxurious moustache and white beard.'

'Not someone who would blend into the background then.'

'No, I've no idea why they didn't imprison him or shoot him dead. People died for lesser things than breaking the curfew. Sometimes I wonder if they admired his noble bearing and absolute civility to everyone he met. Or maybe he reminded them of their grandfathers back home. Who knows?

'I visited him once when he lived in an apartment with his daughter-in-law and granddaughter, but they didn't make me welcome and there was a lot of unpleasantness over money and antiques I inherited from my mother which had mysteriously disappeared.

'Anyway, my grandparents had four children: a daughter Haneczka born in 1889, a son Jerzy born in 1894, then my father Stanislaw born in 1898 and another son Tadeusz born in 1900. They also looked after a young boy from a humble background called Jan Zieja, who became a priest and is a living saint. He is the truest Christian you could ever hope to meet, but that's another story.

'My father, or Stas as his family and friends called him, studied law and political sciences at Warsaw University. He must have inherited some of his father's love for words because he went into journalism. At one point he worked on the Illustrated Daily Courier.'

'Truly? My mother loved that newspaper. There was a writer she particularly liked – perhaps it was your father? Imagine that. She used to settle down of an afternoon with a glass of tea and enjoy half an hour of peace and quiet reading its pages. There was hell to pay if you disturbed her during her special time.'

'What a coincidence. I'm not sure how long he worked for the paper but his career prospered, and he became the Editor In Chief of the Morning Express in Warsaw. Later, and I'm guessing this resulted from his turbulent home life, he became the editor of the Red Courier.'

'Wasn't that the evening paper with the red masthead?'

'Yes, that's the one. Don't tell me your mother read that one as well.'

'No, my father. He used to buy a copy at the station before heading home from work and I would look through it sometimes, though, to be honest, the adverts interested me more than the articles.'

'Tata loved his job and from what I've heard he excelled at it, well at first he did; later things took a turn for the worse. I wish you could have met him, Renata. He was a brilliant man: erudite, opinionated, a witty raconteur and convivial host. He loved poetry, especially the works of Cyprian Norwid, and he wrote poetry himself. You would have liked him, I'm sure, and he would have taken to you immediately.'

'He sounds an amazing man.'

'He was. He really was.'

Renata reached for her friend's hand as she remembered her father.

'I'm not sure when he married my mother or even how he met her, but her maiden name was Wanda Gloszkowska and her Coat of Arms was Jastrzebiec.'

'Goodness Marta, do you think the lice know they're feasting on such fine blood? They should feel honoured.'

Marta grinned.

'It's amusing how important these things were in the past. It seemed to be instinctive that if you knew somebody's name you also knew their Coat of Arms. I wonder if such details will remain important?'

'People find it hard to let go of the past at the best of times and we've all been through the worst of times. Perhaps that will make genealogy even more important and people will want to identify themselves with their ancestors more than ever.'

'Perhaps.'

'Tell me more about your father. Was he handsome?'

'He was, not that I'm biased.'

'Of course not. And what about your mother? Was she beautiful?'

'Yes, they made a striking couple, and they lived the good life. A considerable salary funded champagne and caviar, tailored clothes, servants, trips to the theatre and concerts, everything they needed or thought they needed for their happiness, including the arrival of their beloved daughter, me.'

'So your parents loved each other at the beginning?'

'Yes, I have no reason to doubt it.'

'Oh, that makes it so much worse.'

'It does. Now that I've started talking about my family all these memories are crowding into my head. I was having a nap, sleeping in a pram or a cot outside in the garden – this must have been at Hortensia Street – and a storm broke out. It must have happened suddenly because I was alone when the thunder and lightning started. The branches of a tree are swaying above me and I wonder now if lightning struck the tree? Anyway, they came running to fetch me, but by then I was screaming blue murder.

'As you know, I'm still terrified of thunderstorms and want to hide in some dark cupboard until it's all over. It's bizarre after everything we have been through in the camp that I'm so frightened of a natural phenomenon. I can't say which I find worse: the flashes of lightening or the sound of the sky falling in.

'Another memory is when I kept getting terrible sore throats, and the doctor decided that I needed my tonsils removed. In those days they used to do that operation without anaesthetics. Can you imagine it? At first, I opened my mouth willingly, and they got the scissors or whatever instrument they used inside my mouth and cut out the first tonsil.

'They didn't get the second one. I screamed and screamed mostly from the pain, but also from the outrage of it all. When they tried to reason with me, I clamped my mouth shut. Mama tried pleading and bribing me with treats, but I was adamant and they gave up.'

'Goodness, Marta, you have had the most extraordinary childhood. Did you continue to suffer from sore throats?'

'I can't remember but I guess it must have cured the problem to some extent because nobody ever mentioned my tonsils again.'

'No, they wouldn't dare.'

'Time we got back to my family. Let me tell you about my uncles. The oldest, Jerzy, became a government minister in charge of home affairs; he married a woman called Wanda Dowojna-Sylwestrowicz, and they had a daughter Krystyna. The youngest, Tadeusz, joined the Army and married a woman called Zofia Hubicka and they had a daughter Alicja.'

'So that means all three brothers had just one daughter each.'

'Yes, you're right. Krystyna and I were born in the same year; Alicja came along seven years later and everyone acknowledged her to be the most beautiful of the three cousins.'

'What's happened to them?'

'Well, I imagine Uncle Jerzy would have escaped to safety, his family too, when the Germans invaded. I guess he's part of the Polish Government in Exile in London. I don't know where Uncle Tadeusz is now, but his wife and daughter are still in Poland, at least I assume they are. They were the ones living with my grandfather.'

'What about your parents? What happened to them?'

'Stalin's henchmen murdered Tata at Katyn; my mother died when I was thirteen.'

'Oh I'm so sorry, Marta.'

'It's all right, Renata. I've grieved for them in the past and I miss them all the time, but the pain isn't the same anymore.'

'So what about your Aunt Haneczka?'

'Ah well, she is central to this story, but we'd better save her for our next escape.'

'Oh, must we?'

'Who knows how many more Sundays lie ahead.'

'I guess so. Oh Marta, thank you for doing this. I feel I've been living a different life just hearing about your family.'

'And you must tell me about your family.'

'Boring.'

'Mm, there's a lot to be said for boring.'

Boredom would be a privilege in this environment: yawning and stretching and looking around for alternative activities; it would mean time to consider and assess, to exercise choice as a human being instead of obeying commands like a slave.

So much of their life was experienced on a knife-edge. There was nothing dull or blunted about their existence: everything was extreme, intense, concentrated, from the hunger in their stomachs to the cold numbing their limbs to the fear stalking their every move.

21

'I'VE BEEN LIVING WITH your family all week. I can't wait to find out more.'

'In that case we must move onto my Aunt Haneczka who lies at the centre of this whole tale. She was a remarkable woman. Intelligent, erudite, a true patriot, she lived several lives all at once and still found time to read a book or go to the theatre. Do you know what I mean?'

'Yes, very much so. I used to be friends with a girl at school like that, always doing something, going somewhere, joining something or other and she still achieved top grades in all her subjects.'

'That sounds similar. Aunt Haneczka became one of the first women doctors in Poland. She completed her medical studies at the University of Lausanne and worked as a surgeon at the Hospital of the Holy Spirit in Warsaw. During the Great War she operated in two of the Red Cross Hospitals; one at Brest-Litovsk but I can't remember where the other one was.

'Towards the end of 1917 they put her in charge of the press department of the First Polish Corps in the East.'

'That's a change of direction.'

'Another of those several lives lived all at once. Aunt Haneczka was a social and political activist no matter what else she did.'

'Your family must be very proud of her.'

'There's still more to admire because the Polish Military Organisation working for Poland's freedom sent her and her husband Stefan to work undercover in Moscow, Kiev, St Petersburg and then in Finland and Paris. For that undercover work they awarded her the Cross of Independence with Swords and the Silver Cross of the Order of Military Virtue.

'The Virtuti Militari? Heavens. There aren't many women who get awarded that.'

'When she returned to Poland, she worked in the High Command of the Polish Army and then in the office of the Civil Head of State and in 1930 she became a senator.'

'Was she beautiful?'

'More striking looking than beautiful, a handsome woman rather than a pretty one, although she was thirty years older than me so perhaps I'm not the best person to comment on her looks.

'My last memory of her was in Warsaw when she worked night and day to staunch the fires started by all the bombs. I really admired her for that because I couldn't stand it myself. After only a few days I had to get out. I'm such a coward.'

'No wonder. I imagine the bombing resembled one enormous storm with fires like lightening and explosions like thunder.'

'Mm I never considered that. Actually, Renata, that makes me feel better. Perhaps I'm not such a coward, more a victim of my childhood trauma.'

'Don't say that, you're not a coward at all. Nobody who survives this camp day after day can be called a coward. Besides, I don't suppose getting out of Warsaw was easy.'

'No, the roads were full of people trying to leave and the Luftwaffe were merciless, dropping bombs on refugees, flying low and strafing women and children as they ran into the fields and dived into the ditches.'

'A taste of what they had in store for us.'

'Indeed. Only this isn't helping us escape, so let's change the subject.

'What I don't understand is why your aunt is central to your story.'

'Ah, because instead of reaching the dizzy heights of a senator, she could so easily have become a social outcast.'

'Why?'

'Because in 1915, while still single, she became pregnant with a married man's child.'

'What a delicious scandal. Oh dear, I am sorry, Marta, I shouldn't have said that. It's your family after all.'

'No, it's all right. A man called Stefan Hubicki, a bachelor some ten years older, also a doctor, stepped in and married her and averted the scandal. Do you remember my uncle Tadeusz married a woman called Zofia Hubicka? Well, Stefan was her relative. Now whether the family put pressure on him or whether he was an honourable and decent man who wanted to help a colleague or whether he had always admired her from afar, who knows? But in whatever way the marriage came about, he accepted her son, Andrzej, as his own.'

'And the married man who made her pregnant?'

'Are you familiar with the architect who designed the Sejm Meeting Hall and who helped to restore the Royal Castle after we regained independence in 1918? He was one of the founders of the Society for the Preservation of Historical Monuments.'

'No.'

'Well, the man I am referring to is Kazimierz Skorewicz. Apparently he graduated from the St Petersburg Institute of Civil Engineers and became the city architect of Baku, the capital of Azerbaijan in the Russian Empire, before he returned home to Poland.'

'Pity he didn't stay there in Baku.'

'Indeed.'

'You know what I really hate? There he is this successful architect, but it could be a man in any profession, and he has his fun and then he walks away from it all leaving your aunt, but it could just as easily be any other woman, to face the social disgrace he's responsible for.'

'Well, it's always been different for men. Although to be fair, I'm not in a position to say exactly what happened. Maybe she fell in love with him and instigated the affair if not the actual pregnancy. Whatever the circumstances, my family found out and her brothers, including my father, vowed to avenge their sister and make him pay for his misdeed in a way that would cause him maximum social disgrace.'

'No. How on earth would they be able to do that?'

'By seducing his daughter and causing her ruin.'

'Oh my God, like Natasha Rostova in War and Peace.'

'Renata, you are a constant surprise. So you've read Tolstoy?'

'I loved that book and spent a whole summer with my nose stuck in its pages only emerging for meals or to help round the house when my mother forced me to. When that beast Kuragin kisses her and plans to abduct her, I thought it was the end of the world.'

Marta couldn't help laughing at the contrast between Renata's imagined apocalypse and the reality of their daily extermination.

'You know, Renata,' she said, smiling at her friend, 'we started this weekly escape to help you, but I think it's helping me every bit as much.'

'Then I'm glad. Now come on, what happened next?'

'Well, they assigned my father the task of seducing Maryta, but when he met her, it was a coup de foudre. They both fell head over heels in love with each other.'

Renata pressed her palms to her cheeks, her mouth slack. 'This is amazing.'

'I told you the story was incredible.'

'What about your poor mother caught up in all this? Presumably she knew nothing about this proposed seduction?'

'No, I can't imagine for a second she would agree to it. And it was a terrible thing to do; Maryta wasn't to blame for her father's indiscretions.'

'No, and it was your mother, and you who suffered.'

'What are you two talking about?' Their blokova had wandered over to their bunk and now stood close to Renata.

'Oh, about men and their foolish ways,' said Renata, focused on a louse.

The blokova spat on the ground, folded her arms and leant on the bunk post.

'Men? Huh there isn't one I wouldn't have strangled at birth, the pathetic, disgusting creatures. Now, if you want to experience true relationships, I'm more than happy to enlighten you.' She let her eyes linger on Renata.

'Thank you, I appreciate the offer, but I wouldn't dream of upsetting your special friends because I've heard the loving way they talk about you. Besides, information gets out and if my fiancé ever found out, he would kill me, even inside a concentration camp, I promise you that.'

The blokova sniffed and considered arguing further but the devotion of her acolytes mollified her.

'If you ever change your mind…'

'You'll be the first to know, blokova. Thank you again.'

'Wow you handled that brilliantly,' said Marta.

'God, can you imagine it? As if our life wasn't foul enough without having to service the blokova nightly. It's not that I object to what other people do; it's being coerced into something that should be private and voluntary. Do you mind if we go out for a brisk walk? I need to clear my head.'

The following Sunday, Renata was eager to find out more.

'We reached the point where your father and Maryta had fallen in love with each other, so what happened next?'

'There must have been a period of uncertainty and, I hope, of conscience for my father. All I remember is that it devastated Mamusia, and she kept saying 'Pray that your Father doesn't leave us.' Remember I was so young I didn't understand what was going on.'

'Oh, that is so sad. How awful for you to feel your mother's happiness depended on the success of your prayers.'

'I doubt I could have articulated that thought but you're right. It was a terrible burden to place on a child though I am sure she didn't mean to. She was a loving mother, but she was also still very much in love with my father.'

'What a man to inspire such love and devotion from two different women.'

'In my eyes he was just my Tata. It wasn't until I was much older that I appreciated him as an individual; I guess that's true of all children.'

'Yes, you're right. My father seemed a distant figure in my childhood, and when I grew up, the war broke out. He enlisted and now I have no idea where he is or even if he is still alive. What a waste it all is. Anyway, let's get back to your parents.'

'I don't remember how long the uncertainty continued for, weeks or months, but eventually Tata and Maryta set up home together. That's when they sent me away to boarding school, one run by the Ursuline nuns. I hated it there, loathed it with a passion. The nuns did their best, but all I wanted was to get back to my home and my beloved mother. My father too, but at that age it's your mother who's most important. Hence my naughtiness and always getting into trouble. It was my childish way of saying I wanted to be with her.'

'Why didn't you stay with your mother?'

'She had to work as a seamstress to support us.'

'But surely your father paid alimony for you after the divorce?'

'Actually, I've been wondering about that. People bandied about the word divorce, but the conversation always stopped dead when I walked in so naturally I assumed that's what happened. But perhaps they only separated. My mother was a staunch Catholic so I wonder now if she would have agreed to a divorce. She would have been dead set against it on religious grounds alone, never mind her personal feelings.

'Also I don't remember any wedding ceremony for Tata and Maryta. I suppose they might not have invited me, but there were no photos in their apartment and none of their friends ever mentioned one.'

'Perhaps if your mother had agreed to a divorce, a financial settlement would have enabled you to stay at home.'

'Perhaps, but then the Church would have deprived her of Holy Communion and that prospect was more devastating for her than being unable to keep me at home.'

'Either way, they avenged your aunt.'

'Yes, you're right, it must have been a disgrace for Maryta's father to see his daughter married to a divorced man or even worse to see her living in sin with him.

'Living in sin.' Marta snorted. 'And now here we are in the seventh circle of hell and all I can think is: Does any of it matter?'

'Oh Marta, I've made you mournful, I'm so sorry, I didn't mean to do that. Tell me something of your life at school. Did you make any friends there? What else did you do to warrant being expelled?'

Marta remained sorrowful for several minutes, but when she glanced up to see Renata's hopeful face, she shook herself out of her despondent mood.

‘Let’s leave that for another Sunday. It would do us good to get out of here for five minutes.’

‘Good idea, we’ll do that,’ said Renata, as she hitched up her shoulders and gave a feeble smile.

22

'THE THING I REMEMBER most about boarding school, except for the mice in chapel, was bath time.'

'That's a strange thing to remember.'

'The bath time was even stranger, believe me. We all had to wear these long vests under our school uniform and when we got into the bath, we kept them on.'

'What?'

'It's true. The nuns used a flannel to wash us under the vest.'

'But it would be sopping wet?'

'It was and I remember thinking I never kept my clothes on when I had a bath at home.'

'Why did they do it?'

'I suppose they had some bizarre notion about the human body being sinful. They must have whisked off the wet vest and wrapped us in a towel and dried us off but I've no recollection of that at all.'

'What a narrow-minded approach to life. But with that background it must have been an agony for nuns to go through that humiliating reception at Ravensbrück.'

'I don't recall it being fun for any of us.'

'Whoa. I meant nothing offensive. It was appalling for all of us, but you have to feel a special sympathy for nuns who have taken a vow of chastity and can't bear to see a child's innocent body to face scrutiny by those pigs of men laughing and jeering.'

'No, you're right. I don't know why I reacted like that. Perhaps I'm still blaming the nuns for my incarceration in boarding school.'

'Easier to blame them than your parents.'

'How true. Have you considered studying psychology when you get out of here?'

'No, I'm setting up a restaurant with a menu as long as your arm and plates the size of wagon wheels. God, can you imagine it? Having enough to eat? Going to bed with a full stomach?'

'No, I can't anymore.'

But Renata, eyes closed, mouth watering, had entered her fantasy world of food.

'The soup will be so thick with vegetables and meat and pulses you'll be able to stand your spoon up in it.'

'Renata stop it. It's hours before we get our evening rations. And I'm sure it makes it worse to keep obsessing about food.'

'Do you? But you're the same aren't you? Don't you think about food all the time?'

'No, I don't. I dream about food, I admit it, but when I'm awake my biggest desire is to wallow in a luxurious bath, get rid of all these vile fleas and lice, step into a freshly ironed nightgown and sleep in a comfortable bed with clean linen, a thick duvet and a pillow to rest my head on.'

'Mm tempting as a second choice, but not as good as mine.'

Conversation often turned to food with inmates exchanging recipes and memories of meals prepared for special occasions. Sick of hearing the subject, Marta determined to make her friend focus on something different, so she returned to her schooldays.

'At some point my mother gave up trying to send me away to boarding schools, and I returned home and attended a local school. With my life back to normal, I found I enjoyed school. Well, perhaps I should qualify that, I enjoyed the subjects that interested me and I excelled at, language and literature above everything else.

'Best of all I became friends with a small group of girls and we did everything together. We used to play 'Truth or Dare'. On my God, Renata, that was so exciting. We were honour bound to tell the truth in response to any question or undertake the dare if we didn't want to answer. I tell you we used to sweat in those games wondering what questions the others would dream up. The dares were daunting as well so the choice between them wasn't easy.'

'How old were you then?'

'Fourteen or fifteen, I guess. We were good friends and loyal to each other, but I have to tell you their parents didn't approve of me. They regarded me as a bad influence which I always considered most unfair. After all, I never made my friends do anything they didn't want to do. If they did something, like a dangerous dare for example, then why did I get the blame? They could always have told the truth instead.'

'Perhaps it was your rather exotic family background they really disapproved of.'

'That's possible. I've just remembered a time when I tried to get one of my friends to break my leg.'

'What? You are joking, aren't you?'

'No, honestly, I couldn't face going to school that day, perhaps I hadn't completed an assignment, or I was in trouble for some other reason. I decided a superb excuse for my non-appearance would be to break my leg. So, along with my friend Krysia, we went to the railway sidings where there were plenty of sleepers lying around. I knelt on one of them and I told Krysia to keep jumping on the back of my leg.'

'Oh, for heaven's sake, how was that ever going to work? And you're supposed to be the intelligent one?'

'Seemed a good idea at the time,' said Marta, a little petulantly. 'Besides, I was a lot younger, probably just eight or nine.'

Renata snorted in derision. 'Bet you had a few bruises to show for your good idea.'

'Yes, all right, there's no need to go on about it.'

'I wasn't.'

'Humph.'

Silence followed while both women examined their clothes for lice with studious attention until they caught each other's eye and giggled like small children.

'I'm quite convinced now that my parents didn't divorce, but I'll tell you who did.'

'Who?'

'Aunt Haneczka.'

'Never.'

'Yes, it's true. The marriage to Stefan didn't work out and it must have been a real divorce because Aunty married Henryk Szlendak in 1938.'

'Was Andrzej ever aware of his background?'

'I honestly don't know. He was a pilot and died in the early days of the war and Aunt Haneczka died in 1941 so I guess we'll never find out. Anyway, let me tell you about my mother's death. At the age of thirteen, I developed scarlet fever. Mama nursed me and then caught the disease herself. She developed complications, and they admitted her to hospital. When I went to see her, she said: 'Tusienku, you have such beautiful eyebrows; never let anyone mess with them.' Those were the last words she ever spoke to me. Two days later she died.

'The official cause of death was scarlet fever and its complications, but everybody said she died of a broken heart because she didn't want to live without my father.

'My beloved Mamusia dead. Nobody can ever replace your mother and nobody ever did. That's when I started smoking. One of my parents' friends, seeing me devastated, offered me a cigarette, and I became hooked straightaway. If you offered me the choice right now between an extra ration of bread and a cigarette, I would take the cigarette. God, I can't tell you how I miss having a smoke.'

'I tried smoking once, but it made me throw up.'

'Then you're lucky. It's one less thing to miss. Anyway, after my mother died, my father took me to live with Maryta and him and she looked after me with great care and love.

'She made me an off-white dress for the funeral and tied up my hair in a huge black bow. Mamusia had requested that my father place red roses around her face in the coffin. Somebody did, but it wasn't him; he didn't even come to the funeral. I walked behind her coffin on my own.

'They buried her in the Powazki Cemetery in Warsaw between two fir trees. Masses of people turned up to pay their respects, but not the one person she would have wanted there.'

'Oh Marta, how sad.'

'I miss her every single day.'

'So what was life like with your father and Maryta?'

'Not good to be honest. He started to drink heavily and eventually lost his job as editor. Whether he felt guilty about my mother or whether he and Maryta were falling out of love, I can't say, but they used to have terrible arguments. In fact, they used to get me out of bed at night to take sides. I remember leaning against the wall thinking how stupid and petty their disputes were.'

'How selfish.'

'Yes, I guess. They couldn't carry on like that and eventually they split up. By then I was getting on with my life and busy working for my final examinations to graduate from school and go to university. The world beckoned, and I was more than happy to embrace everything it offered.

'There is one other incident I remember from that period. It's hard to believe now when you look at my wispy scarecrow head, but I had the most fantastic, chestnut coloured hair which I wore in two plaits. They came down to my bottom, and they were a complete pain because they were so heavy.

'One day, in a fit of rebellion or just to assert my independence, I made an appointment to the hairdressers and had the lot cut off. There was so much hair they sold it to a wigmaker so I made money too.

'What a relief it was to shake my head and feel the bounce of my new bob! I returned home so proud of myself and do you know what my father said: "Oh Marta, what have you done? Your one beauty." Almost exactly the same words spoken to Jo when she cut off her long hair in Little Women. Do you remember that book? "Oh Jo, how could you? Your one beauty." He had a point, I suppose, but I never regretted doing it. And Maryta said I looked modern and grown up which was just what I wanted to hear.

'I did some strange things growing up. For example, I used to drink loads of vinegar.'

'Yuk. Why did you do that?'

'Because I wanted to be pale and interesting and I read somewhere that drinking vinegar would get rid of my rosy cheeks.'

'That's mad. My mother used to pinch my cheeks to give me a little colour in them, saying it would make me look healthy.'

'I used to pinch my eyebrows together to create frown lines.'

'Why?'

'To make me appear intellectual.'

'I wish I'd known you in those days. All my friends seem boring in comparison and their parents even more boring.'

'I'm sure Maryta would have settled for boring instead of all those pointless arguments. I'm not sure what happened to her after they split up, but my father married a woman called Blanka, which surprised everyone, and life settled to a large degree until war threatened. He was an officer of the Riverine Flotilla of the Polish Navy, stationed in Pinsk on the River Pina, and they mobilised his reserve battalion on August 31.

'Shortly after war broke out, I made my way to Pinsk to find him, but it was already too late and I never saw him again. There was a card from him, posted in Pinsk, which ended with the words 'Stick together'. I'm not sure whether he meant that in a spiritual sense or whether he meant Blanka and me, but I never saw her in Pinsk, although she had gone there to be with my father.

'I heard from him once more in 1940 and then nothing more until 1943 when I was sitting on the toilet reading the paper and saw his name in the list of people murdered at Katyn.'

'Oh God, what a terrible way to find out.'

'That's the truth. It was the most terrible shock and I still can't bear to think of him dying in that dreadful way. That's why I don't understand why our communist friends are so delighted at the prospect of liberation by the Red Army. To me it would be an unmitigated disaster.'

The Sunday Escape Committee, as they called themselves, continued to meet well into the Spring of 1945. When Marta had exhausted her many tales, Renata was supposed to take over, but she seemed reluctant to talk about her family. So they started on the books they had read and spent hours arguing over characters and plot lines and how they would have behaved in similar circumstances.

The camp regime did not alter, but everyone detected a new nervousness among the aufseherinnen and SS officers; at the factory, they increased quotas, but talk of an end to the war became a regular, if whispered, feature of each day.

Then, out of the blue, the Ober announced that inmates could leave for another camp or stay at Finow. They had to choose immediately. Marta and Renata looked at each other in panic. What should they do? The Russians were approaching fast, and that made all the difference. In those few seconds of weighing up alternatives, they took the risk and climbed into the trucks.

'Have we done the right thing?'

'Too late now.'

When fuel ran out, the guards forced them to march along endless roads. They slept as they walked and encouraged each other when their legs turned into lead and all they wanted to do was lie down and die. Some did and were dispatched with a shot to the head. The crack of a revolver was enough to make them continue.

Sometimes they ate bread and water, more often nothing. At night they slept in the ditches and carried on in the morning. Numbers dwindled as the stragglers were shot or failed to get up in the morning, death reaching them before the SS bullets.

When they reached the sub camp at Hamburg, the Germans were running about in a panic and glanced at the new arrivals in terror. Clinging to each other they made their way to the nearest hut and collapsed exhausted onto the bunks. As the hours passed, Marta became aware of a change of atmosphere, of different sounds reaching her ears, of strange voices she didn't recognise.

A camp inmate kept them updated: the Germans have vanished; the British Army is here; the war is over.

'We… should… be… celebrating.'

She dragged every whispered word out of her larynx. Renata moaned in response. Asleep or awake they barely moved.

A rich, meaty smell wafted in through a broken window and teased their nostrils transporting Marta back to her childhood watching their cook prepare stroganoff in the

Polish way. She salivated at the chunks of beef sizzling in the pan; her eyes prickled as the sharp knife sliced through the onions; she pinched a cucumber pickled in dill before the cook shooed her away.

This was like the dreams of food they used to have in the camp with the added satisfaction of aromas making them seem real.

Her eyes shot open.

'Renata, listen, this is important.' She cried with the effort of speaking urgently.

'Only eat bland food. Anything else will kill you.'

'No... strength... to... eat.'

She thanked God, knowing how Renata's thoughts revolved around food. Outside emaciated bodies passed out and died in an instant or lay clutching their stomachs in agony as they feasted without restraint on the rich stew prepared by army cooks.

The pity of it all struck her. People who had survived so much denied a future through someone's good intentions. It was such a human action, after all, to try to feed up those who had nothing. To show love through food.

Marta lay on her bunk and observed the soldiers, many openly tearful, who ventured inside the stinking huts to help the bed-ridden with water and, after their initial error, small quantities of rice or potatoes.

What a strange creature man was. Here were hardened soldiers who must have witnessed terrible scenes on the battlefield yet, for all that, could find it within themselves to weep with compassion. Yet other men, endowed with the same intelligence, the same type of military training, had not only inflicted the suffering on them in the first place, but mocked them as they did so.

Among the victims of this misery she had witnessed so many responses ranging from the bestial and criminal to the enlightened and kind-hearted. What caused the difference? Was it religion? Sometimes it was. Friendship or kinship? It certainly played a role in her survival. Was it upbringing? Well if it was, it had nothing to do with class, she was sure of that. Was it nationality? She had mostly been proud of her fellow Poles in the camp, but then again two Ukrainians, whose nation proved so helpful to the Nazis, had procured food and then medicine for her.

Would she ever be able to figure it out? No, mankind was a puzzle: a terrifying, awe-inspiring, ridiculous conundrum.

Long periods of sleep and better nutrition saw the friends get better. Minds raced ahead of bodies as they revelled in the knowledge the war had ended, Hitler was dead and they were safe in the British zone of control. Both wept at the thought of their beloved Poland under Soviet control.

'Maybe it won't be so bad.'

'You think?'

As the weeks passed, they grew impatient with life in a concentration camp, surrounded by painful associations, and leapt at the chance to move to Wentorf, 20 miles east of Hamburg, and its displaced persons' camp.

WENTORF
1945

23

'WILL YOU LOOK AT this place? I've never seen anything like it. I was certain we'd end up in another basic camp with wooden barracks, not these fancy brick buildings.'

Renata peered round the tarpaulin wide-eyed as the truck drove into Wentorf DP Camp.

'You'll fall out in a minute.'

'Don't you want to see?'

Marta rubbed the back of her neck, hoping the tightening sensation wouldn't result in another headache.

'Time enough when the truck stops.'

'What's the matter?'

'Nothing.'

She attempted a smile and gazed into the drab interior at their travelling companions. Renata touched her on the arm.

'Come on, Marta, tell me what's bothering you.'

'Oh nothing, I suppose. I was just remembering how we used to say change was always change for the worse. It was almost like a camp motto.'

'Oh, Marta, not anymore. Or at least it doesn't have to be.'

'No, you're right. I'm being miserable.'

'You need a cigarette.'

'Ah, how well you know me.'

The truck came to a halt outside an administration building and the driver, a young private, jumped out and helped them down from the truck. They were slowly regaining their physical strength but despite their increased rations they were still stick thin and tired easily and were glad of his assistance. An interpreter travelling with them told the group to wait while he went inside.

The soldier sauntered up to Renata and chatted.

'You've got an admirer,' said Marta, blowing smoke into the air and grinning.

'Yes, but I don't understand a word he's saying.'

'Neither do I.'

Eventually, the young man took hold of her hand, shook it vigorously and ran back to the truck before reappearing with a packet of cigarettes and half-eaten bar of chocolate which he thrust into her hands.

'For you. Good luck.'

Renata beamed her thanks and waved as the truck drew away.

'Chocolate! Do you think it would be all right to eat it?' she said, snapping the remainder in half.

'No, please keep it all for yourself. However, if you're not in need of that packet of cigarettes?'

'They're yours. No need to ask. So what do you think about the chocolate?'

'Perhaps just a small piece at a time.'

'Oh good,' said Renata who already had a chunk halfway to her mouth.

The rest of their group had started to move inside the building and they joined them. As they waited their turn to be registered, they noticed a large pin board with hundreds of handwritten notes, all of them seeking information about missing relatives. Marta walked up to it and read the messages under her breath, her fingertips caressing the names. After several minutes she returned phrasing her own request in her head.

'My God, how depressing is that. Talk about looking for a needle in a haystack.'

'True, but we have to take every opportunity we can. You never know who might read it.'

'I gave my details to the Red Cross when they visited the camp just before we left. That's good enough for me.'

'So did I but I don't want to miss out on any chance for information.'

'Suit yourself.'

'Why are you being like that, Renata? Surely we all have to do whatever we can and not just leave it to the Red Cross.'

'But look at that board. There's no organisation to it. They're not in alphabetical order or geographical order. They don't even have a date to say when they were first pinned up. It would take you days just to read them.'

'Yes, you do have a point. Perhaps we can suggest some changes to the people in charge.'

Renata scuffed the toe of her shoe along the wooden floor and looked past the queue to see how much longer they had to wait.

An hour later, with their paperwork completed, they headed out with instructions on how to find their sleeping quarters.

'Right, if I've understood that correctly we need to go to the end of this road, turn right and then it's the second building on our left.'

'I'm glad you took it all in. I'm hopeless at directions.'

'So now you've had a chance to examine our surroundings, what's your opinion of our fancy new camp?'

'Fancy? The buildings are monstrous, ugly and unimaginative, in a word, German.'

'Yes, yes, I agree, but still impressive in their own way. What are they – four, five-storey high? I wonder what it used to be. It's too uniform to be a town and yet the roads are better than the ones we had back home in Plonsk. And it doesn't seem to have sustained any bomb damage either. Why don't you ask? Please?'

Marta sighed and returned to the reception desk, glancing again at the notice board.

'It's an army camp, or was.'

'Yes, that makes sense.'

'Can we go now?'

'Goodness you are in a bad mood.'

'I'm just tired. Right now all I want is to be home and we're a long way from that.'

'That's true but you've got to admit it is a change for the better.'

'Yes, it is.'

By the time they found their beds and introduced themselves to their neighbours, it was time for supper and they made their way to a meeting room on the ground floor where large urns of cocoa and slabs of bread were set out for all the latest arrivals to the camp.

'The cocoa is watery, but it's sweet and there's plenty of bread to go round.'

'Yes, we won't be going to bed hungry, that's for sure.'

In the middle of the night Marta sat bolt upright gasping for breath. Renata, her face illuminated by moonlight, was sitting on the edge of her bed staring into space. She leapt off and hugged her friend.

'What's the matter? Are you all right?'

Marta was shaking uncontrollably, her heart racing, her face ashen.

'I was back there,' she whispered. 'In the camp. Dead bodies pressing me down. I couldn't breathe. They were suffocating me.'

'Shh. It's all right. It's all over. The British Army liberated us, remember?'

Marta gave a lopsided smile and tried to keep her voice light.

'Yes, they liberated us, Renata, but will we ever be free?'

The two friends sat in silence clinging to each other.

'Anyway, what are you doing still up?'

'I couldn't sleep. The bed was too comfortable.'

'Yes, I know what you mean. Perhaps we should sleep on the floor?'

'Definitely not. I want to get used to comfort of every description.'

Marta smiled.

'Well let's give it another try.'

In the morning she woke tired and deflated. She looked around the dormitory. Renata was still asleep in the next bed. Other women were getting up, heading to the showers and toilets or pottering about.

She watched as a woman on the other side of the room removed all her belongings from a small canvas bag, laid them on the bed and then returned them one by one before starting the process all over again. It seemed like a prayer in motion.

The neat rows of iron bedsteads and utility cupboards made her imagine the soldiers who once inhabited these barracks. She remembered the Wehrmacht troops marching into Warsaw, uniformly blond and blue-eyed. Later they became a more motley crew.

How she'd hated seeing their arrogant faces, hearing their barked orders, smelling her nation's defeat in gunfire and blood.

Renata stirred.

'Shall we get up?'

Marta nodded and swung her legs out of bed. Would she ever feel at ease here? Was it possible on German soil? And when she left here could she make a home for herself anywhere? Would Ludek understand what she had been through? Would anyone?

Breakfast in the canteen was a noisy affair. They clutched at each other as they walked up to the serving hatch to collect their coffee and bread past tables of men and women sitting together talking, bickering, swapping tales, even laughing and joking.

It didn't seem real. They'd walked into a newsreel or onto a stage. It had been so long since they'd experienced anything like this. They found themselves a space at one of the long tables and ate without talking, their wary eyes taking it all in.

More and more people kept joining the queue for food and the continuous rumble of voices was interspersed with the chink of cutlery and plates and orders shouted across the kitchen behind them. They cleared their utensils and walked out into the fresh air.

'Do you suppose that's why they gave us supper in a room on our own?'

'To give us a chance to get acclimatised? Yes, probably. I must admit that was too noisy for my liking. It would be lovely to sit out here for a while and enjoy the peace and quiet.'

'But you are coming to the induction meeting at ten?'

'I guess so.'

'You seem reluctant.'

'I'm dreading hearing the rules. You can't do this, you have to do that, make sure you've got this, don't forget to do that.'

'I'm sure it won't be that bad. They all seem quite relaxed so far.'

'Mm, but will it last? We are in Germany after all.'

'Yes, but under British protection, don't forget that.'

'There, you're doing it already.'

But they both grinned; humour lightening their spirits as it had done so often in their friendship.

The induction meeting was less about rules than the opportunities available to them. There were classes in all manner of trades as well as schools for youngsters, everything to help them reintegrate into society. The man leading the session put up a map of the camp and they gawped at the facilities: a radio broadcasting centre, a cinema, a sports field, a hospital, a chapel. There was even, of all things, a windmill.

The camp had opened at the beginning of June and already there were thousands of people there, mostly Poles but also Lithuanians, Latvians, Yugoslavs and Jews from various territories.

'I wonder if I should take up tailoring classes,' said Renata, after they left the session.

'My mother used to say people were scared of doing alterations for themselves so it was a good way to earn money. Actually, even if I say so myself, I'm quite good with a needle and thread already but it would be useful to have a certificate to show people. What about you? Is there anything you'd like to do?'

'I'm interested in getting involved in the camp newsletter. I don't suppose it'll help me get a job but it'll be the first creative thing I've done for ages. It might lift me out of this mood of despondency I keep falling into.'

'Poor Marta. I do understand what you mean. I assumed it would be easy once we left the concentration camp behind but it's followed us here, hasn't it? I seem to veer from enthusiasm and joy to lethargy and wondering what the point of anything is.'

'Perhaps having a routine and a purpose to our day will make all the difference. I certainly hope so.'

Later that same day Renata entered the administration block to sign up for the tailoring classes.

'Are you sure? That would be rather unusual,' said a rather officious middle-aged man peering at her over his glasses.

'Quite sure, thank you.'

'Only we do have a millinery and toy making class run by Mrs Antkowiak which is very popular with our women residents.'

‘Is it against the rules?’ asked Renata, crossing her arms and glaring at him.

‘No, not at all, if that is what you wish.’

‘I do.’

When she joined the class the next day, she understood his hesitation: she was the only woman. The men were friendly and welcoming and the tutor, if he noticed her sex at all, made no comment. He seldom looked his students in the eye, focusing exclusively on the work, folding sheets of old newspapers as he explained various techniques, stroking the samples of material as he examined their stitches.

‘I’m enjoying it,’ she told Marta as they compared notes after their first week at the camp.

‘One of the men is absolutely hopeless. I can’t imagine he’ll pass the course. I keep helping him whenever I can but he’s all fingers and thumbs.’

‘Have you considered that you might be the one putting him off?’

‘What do you mean?’

‘Well you are very attractive, Renata. Perhaps he’s falling in love with you instead of his work.’

‘Oh don’t be silly. I haven’t got time for any of that,’ she said, blushing a deep crimson all the same.

Marta introduced herself to the small editorial team putting together a weekly newsletter for the Polish inhabitants which they called “Ostatni Etape” or “The Last Stage.” They were pleased to have an extra pair of hands and interested in the suggestions she made for future articles. She felt she had found her niche in the camp and the fact that they were all such dedicated smokers added to her feelings of warmth; meetings always took place in a cosy fug.

As the weeks turned into months, both women began to flourish. A casual observer would have noted a new vigour in their movements, a sparkle in their eyes, and a readiness to smile that masked their recent history. They made friends and were soon part of the noisy groups that sat in the canteen eating their meals and chatting away.

'Why are you looking at me like that?' said Marta as they were getting ready for bed one night.

'It's just that dress. It really doesn't do anything for you. Would you mind if I had a go at altering it for you?'

'Be my guest. I was going to wear my skirt and blouse tomorrow, anyway.'

'Mm, well that doesn't do much for you either but one thing at a time. Put it back on for a moment. I asked my tutor if I could borrow a sewing kit for the weekend so if I pin it up now I'll have it finished for you by tomorrow night.'

Marta had one fitting the next day and after a few minor adjustments the dress was finished.

'You've done a lovely job. I can't wait to wear it tomorrow.'

'Thank you. It was a pleasure.'

The next morning Marta seemed taller; she walked with wider steps, swinging her arms. The tailored dress emphasized her newly emerging figure and boosted her confidence. A wolf whistle as she walked into the canteen made her laugh out loud and give a wave.

'This is the first time I've felt like a woman in I don't know how long.'

'You do look marvellous.'

'Thank you. It actually makes me want to do something about my appearance now. People on the hairdressing course are looking for models to try out their skills so I might go along to that.'

'You should.'

A few nights later Marta sat on her bed, staring down at her hands.

'What's happened? What's wrong?'

'I'm going to have to visit the dentist.'

'Why?'

'Look.'

Marta opened her hand to reveal three white teeth.

'They fell out when I was brushing them. I'm going to have to wear dentures, aren't I?'

'We all are. All my teeth are loose too.'

'My family despised people with false teeth.'

'Mine too. False teeth belonged to people who hadn't bothered to brush their teeth and if they didn't bother with their teeth... well you can imagine the rest. And yet we tried so hard in the camp, didn't we? Washing in freezing cold water in the middle of winter, rubbing our teeth with a stick, doing everything possible in the circumstances.'

'Yes, we did. I realise it's not our fault, but it's going to take some getting used to.'

'Try to remember the positives: at least we won't be standing naked while he looks in our mouths like we had to in the camp.'

The dentist confirmed there was nothing he could do to save Marta's remaining teeth and set about fitting her for dentures.

'Nearly everyone from the camps is being fitted with dentures. I don't suppose you'll find many natural smiles in Wentorf,' he said.

Once she left his surgery, she discovered he was right. Everywhere she looked men and women were wearing dentures or revealing gaps when they smiled. It made her accept the situation. With so many people wearing them, surely her family and friends would understand?

'At least there's one good thing about these,' she said, comparing her pristine dentures with Renata's.

'What's that?'

'I've finally lost that gap between my front teeth. I did so hate it growing up.'

24

MARTA VISITED THE NOTICE board in reception on a daily basis. Her own request for information about Ludek Golab, last seen in Krakow, June 1944, was pinned up with all the others. She didn't expect a response in all honesty but checking the board took on the role of a pilgrimage. It was her prayer to the future, for herself and all the others seeking their relatives and friends.

She had also written a short letter and sent it to his family home. Unlike the articles she produced quickly and fluently for the camp newsletter, she had been stumped for words.

I am alive. Write to me. I love you.

It said everything and nothing. She longed to see him, to gaze into his eyes, to hold him close. She couldn't imagine telling him her story. Words had connected them as intimately as touch but the right ones didn't exist, not any more. Love had once bound them together through joy and sorrow. Was that the answer? She believed in love. Love would find a way. Wouldn't it?

She moved aside to let another woman pin up her notice while she considered writing an article about the Red Cross search for missing relatives and how it worked. The article could end with a plea for volunteers to organise this board in a more logical way.

'Do you suppose it works?'

'We have to hope so,' said Marta. 'Have you informed the Red Cross as well?'

'Yes.'

'Who are you looking for?'

'My cousin. She decided to hide at the start of the war. I'm not hopeful, to be honest, but if anybody had the ability to survive the last six years it would have been Rachel. She had that kind of spirit.'

'You said Rachel, not Rachel Goldstein by any chance?'

'No, she was Rosenberg by marriage and her maiden name was Jacobson.'

What was she expecting? Coincidences like that only happened in novels. Besides, the last time she had seen Rachel she wouldn't have given her much chance of surviving another week let alone a year.

'Why do you ask?'

'I met a Rachel Goldstein when we were both prisoners on our way to Ravensbrück concentration camp. She had been in hiding too but the elderly couple sheltering her left to visit their daughter and never came back. When the food ran out she managed to join a partisan group but they were caught in an ambush.'

'At least she managed to fight back.'

'Yes, I hope that gave her some comfort.'

'None of our family wanted Rachel to go into hiding. They were convinced we should all stick together, but she was right to do it, wasn't she? All the others are dead now.'

'I'm so sorry.'

Her sympathy was inadequate and yet she sensed the woman wanted to talk.

'What are your plans for the future?'

'Let me see, Monday I'm getting married.'

'Married? Oh my goodness, many congratulations, I mean mazel tov. What a joy to have a wedding to celebrate.'

'Thank you. I've only known Isaac for a few weeks. We met here in the camp but we're already very fond of each other and times are so different. It's not as if I can ask my mother to arrange for a matchmaker.'

'No, indeed.'

'And then we're off to Israel. We want to be among our own people where we don't have to worry about being Jewish. It'll be a whole new start in a new country, our country. I can't wait and then we hope and pray there'll be more of us.'

She caressed her stomach, a smile playing on her lips.

'You're not...?' asked Marta eyes opening wide in delight even as her guts contracted in a painful reminder of loss.

'No, not yet, but I'm certain it will happen even though the doctors said we shouldn't burden our bodies with pregnancies after all the starvation and ill-treatment.'

Marta nodded. She had been told the same thing during her medical shortly after arriving at Wentorf.

'But God will decide that, not me, and certainly no goyim doctors.'

Marta smiled.

'I wish you as many healthy, happy children as you wish for yourself and I shall pray that everything goes smoothly for you and Isaac in the years ahead.'

'Thank you.'

The two women hugged as if they'd known each other for years. Marta watched her walk away and give a little wave.

She moved aside as someone tacked a notice onto the board, offering up a prayer for her new friend. Euphoria surged through her body; she convinced herself the future was bright for all of them but when she remembered her dead son, her elation died as quickly as sea spray hitting sand.

A pin dropped to the ground followed by the soft thud of a folded envelope. Marta picked both up and found a better place to pin them back up more securely. She read the notice: Looking for family and friends from Katowice and surrounding area. Karol Lewandowski, aged 28, Building 4, Wentorf.

Hundreds of notices, thousands of stories, millions dead. It was too much to take in. Easier to write articles, swap clothes, share the few cosmetics that came their way and wait for whatever the future would bring.

She wandered across to the canteen where she had arranged to meet Renata after her class. She was sitting with a group of their friends. Marta collected a plate of food and joined them. She always ate her meals with care and attention, delighted to use a knife and fork again, and make conversation. It was a welcome return to civilised behaviour.

'Did you hear this morning's radio report? They say there is widespread malnutrition, even starvation throughout Germany,' said Pawel who was taking an electrical training course.

'Good. Let them starve,' replied his fellow student Antek. 'What? Why the disapproving faces? Anybody would think I'd dropped a stinker.'

'How is starving the Germans going to help anyone?'

'It makes me feel better, for one. Why shouldn't they starve after what they did to us?'

'Yes, but it's always the women and children who suffer the most.'

'And you think they don't deserve to? You imagine it was just career Nazis who were responsible for slave labour and all the concentration camps? Well let me tell you they all bloody knew what was going on. Men, women, children, the old, the young, the sick, the fighting fit, everybody realised exactly what they were up to.

'And I'll tell you something else. I find it easier to forgive, not that I intend to, a Hitler or a Goering or a Himmler than I do the ordinary people who stood by and watched it happen. They were maniacs, psychopaths, arguably not responsible for their actions, but Mr and Mrs Average? They can burn in hell for their silence and their apathy.'

Antek thrust his chair back and strode out the canteen without a backward glance.

'Oh dear,' said Renata as they all sat stunned by the outburst.

'He has a point, though, don't you think?'

'Maybe. But I'd like to believe we could move on from "an eye for an eye" and learn something from the horrors we've all been through.'

That night Marta watched as Renata tossed and turned. Sleep eluded her as she remembered the crows and the ordinary German women working in the munitions factory.

Were they equally culpable? Moans and muffled words came from the next bed. She forced herself up to comfort Renata but stopped short of her bed, her face crumbling, as she saw the piece of bread clutched in her fisted hand.

Days passed before Renata raised the subject again.

'Do you still hate them?'

'Who?'

'The crows.'

'No, not really. Don't get me wrong, I wouldn't want anything to do with them, but hatred is too strong a word. It helped me cope in camp to imagine taking my revenge on them but now I mostly wonder how they could behave like that? What turned them from human beings into… into what? How would you describe what they became?

'They saw us as vermin but why? We didn't look any different from them, at least not at first. And what did they see when they looked in a mirror? What do they see now? Did they not realise what they were doing? And if not, what would have opened their eyes?

'I keep remembering all the things we witnessed, good and bad, beautiful and ugly, depressing and inspiring. How can it be that in the worst place on earth, full of cruelty and bestiality, we also found courage and friendship, generosity and love? What does that make mankind?'

'Unfathomable, I guess.'

'I guess.'

'What about ordinary Germans? Mr and Mrs Average as Antek described them.'

'I don't know, Renata. He says they stood by and did nothing. But were we any better when they came for the Jews?'

'Judge not lest you be judged?'

'Exactly. Who knows what it was like for ordinary families? What chance do ants have when an anteater visits their nest?'

One Sunday morning the two friends strolled out of the dormitory, arm in arm, and made their way to a favourite bench positioned near a small expanse of lawn. Marta lit up and toyed with the cigarette packet that was never far from her side; Renata leaned back as the late autumnal sun warmed her face and limbs.

'Do you suppose we'll ever be normal?'

'Don't you feel normal now? Sitting here, enjoying the peace and quiet?'

'Oh, I don't know. We seem to do normal things, behave like normal human beings, but I can't get my head round things. Over a year has gone by since I was arrested and yet it seems like a hundred years and more. One minute I had a life, then a prolonged nightmare and now here I am with no life at all.'

Renata sat upright.

'What's brought this on? Of course you have a life. Count up all the food and clothes and comfortable beds and the friends we've made since coming here. There is nothing to stop us laughing or crying or shouting or walking out of here any time we want to. If that's not life then what is?'

'But it's not the life I had. Not with my family, my fiancé…'

'Your what?'

'My fiancé, Ludek Golab. Well, I say fiancé, it wasn't official, because of the war and working for the Home

Army, but Ludek was the love of my life and I of his. There was never any doubt about that.'

'I don't believe this. Do you mean to say you kept me alive with tales of your family and it never once occurred to you to mention your fiancé?'

'Oh Renata, I couldn't. He was the reason I ended up in Ravensbrück. The Gestapo caught me carrying a gun for the resistance, but I wasn't in the Home Army myself, Ludek was. On June the 11th 1944, he woke up with a premonition that something would go wrong. So I persuaded him to let me courier the gun in his place. And he was right. The Gestapo were as good as waiting for me.'

'Explain to me, Marta, why did you do it? Why put yourself in so much danger?'

'Love. I did it for love. Ludek would never let his colleagues down and I was convinced I would get away with it, which, in a way, I did. I got through all the interrogations without mentioning his name once and I had to carry on protecting him by keeping him a secret from everyone, even from you.'

'Did he know you ended up in Ravensbrück?'

'I'm not sure. But I've always wondered why, if he knew, he didn't send me any parcels there. He did while I was being held at Montelupich Prison in Krakow so it seemed strange that he didn't continue doing so.'

'Do you suppose he's still alive?'

'Yes, I do. We were so close, Renata, it doesn't seem possible for him to have died without my sensing it, without my knowing it in here. When the Red Cross came to the camp, I gave them all his details, and I've written to him from here, so we'll just have to wait and see.'

'Oh, you poor thing, no wonder your mind is in turmoil. What will you do if he is alive?'

'That's the only important question. Perhaps that's why I'm so unsettled all the time. I want to be with him more than anything else in the entire world. And yet the prospect of returning to a Poland that's no longer free terrifies me.'

'Yes, I understand that.'

'It's not just about the Soviets, though that is bad enough, it's the notion of being restricted in any way. We were in a prison of our minds as much our bodies...'

'You don't need to tell me that. If we hadn't had our Sunday Escape Committee, I dread to think what would have become of me.'

'Going back would be like entering another prison, maybe one without walls or barbed wire but still a prison. Look at the way they blame Katyn on the Germans. Imagine going back and not being able to talk about what they did to my father and to all the others. That would be another prison of the mind and I'm not sure I could stand it.'

Renata gave her a hug.

'I wonder if Irenka survived the camp.'

'Who?'

'Irenka. Did you never meet her?'

'If I did, I don't remember.'

'Oh, you wouldn't have forgotten her. She drove Danuta to distraction. Irenka was a communist and very proud to be one and always boasting how their comradeship would defeat the Nazis and lead to a wonderful new world. She's probably running Poland as we speak.'

'Sounds terrifying.'

'To be fair, she had useful information about how to survive in the camp. While I didn't like her, she helped us in those early days when we were all shell-shocked.'

'What made you think of her?'

'I don't know… the knowledge of communists being in charge, I suppose.'

Two weeks later the postman did his morning rounds in the canteen, taking the opportunity to pick up a free breakfast, before depositing any unclaimed letters in reception.

'Letter for Miss Paciorkowska.'

Marta blanched even as she put her hand up to identify herself.

'Is this it? Is this the information about Ludek?'

The Krakow postmark and the familiar Greek alpha left her in no doubt.

'It's from Ludek.'

'Do you want me to go away?'

'Yes. No. Yes.'

'Read the letter and I will wait on the bench outside.'

'Thanks.'

Marta sat staring at the envelope before taking a deep breath and opening it with her knife. When she pulled out the sheet of paper and started to read, a frown deepened between her eyes.

She took out a cigarette. Minutes passed as she breathed in the nicotine and clenched and unclenched her fist, biting at her fingers, rubbing her forehead.

She re-read the letter and hurried out of the canteen.

'Marta? Where are you going? Are you all right? What did the letter say?'

Turning she looked at her friend distractedly.

'I don't understand it.'

'What do you mean?'

'The letter makes little sense.'

'How so?'

'Here, read it yourself.'

Marta stared at the ground, a new cigarette already lit.

'Ah, I see what you mean.'

'He says he's so glad I'm alive because I can help him prove how they betrayed him. The letter is all about him and his betrayal and his theories about how it happened. It reads like garbage, like a stream of invective. I don't seem to exist except as a means to an end. And he sounds so angry. Look at the way he's pressed his nib into the paper with such force. I tell you I don't recognise the man who wrote this letter. This isn't my Ludek.'

'Oh Marta, perhaps this is a sudden outpouring of madness: a kind of release of all the tension and guilt he's built up during the last year. He's poured it all out like draining an abscess or getting rid of a poison. If you write back to him, ignoring the contents, he'll reply as a different person.'

Marta considered Renata's words and nodded.

'Yes, perhaps you are right, I'll do what you suggest.'

She sent another letter, full of love and hope, that same day. She didn't recognise the address Ludek had written on the envelope but imagined he had moved for safety reasons after her arrest.

When she received his reply her disappointment was acute. The new letter still talked of betrayal and conspiracies but now he attacked her, questioned her loyalty, spurned her love, suggested she had something to do with his incarceration. What did he mean? Was he in prison? Had they caught up with him while she was in Ravensbrück? Were these the ramblings of a man broken by torture?

Renata struggled to help her friend in her misery and then succumbed to her own as the Red Cross confirmed her brother had perished in Auschwitz. Of her family in Plonsk there was no news.

Preoccupied by their own thoughts they had little to say to each other in the ensuing weeks and even less when they attended the camp interviews to determine their future, realising the close friendship which had sustained them for so long was coming to an end.

'What are you planning to do?' asked Renata, as they watched the sun go down.

'I don't know.'

'I've made my decision.'

'What is that?'

'I can't return home, Marta. Even if my parents are still alive, I am certain they will blame me for Jurek's death and I have sufficient guilt on that score.'

'But they will be so glad you survived.'

'I'm not sure that's true. I never told you but once my brother was born, I ceased to exist except as a carer or a bodyguard.'

'What do you mean?'

'It was always "Look after Jurek" or "Make sure Jurek is safe". They invested all their hope for the future in him. "Jurek will do this" or "Jurek will do that." If Jurek said something remotely amusing, they fell about laughing. If he made a comment on world affairs, they would nod proudly and repeat his comments to all and sundry. If I did the same, they told me not to show off. If I asked about my future, they just laughed and said "Oh you needn't worry your pretty little head." The implication was clear, yet I was the clever one, the one who did well at school, while Jurek just messed about.

'I loved my brother, truly I did, but it was hard to live life as a second-class citizen just because I was a girl.'

'I can't imagine what that would be like. I've never seen being a girl as a handicap in any way.'

'No, your aunt was such a strong role model, not just for you but for all your family.'

'True, but even without my aunt I don't imagine anybody in our circle would regard a girl as less important or valuable than a boy.'

'No? Well my parents did. They will say I failed them and Jurek by not taking better care of him. The irony is that it was all Jurek's idea to go out painting the walls. I could no more have stopped him than I could have stopped the wind.'

Now she understood her friend's ambivalence about the notice board.

'So what will you do?'

'Well, the next three boats due in port will head for America, Sweden or England. I've nobody in any of those countries but, hey, America has Hollywood, and that's good enough for me.'

'Yes, I can imagine you in Hollywood. Think of all the costumes you could make with your skills as a tailor. My dearest friend, I shall miss you so much.'

'I will miss you too.'

'How long do you have before you leave for America?'

'Two weeks.'

A few days later Marta received a letter from Ludek's brother confirming her worst fears. Ludek had been diagnosed with schizophrenia and was now living in a mental hospital just outside Krakow.

'I am so sorry. It seems such a cruel blow after everything you suffered for love.'

'I have no regrets. I still love him with all my heart, but I can't go back to Poland now. He's solved my problem for me. Would I have gone back if he had been well? I'm not sure, but as it is, I don't have to make that decision any more. He is no longer there, not the Ludek I remember and fell in love with.

'But I will say this: I will never marry or become involved with another man for as long as he lives. That is my pledge to him.'

'Oh my God, that is so romantic.'

'It's the least I can do as a tribute to the love we shared, a love that meant more to me than life itself.'

'And what about life? Your life? What will you do now?'

'I've family members in England so it makes sense for me to go there and resume my education, complete my degree in psychology and then fulfil my ambition to work with problem children.'

'Will we ever meet again?'

'We must. Whatever happens in our lives we must promise to meet up one day.'

'It's a promise.' And the two friends shook hands on it and hugged with all their might.

After Renata left for America, Marta had to wait several weeks before the authorities finalised her own transport to England. She lifted a small suitcase onto her bed. It was leather, scuffed on the corners and musty inside, but solid enough to sit on unlike Renata's cardboard one. She filled it with clothes and a spare pair of shoes; everything donated by Wentorf's welfare department.

Had some of it come from concentration camp stores? They must have amassed huge quantities of clothing. She was curious what had happened to the colourful skirt she had worn on the day of her arrest. Would she even recognise it now?

She put on a winter coat that was much too big for her and wandered across to the administration building. Dozens of people milled around the reception area waiting for the next transport to the docks. Marta ventured outside to have a smoke. She joined a group sheltering round the corner away from the biting wind. They were exchanging destinations: London, Scotland, Leeds, Cornwall.

A lanky man with intense brown eyes and long, slender fingers suggested they should all keep in touch, set up an association of survivors, a club of sorts. He looked directly at her as if challenging her to organise it then and there.

She lifted her chin and blew smoke into the air before looking away. Swapping tales of the crows over tea and biscuits? She didn't think so somehow.

She stubbed out her cigarette and heard the rumble of wheels in the distance. Two buses turned into the road and rolled towards them.

This was it. There was no going back. It was time to start a new life.

Turmoil and excitement, fear and joyous anticipation tumbled around inside her. What would her life be like? Memories of the camp still came unbidden at odd times of the day or night and left her breathless with anxiety, tears smarting in her eyes; yet she knew she had been so lucky through all the disasters of the last year, surviving where so many had perished.

She tried to imagine a bright future, surrounded by family and new friends, working at her studies and undertaking her chosen career, helping others lead useful, pain-free lives. If she could no longer have the love of her own life, she would devote herself to filling other lives with love instead.

And one of the first things she would do, she decided on a whim, was lie about her age. Well, why not? They'd stolen six years of her life why shouldn't she make up for some of that time?

She imagined Renata's outraged reaction to her plan. She could be very – what? – innocent, straight-laced, honest perhaps? God, she would miss her friend so much.

Marta picked up her suitcase and stepped onto the bus. She found a seat by a window and looked out. As the bus moved off, she took out a piece of paper from her pocket and held on tight to Our Lady's Dream

The following article was written by Marta Paciorkowska and published in 'The Last Stage' issued on the 25th December 1945. It was the last newsletter she worked on in Wentorf DP Camp and the final lines of the article refer to a future with her fiancé, a future she knew would never happen, even as she wrote the words.

The festival of Christmas Eve, or Wigilia, is of special importance to Polish people who value its traditions and customs as well as its religious significance.

The main celebration of Wigilia is a solemn, family supper which starts as soon as the first star, symbolic of the Bethlehem Star, appears in the sky. This is the moment when family members share the Christmas wafer or oplatek, wishing each other health, joy and good fortune for the coming year. The oplatek, made of flour and water, symbolises the bread Christians share during the celebration of Mass.

After a day of fasting, the meal which follows the sharing of the oplatek is a feast of vegetarian and fish dishes, usually twelve in number to symbolise the twelve apostles. An extra place is laid at the table for the unexpected guest in accordance with the Polish tradition of hospitality.

After the singing of carols and the exchange of presents, the festival ends with attendance at Midnight Mass.

TWO CHRISTMAS EVES

Tiny, glittering sequins on a navy blue background: millions of stars above us. The moon, cut from silver paper, hangs so low that you could surely reach out to it just by standing on tiptoes. The earth and trees are covered by fluffy blue cotton wool snow. A beautiful night. A night which forms the backdrop of a fantastical theatrical scene.

The main actors are not on stage yet – only the non-speaking parts are there. Motionless, silent, long lines of ghostlike women. In identical simple striped costumes, they wait for the start of the performance. Each one knows her role. Though what is the role of an extra?

'Tonight will be a short roll call and there's sure to be extra rations' Mika whispers to me as we stand in our rows of ten in front of the block, just as we do every night.

'Why?' I ask, brought back to reality.

'You don't know?! Because it's Christmas Eve.'

'Ah yes...that's right...I forgot.'

Christmas Eve...So, in Poland now they are sharing the oplatek...they're lighting the Christmas tree candles... sitting down to the meal...I know: there is one extra place laid at the table; there is, after all, a constant, unceasing hope that I shall return. Oh but what an immense pain, beyond one's strength, and how hard it is to hold back the tears when you're missing a loved one at the Christmas Eve table.

As for me? No – I don't cry. I find within myself neither grief nor homesickness. Nothing. With blank hatred I observe bellowing, drunken Ruth take the roll call and I think only of when I'll be able to lie down. But waiting for us inside the barracks is a completely unfestive surprise. They haven't brought any bread, or maybe simply our merrymaking overseer didn't fancy distributing it today.

'So much for your bigger rations' I tell Mika my sardonic laugh disappearing into the uproar of other voices. All of them are talking simultaneously, impotent rage and hunger reduces some to tears – others swear loudly. After a time peace descends. Somebody tries to strike up a carol – a few others join in. 'Silent night, holy night.' But these words in the cold barracks seem too painfully ironic. Voices break… they stop mid verse and don't try again. Huddled with my knees under my chin, I cover my head with a blanket and try to warm myself with my own breath. I don't think and I don't reminisce. I am in the depths of degradation where I feel nothing beyond the physical pain of hunger and cold. On my palate I keep a crust of bread, already softening, and I try to sleep. Sleep is often a remedy for life. Maybe I'll dream of a real Christmas Eve.

* * *

A year has passed and Christmas is approaching. It won't be a happy one. A full stomach allows one the luxury of yearning for other, past Christmases spent with those closest to us. The words of a carol bring Poland to heart – the warm interior of our home with the Christmas tree lit up, white linen on the table. And as the Star of Bethlehem reveals itself in the sky, I will more than ever, feel your absence, your warm words when you shared the oplatek with me. Do you remember? We felt so strangely awkward – tears swam in our eyes but of course we were embarrassed to admit to them. And we covered up our emotion by an assumed ease of manner. Tonight it's Christmas Eve without you and I'm crying. It's nothing. It's good. Through these tears I'm returning to humanity. I am able now to reminisce, I am able to think about you. And today we will find one another again in our thoughts as we once again send Christmas greetings from afar.

And next Christmas, we will spend it together. For certain, I believe it. And then together we will sing, maybe a little out of tune, but with great joy 'GLORIA, GLORIA IN EXELSIS DEO!

BACKGROUND NOTES

At the end of the First World War, Poland re-emerged as a sovereign state following 123 years of subjugation to foreign powers. In 1795 the country was divided between Austria, Prussia and Russia and ceased to exist on the map of Europe. Five generations lived under three different conditions of political oppression, but their desire for freedom was never extinguished. Civil disobedience, uprisings, military conflicts and various political developments such as the creation of a small, semi-independent Polish state, the Duchy of Warsaw, by Napoleon Bonaparte following his defeat of Prussia, all helped to foster the belief that independence was possible.

The period between the two world wars was an exhilarating time to be alive: there was an explosion of brilliance in the sciences as well as the arts, with Poles at the forefront of European developments in philosophy, mathematics, economics, linguistics and anthropology. Polish writers, poets, dramatists and artists of seemingly infinite talent and variety found enthusiastic audiences in their homeland and further afield. Intellectual and cultural life thrived and Marta's family, affluent and well connected, were active participants.

Politically, too, these were interesting times as the new Polish republic sought to find its feet after the devastation of the First World War – most of the fighting on the Eastern front took place on Polish fields – and with the lack of an integrated infrastructure inherited from the separate partitions. Parliamentary democracy, albeit with frequent government changes, lasted until 1926 when the popular military leader Jozef Pilsudski staged a coup; his authoritarian regime continued until his death in 1935 and was upheld by his allies and subordinates until the outbreak of the Second World War.

Hitler invaded Poland on the 1st of September 1939. Shortly afterwards Britain and France both declared war on Germany but left Poland's forces fighting the Nazis on their own. This they did with typical heroism and not a little military skill, inflicting heavy losses on the enemy and keeping it in check for longer than anyone expected. Then on the 17th of September Russia invaded Poland and soon all was lost: the country was partitioned once more and effectively ceased to exist.

This much is well known; what is perhaps less well known is the ferocity with which both sides sought to destroy the Polish people. This was no ordinary war, no ordinary occupation: both sides carried out atrocities designed to reduce the Poles to a leaderless nation of slaves who would serve their new masters' purposes or be obliterated at will.

Nearly one in five of the pre-war population of Poland, over six million people, died in the conflict. Under Russian occupation an estimated two million Polish citizens were arrested and deported to the Gulag Archipelago; within a year, at least half were dead from the extreme cold and starvation. The Nazis, meanwhile, designated Poles as sub-humans or Untermenschen who occupied land they required for their living space or Lebensraum. Poland's elite – the term was broadly interpreted – was to be extinguished either through large scale executions, such as those that took place regularly in Pawiak Prison or the Palmiry Forest, or through hard labour and starvation in the network of concentration camps.

Mass deportations of civilians to make way for German colonists were accomplished with typical brutality and disregard for life. Blond, blue-eyed children who met Nazi racial criteria were sent to the Reich for Germanisation. In addition, there were regular street round-ups where truckloads of men, women and children were sent to Germany as slave labourers.

Those who managed to evade death or deportation found daily life a struggle. There were no jobs for the intelligentsia and they had to turn their hand to anything that became available. All Poles were expected to manage on greatly reduced rations, more so than any other occupied people. So, for example, in 1941 the citizens of Warsaw were allowed 669 calories a day while Jews were allocated a mere 184 calories a day. Since both were racially inferior, the Nazis reasoned, they required less food.

Clothes, which could only be purchased using coupons, were also in short supply and very expensive while the German monopoly on leather and rubber meant that shoes were impossible to repair and could only be replaced with wooden clogs.

In their bid to destroy Polish history and culture, the Nazis closed all scientific, artistic and literary institutions as well as all secondary schools and universities. Some elementary schools remained open for the purpose of giving pupils a very basic education and teaching them enough German to obey orders. The teaching of history was specifically forbidden and history books were confiscated while any monuments to Polish heroes were torn down.

The Catholic Church, almost synonymous with Polish nationalism, was persecuted throughout the country. Churches, seminaries, convents and monasteries were closed down in large numbers and thousands of priests and nuns were sent to concentration camps, into forced labour or killed outright. Krakow, which formed the capital of the General Government area, was treated more leniently with churches being controlled rather than obliterated.

Needless to say, the Poles did not take this new oppression lying down. Resistance was almost universal and ranged from acts of sabotage in the workplace to the active maintenance of an underground cultural life. Education for secondary pupils and university students was provided in secret; actors gave readings and performances in private homes; newspapers and pamphlets were issued by an underground press; welfare organisations were set up to help the Poles and, uniquely in occupied Europe, to help the Jews; smugglers brought in regular supplies of food from the countryside into the towns to prevent widespread starvation.

Many examples of resistance were ordinary actions by ordinary people united in their hatred of what the Nazis were doing to their country. There were also various resistance organisations whose foundations were laid before the end of the Nazi invasion of Poland in September 1939; the most important of these was the Home Army which eventually subsumed most of the other organisations to form one of the largest, if not the largest, resistance movements in occupied Europe.

Ask almost any Polish family about their history and they will tell you amazing tales of heroism, of survival against the odds, of colourful characters in their past. So why single out my mother's story?

Firstly, because her family history seems uniquely dramatic, even outrageous, and it feels a shame to see it lost for want of writing it down. Truly, it belongs in the category of 'you couldn't make it up' stories.

Secondly, because she was one of the survivors of a Nazi concentration camp and it remains vitally important to continue to bear witness to their experiences, to ensure that the horror they underwent is never forgotten. People say that her generation didn't want to talk about the war, but she wanted to tell her story and was initially rebuffed: the war was over, everybody had suffered, nobody wanted to know. By the time people were interested enough to ask, she had learnt to be silent.

I used the format of a historical fictional memoir to tell her story because it enabled me to flesh out the bones; I knew the outline of her arrest and imprisonment and many individual details but not the complete picture. I knew, for example, that she had learnt German in the six weeks that she was first imprisoned on suspicion of being Jewish and that she did so with the help of fellow prisoners. Creating the character of Pola enabled the narrative to flow and to bring in other details, such as the Polish Catholic prayer entitled 'Our Lady's Dream,' which my mother learnt in prison and turned to throughout her life.

The brutality of life in Ravensbrück concentration camp, a camp specifically designed for women, has been documented in various places, most recently and comprehensively by Sarah Helm in her book, 'If This Is A Woman'. While the incidents described in this book are true to that life the conversations and reactions of other prisoners have inevitably been imagined. Although my mother wasn't a saint, she did, remarkably, share her bread ration with a fellow prisoner and refused to fight over food.

The fictional character of Inspector Bauer – I simplified organisational titles – and his family enabled me to explore questions I continue to be interested in: was it possible to live in Nazi Germany and not know what was going on? What does it mean to lead a moral life in any totalitarian regime? How would I have behaved in similar circumstances? And in our own times, can any of us claim to be virtuous living in a free and democratic country yet knowing that torture is practised further afield and doing nothing about it?

True to her vow Marta remained faithful to her fiancé, Ludek Golab, until news of his death reached her. In 1952 she met and married my father, Tadeusz Wielogorski, a handsome, courageous army officer, recipient of Poland's highest military decoration for heroism on the battlefield, the Virtuti Militari. At long last she was able to fulfil her dream of having children and in due course gave birth to a son and a daughter.

ACKNOWLEDGEMENTS

My thanks to everyone who read the first drafts for their kind words and helpful suggestions: Janet Hurton, Phil Parker and especially Mick Jeffs who kept me on track in the early days.

I am indebted to Barbara Dresner and Geraldine Parker whose insightful comments proved invaluable. Barbara also translated Our Lady's Dream and polished my own translation of Two Christmas Eves.

Last but never least, my husband, Mike, my soulmate, without whom this book would not exist and who gave endless encouragement and support.

There are many excellent books about Poland's history and the Second World War but I found the following particularly useful: Berlin at War by Roger Moorhouse; The Third Reich in Power by Richard J. Evans; The Gestapo by Frank McDonough; The Forgotten Holocaust by Richard C. Lukas; Heart of Europe: The Past in Poland's Present by Norman Davies.

Inspiration also came from A Girl Called Judith Strick by Judith Strick Dribben; Alone in Berlin by Hans Fallada; Ravensbrück by Micheline Maurel; And I Am Afraid of My Dreams by Wanda Poltawska. I was pleased to find confirmation of my mother's memory of being washed in a long vest in The Last Mazurka by Andrew Tarnowski.

I also benefitted from the wisdom of The Literary Consultancy and the Jerry Jenkins Guild.